MW01488117

# Light of Day

## Daylight Book 1

**By K.M Thompson**

**Publisher: O'Connor & Collins Publishing Ltd**

**Literary Editor: Gypsy Heart Editing**

**Book Formatting: Josh Hilden**

**Cover Designer: Gypsy Heart Editing**

*For my amazing Husband,*

*You are the most patient and*

*understanding man I've ever met.*

*Happy first wedding anniversary.*


*I love you baby xXxX*

# Table of Contents

# Dana

# Chapter 1

"No, no, no, and no." One piece of clothing after another comes flying out of my wardrobe until nothing is left. "Why can't I find anything to wear... argh?"

"What's up sweetie?" My roommate James Ward pokes his head around my bedroom door.

James and I have been friends since Mrs. Jenkins class in year five at school. I love him so much, he's like a brother to me. He's been a constant in my life, a rock, supporting me through everything and anything. Considering he's had his fair share of crap thrown at him, he has never failed me, for that I will always be truly grateful.

"I have nothing to wear for my first day

tomorrow. Everything clashes with my hair." Landing my dream job as a photographer for the prestigious lifestyle magazine *Mode* had been nothing short of a miracle. How I managed it after the bag of nerves I was at the interview I'll never know. Rambling on about how much I wanted to be out in the world, taking photos of things people see as ugly and making them look beautiful, I was surprised to receive the phone call to say the editor had met with the boss and he loved my work. Tomorrow I will be meeting the owner of the publication, something I'm dreading. Someone who has all that power to oversee the running of over twenty magazines has no time to be nice to the little people like me. Now to top that off I can't find anything that doesn't clash with my copper red hair, seriously what clothes have I been wearing all my life to only just notice this.

"Dana, you have to be kidding me." James walks over to the massive pile of clothes on my bed and starts going through them. "There has to be something in here you can wear, you didn't throw away all your clothes before we moved, I wouldn't have let you. Let me look."

"Go for it, there is nothing that says classy and sophisticated yet casual and breezy. This is hopeless."

Just then, James holds up a green sleeveless turtle neck jumper with a pair of gray suit trousers.

"Wear this with the black flat dolly shoes. Perfect." James smiles.

"How do you do it?"

"Dana sweetie, I'm a genius when it comes to fashion, you know this. Want me to do your hair for you in the morning?"

"What would I do without you?" I smile at him.

"You're never going to find out," he says, kissing me on the top of my head. I scuttle off to get myself in a nice hot relaxing bath, ready for an early night. James smiles his million pound, megawatt smile, and heads to the kitchen.

"Want a glass of wine, lovely?" James shouts through.

"Oh! Yes please!" I reply.

James enters the bathroom without knocking and places the glass on the edge of the bath and walks back out after I thank him. James is stunningly good looking and really needs to come with a warning. With his short jet black hair, chiseled facial features and stormy gray eyes, he's every woman's ideal man, just a shame he's gay. I wouldn't be letting him in the bathroom with me naked in the tub if he weren't. On the plus side, I have an amazing friend who I know will never flirt with me or put me in any awkward positions, and he is also great when it comes to fashion, hair, and make-up, not to mention some of the more fucked up stuff. Seriously I don't know what I would do without him.

Removing myself from the depths of the bath, I dry off,  rub body lotion on myself, get into track bottoms and a comfy t-shirt and go in search of James and the rest of the bottle of wine. Walking down the hallway I can smell James cooking sausages, God I love this man.

10

"You know the way to a woman's heart." I flutter my eyelashes at him in a mock attempt to flirt. Picking up the half empty bottle of white wine, I pour myself and James another glass.

"Damn. So that's why I can't get a man, I've been doing it all wrong," he says smiling at me. It's so easy to be around him, I couldn't imagine a time when I didn't need him and hated the six years I lived without him.

"Surely not. Anyway, you have a man, sorry I mean two men. How is Andy? And have you called Lewis yet?" I'm wondering how he will react to this line of questioning. He left Lewis behind in London when we moved to New York with my Mum and Richard, four weeks ago. A decision I think he made for me, but he told me he was doing it for himself. Lewis hated that I was always James' priority, just as he will always be mine. Then James met Andy after only a few days of being here, and now he's struggling with his conscience.

He waits for a beat before answering, "He

misses me and can't wait till he can come out here."

He isn't finished, I can tell there is more, but he doesn't continue. "And, did you tell him?"

"There was just something in his voice Dana, he sounded so sad I couldn't break his heart like that, and I *do* still love him." He turned his back to me, I know he's trying not to cry.

"Do you regret leaving?" I ask trying to hide the guilt I am feeling in my voice.

He instantly turns and walks towards me, pulling me into a hug. "Never Dana. This is where I want to be, here in New York with you." Pulling back he kisses me on the forehead and looks me directly in the eyes. "Don't feel guilty, I'm a big boy and make my own decisions."

"But you can't always put me first Jay, you have to have your own life."

"The only life I need right now, is one where you are in it, okay?"

I couldn't help but smile. "I feel so selfish keeping you to myself."

"Dana we are only twenty-three, we have plenty of time to meet people and get on with life. Let's just deal with our own fucked up heads first, and we will cross the boyfriend bridge when we come to it." Squeezing me tighter, then finally letting go he turns back to the oven to finish cooking the sausages. "Sausage sandwich sweetie?"

"Oh, yes, please. So I won't be meeting Andy anytime soon then?"

"Andy's just a bit of fun, nothing serious, but if you really want to meet him then I'm sure we can arrange something for this weekend," he says with a big boyish grin. He can't fool me, I know this thing with Andy is more serious than he's making out, but I understand he needs to talk to Lewis first.

I smile to myself, thinking just how great life is compared to six months ago. Fighting for my life in intensive care after my psycho ex-boyfriend tried to burn my house to the ground, with me in it. I shudder and shake my head trying to remove the memory and turn to look at James, reminding myself that I'm here because of him. "I love you, James."

"I love you too, sweetie."

As my alarm goes off at six in the morning, I'm reminded that I'm not used to these early mornings. I probably should have continued getting up early after we moved instead of having late nights and lay-ins. Today is going to kill me. After several cups of coffee, two bites of toast, my stomach couldn't handle anymore, I take the risk and enter James' room.

"Wakey wakey, sleepy head," I lull in his ear.

Turning over and burying his head under his pillow he grunts, "It's your first day at work, not mine. Is that coffee I smell?"

I stifle a giggle. He is not a morning person, and I learned a long time ago, that if I'm waking him before seven thirty to soften the blow with caffeine. "You said you'd do my hair for me."

With a final grunt, he heaves himself up. "Give me the coffee."

"You're a ray of sunshine in the morning,

aren't you?" Glaring at me like he's about to strangle me, I jump to my feet and head out of the room calling behind me, "Don't take too much time I have to leave at eight."

Five minutes later he comes into our spacious living area. The apartment we have is rather large, neither James nor I could afford it on our own. This apartment on the Upper West Side is all thanks to mum's husband and the need they have to keep me safe. I had just turned fourteen when my dad died. About a year and a half later, mum met Clay. He was an awful man, he caused a lot of problems for mum and me when she started taking his side on things. I couldn't take much more, and at the age of fifteen, I ran away from home. It took mum a while to realize Clay wasn't all he cracked up to be, but she finally saw it for herself. This epiphany of hers came too late, she had lost me to Grant and the man I thought would be the love of my life. When she met Richard Dalton, he hired all sorts of private detectives to track me down, and I have never been happier to have been found.

Richard couldn't have children and has been glad to take me on as his own, along with James who has no family of his own. Although mum agreed to marry him four years ago, they only married last year as she put off the wedding until I could be there. Richard comes from a wealthy family and is also a successful businessman. Due to expanding his company, he was opening offices in Manhattan and offered to take us with him. A fresh start is what we all needed.

"Why do you have to leave for work so early, I thought you didn't start till nine?" James says, pulling me from my reverie. Wearing only a pair of pajama bottoms with bed head and sleepy eyes. I smile my silent thanks at him for helping me and bring him another coffee.

"Yeah I do, but I have to be in early today to meet this Mr. Day guy."

"Ah the big boss man, have you seen him yet?"

"Nope. I just hope the meeting is over nice and quick, he probably has to do this for all new

16

employees. It must get boring for him having to meet with us when he has a business to run. I can't see him being too interested in anything I have to say." I'm really starting to feel nervous now and slightly nauseous, maybe I should have eaten the rest of the toast.

"You will be okay Dana. It will be over before you know it and then you can get on with what you are paid to do." James gives my shoulders a rub and gets to work on my fiery red hair, curling it and pulling it back and up, he manages to pull off a sophisticated, messy look. I look fabulous if I do say so myself.

Heading to my room to grab my bag and camera equipment I pass by James' room and then pause outside our black room. Touching the handle, I'm grateful we haven't had to use this room yet. We've only been here four weeks, but we are both so happy with our lives that maybe the black room won't be needed anymore and we can turn it into a home gym or something. Wishful thinking on my part as I know we will always need this room, and that we both rely on it. It's not a healthy option, but it's better than the alternative. Grabbing the things I need from my room I hurry out the door and into the lift giving James a big hug and kiss before I leave, with him shouting encouragement at me till the doors close.

Reaching the ground floor, I step out and thank the gods that no one stopped the lift on my ride down, trying to steady my breathing I start to wonder if it was such a great idea getting an apartment on the twenty-second floor. Then again I didn't know I was claustrophobic until I stepped into the lift in our building for the first time. Another one of my phobias I can thank Grant for. Heading past the doorman and out onto the street I start walking to work. Unfortunately, the subway is too packed this time of the day and just sets off a panic attack. I haven't quite worked out how to hail a taxi, so, for now, I'm stuck with walking. On the plus side if I walk briskly to and from work I won't have to visit the gym as much, and I won't feel guilty about getting a blueberry muffin with my coffee at Starbucks on my way to work.

After walking the twenty minutes to work, I look up at the Daylight tower in awe and amazement. It is such a beautiful building nestled amongst other beautiful buildings. There's just something unique about the Daylight that makes it stand out a bit more. If there is one difference I have noticed between London and New York, it's that in New York other pedestrians don't take kindly to you standing in the middle of the pavement doing nothing.

As I enter the lobby I walked into last week for my interview, it seemed different somehow, it kind of feels like I belong here. Walking through the turnstiles onto the main floor, I head for a lift. I hadn't realized how busy the lifts would be at this time in the morning and suddenly became breathless. "You can do this," I quietly mutter to myself. "It's all in your head." Taking several deep breaths, I head to the set of doors that's the least crowded. As they opened, I let everyone else pile in before me. I just hope that my method of being as close to the doors as possible will help, it doesn't. After allowing the car to climb fifteen floors I have to step out and gather myself, this earns me a few stares, but I didn't care, only nine levels to go. As I wait for the lift again, I make a mental note to leave ten minutes earlier in the morning to allow time for this situation.

Twenty-four floors... I've made it! Yes! I mentally congratulate myself. I head into the editor's office to let her know I've arrived and to ask where she wants me. Vanessa Falls' office is very modern and white, it reminds me more of a dentist surgery it looks so sterile. "Hey, sorry to bother you-" she interrupts me before I even have a chance to finish my sentence.

"Not a problem Dana. Nice to see you bright and early, I'll just show you to your desk and then you can head up to meet Mr. Day. I'll have your assignment on your desk by the time you get back."

Vanessa is so uniquely beautiful, with her shoulder length chestnut brown ringlet hair and hazel eyes, she's slim and tall, at least five foot ten without the heels. She looks so at ease with herself. As she comes around her desk I get a good look at her long slender legs, they're beautiful. Following her out of her office we pass several long legged slim model types in little skirts, and suddenly I feel very overdressed... and short.

"This is your desk. Assignments generally come with a three-day deadline, but some may be shorter or longer. When you get back, we will talk about your first shoot, and you can ask me any questions you have then. Right now Mr. Day will be waiting, and he doesn't like to be kept waiting."

Suddenly feeling like I'm a naughty school girl late for class, I make a hasty retreat to the lift and press the call button. As the car arrives, there are only a few people on it, taking a deep breath I step on and press the button for the fortieth floor. We move one level, and six people get on taking the total amount of people in the lift car to nine, and I'm pushed to the back. As I watch the last body enter, I just manage to see him place a key in the panel with the floor numbers on and press the button for the top floor.

The doors start to close as I'm taking deep breaths and close my eyes. It's not working, and I start to panic. Feeling like my chest is about to implode in on itself, I push to the front and start slamming the floor buttons on the side to get the car to stop.

"Are you okay?" I hear a woman's voice ask me.

"I-I c-can't b-breathe," I stutter, placing my forehead on the cold, closed doors. Gasping for air and willing the lift to stop, I become painfully aware of someone's hands on my shoulders. My body feels like it's receiving a jolt of electricity with their touch and it's not helping matters. I tried to shake them off, but they just tighten their hold.

"Calm down and take long, deep breaths." Startled by a raspy, masculine whisper, I still my movements instantly. "I said long deep breaths, not stop breathing." The authoritative sound of his voice makes me pull in a deep breath just as the doors open on the top floor. I scurry out as quick as I can, tripping over my feet and start to fall. I close my eyes ready for the impact, but the ground never comes. Instead, I feel that tingle of electricity go through me again and realized the stranger from the lift is hauling me into an upright position.

"Take deep breaths, slowly, in and out. Rachael, can you get me a bar of chocolate and a can of coke please." Staring at my feet, I realize I'm starting to calm a bit. I choose this moment to look at the stranger who by now must think I'm a complete nut case.

Wow... He has emerald green eyes that look like they sparkle in the light, floppy brown hair and a smile that could melt my insides to nothing.

"Hi there," he says looking into my eyes like he's searching for something. "How are you feeling? Let's take a seat."

Pulling me over to a seat in the reception waiting area, he urges me to sit. "Thank you for all your help. I feel terribly embarrassed."

"Don't be." His smile is so genuine.

"One chocolate bar and one can of coke, sir."

The young receptionist holds them out to me, but my friendly stranger takes them from her.

"Thank you, Rachael. Can you hold all my calls and tell my next appointment I'll be with them as soon as possible."

"Yes, sir." Walking away, I couldn't help but stare, there are so many beautiful women in this place.

"Chocolate or coke?" I'm brought back from my daydreaming by the handsome stranger. "You need sugar."

Looking from one to another. "The chocolate bar, please." I reach to take it, and our hands brush, there it is again, the tingle of electricity. I snatch my hand away. "Thank you, I'm Dana," I say, slightly flustered.

His lips curve at the edges as if he's trying to suppress a smile. "Edward."

Finishing the last of the chocolate, really yummy, but I'll definitely be hitting the gym after work now, I stand to leave. "Thank you again, Edward, but I'm going to have to run. I had a meeting at eight-thirty with Mr. Day, and I'm already five minutes late. I've been told the big boss man doesn't like to be kept waiting. Apparently, he's a right old grump."

"The big boss man, huh?" He has a little chuckle then composes himself. "I'll walk you there, just to make sure you don't faint."

"I'll be all right now, thank you."

"It's not a problem, my office is that way." He gestures the way to go, and I head on.

Reaching Mr. Day's office, my nerves have kicked it up a notch. Knocking on the door and waiting for a beat, there is no answer. Not knowing whether to knock again or not, I'm startled by Edward barging past me and opening the door.

"You can't do that, what if he's on the phone or something?"

Walking straight in, Edward heads around and parks himself in the chair behind Mr. Day's desk. "Where have you been? I've been waiting seven minutes for you." His expression feigning seriousness.

"You're going to get yourself in trouble."

"Take another look at the door, Miss Spencer." As he points to the door, I start to feel light headed again. Please be a nightmare, please, please, please.

EDWARD DAY C.E.O.

Of course, he is.

"Take a seat, Miss Spencer, let's get to know each other." I pick a seat opposite him and stare at my feet, blushing.

"Why didn't you say you were Mr. Day when I said I had a meeting?" I ask feeling rather angry and embarrassed.

"Because it was fun," he said with a wickedly sexy smile, but I was now feeling more irritated. Who does he think he is? So what if he's the boss, surely that doesn't give him the right to humiliate others.

"Well, at least you find it funny. I'm glad you can have a laugh at someone else's expense." His brow knits in the middle, and he recoils at my outburst.

"No Dana, no. That's not what I meant, you misunderstood me." Now it was my turn to look taken aback. "It was fun to talk to someone as me, Edward, and not as the big boss man. You know, the one that's a right old grump." He smirks and rolls his eyes. "You'll be surprised how much people avoid talking to me because I'm the boss." With this, he gives a small sheepish smile, and at that moment he seems a little vulnerable. My heart swells, and I let out a small giggle, and then he does too.

"Oh god, I'm sorry. What must you think of me?"

"That I would like to get to know you more."

Not totally sure of what he means by that statement, I decided to take the safe road. "It was fun, and I don't generally find it this easy to talk to people. Thank you for making me feel so welcome Mr. Day."

"Edward, please call me Edward."

"Okay. What do you want to know?" His smile somehow put me at such ease, but that also makes me wary.

"Where in England do you come from?"

"London."

"Are you settling in well in Manhattan?"

"Yes."

"Such a big talker, I can't even get a word in." His smile reaches his eyes. It's so infectious, I can't help but giggle. "That's a beautiful sound." I'm momentarily stunned by his unprofessionalism but decide he's just trying to calm my nerves. "So how's the first day going so far?"

Looking at the clock, I wonder to myself if he is joking. I've been in the building half an hour and spent the last fifteen minutes with him. "The first ten minutes were great, right up until I stepped in the lift-"

"Lift?"

"Elevator," I reply. He gives me a small knowing smile, and I wonder if he's deliberately being a dick or if he thinks he's just being funny.

"Tell me what happened in the... um... lift." Usually, I would laugh at the mocking, but I was stunned by his unexpected question that I didn't know how to answer.

Lifting my hand and rubbing the back of my neck I let out a deep breath. Some sort of emotion crosses his face, anger maybe, but then it's gone. "I'm claustrophobic," I say blushing with embarrassment at the memory.

"And you got in an elevator?" he asks looking slightly confused, and I understand why.

"Normally I can do a few floors at a time, but then you put your stupid key thing in, and the lift wouldn't stop."

He looks at me like he's contemplating something but nothing could prepare me for his next question. "How did you get the scars on your wrists?"

Sitting in stunned silence while he watches me, I have no answers. "Dana, I require complete honesty from my employees, it's important to me. I asked you a question, please answer it."

Something in his voice told me he wasn't asking for a reply, he was demanding one. "I don't see what my personal life has to do with you."

"It has everything to do with me. It's my job to take care of my employees. Did you try to commit suicide?"

Feeling like I had just been slapped, I stare at his serious face, open mouthed and stunned. "Oh my god. No! Thank you for the meeting Mr. Day," I hiss through gritted teeth. Now he's the one who looks like he's been slapped. "It was lovely to meet you, but I should really get to work." I stand and hold my hand out to shake his. He takes my hand and pulls it to him, lightly rubbing his thumb over the scars. "For the record, it was a long time ago, and I don't wish for my past to cause judgments in my future."

The way he looks at me at that moment was primal, I felt it all the way down in the pit of my stomach, but he stays quiet. I turn to leave, as I open the door I hear him take in a deep breath. The air
30

between us is so charged even I'm struggling to think straight, does he feel it too?

"Dana." His voice is so masculine, I turn to him and see the raw heat in his eyes, he knows he has my attention. "Don't do it again or there will be consequences."

It was a warning. How dare he? This is my boss, and he is a psycho. I've had enough of them to last a lifetime. Straightening up I simply reply, "I didn't plan to."

Arriving back at my desk, I find my assignment. I just want to get out of here. How can a day start off so well and only forty-five minutes in, have me running for the door?

"How was your first meeting with Mr. Day?" Vanessa appears next to me with such a glow. Even if you wanted to hate her, you never could. Do I tell her about the meeting?

I decide against it. "It was all right." I try giving a sincere smile.

"Well, he seems to think so." I must look really shocked because she tries to reassure me. "He just called down. It was all good, I swear. He's looking forward to working with you." Apparently, my attempt at a smile didn't hide my wryness. "Don't look so scared, your first assignment is an easy one. Sightseeing in New York, you have until Wednesday. Now go make those tourist attractions look beautiful, and I'll see you at five."

I feel like I'm in a dream. How did I get this lucky? "Thanks, Vanessa. See you later." I wave goodbye and head to the lifts to start my descent. When I finally reach the lobby, I try and call James to fill him in on this morning's events, but there is no answer. I get his voicemail a further three times, I feel a sudden pang of panic. I decide to swing by the apartment before I start my assignment.

Running through the front door I'm greeted with an eerie silence, where is he?

"Jay, Jay? James are you here?" As I'm nearing the bathroom door I hear the shower, the door is closed. I reach for the door handle and pull down, it's locked. Panic shoots through me. James and I have a rule not to lock any doors in case one of us needs to get to the other. "James! Open the door!" Banging on the door and trying to get to him, I continue pleading. "Please, I'm begging you. We can deal with this together. JAMES!" I hear the lock turn and the door open.

Standing in front of me dripping wet, I know what James was doing. He was trying to forget the pain on the inside, by inflicting pain on the outside. I don't know how long he was under the freezing water, but it was long enough to make his lips and nails turn blue. I grab a towel from the rail and wrap it around him. I pull him to me, to hug him and warm him, we both just stand there for a minute. "First chance I get, I'm removing that god damn lock," I say to him.

Pulling back he looks at me. "Dana." With pleading eyes, I know what he is asking me. He's not ready to talk, he just needs me to help him take the

33

pain away.

"Are you sure?" He nods, and so do I. "Okay. I'll get the belt and meet you in the black room."

# Chapter 2

"Harder, Dana. Please harder!" he shouted at me while holding the rail above his head to support himself. Then with a satisfied cry, I knew I had reached the right amount of force required to push him to the limit, and this would all be over soon.

Listening to him scream - every time I gripped the belt, lifted my arm and brought it down heavily across his back - was so hard. Tears were swimming in my eyes. This was better than the alternative, always. We used to sometimes use a whip to cause a sharper pain, but it was leaving too many scars on our skin, in recent months we've only used the belt. Something I'm grateful for, as the belt causes a lot less damage. James used to self-harm by standing under freezing water till he couldn't take the pain anymore. The problem with this is that he came so close to dying of hypothermia. So I made James a promise, that if he needed the pain to tell me and I would help him do it safely. After he had been discharged from the hospital, I confessed my own self-harming to him.

After what Grant had done, I struggled with emotions. I didn't feel anything, I was just numb. I started going to martial arts classes and contact defense classes. One lesson I sprained my ankle, that's when I felt something again for the first time in months, it was pain, but I felt it, and I knew I was still alive. After that, I sought out the pain in extreme sports, anything that came with the thrill. Anything that came with the fear and the real possibility of danger, but it escalated. Looking at a razor blade one night in the bath, I started thinking about what it would feel like. One thing led to another, and I lost control. I was just slashing away at my wrists, luckily my Mum found me, and she got me the help I needed. I told James how seeing a counselor had helped, but it wasn't enough. So he made me the same promise I made him. After that, we moved in together and made the black room.

"Enough!" he snaps. Throwing the belt down, I grab the dressing gown off the back of the door and wrap him up in it. Leading him to his room, I lay him face down on his bed. I quickly gather the warm water and cotton wool I prepared beforehand. Very gently cleaning the welts and blood on his back, I study the road map of scars from all the previous times in the black room.

"So are you going to tell me what brought all this on?" I wait patiently, I know he will tell me in his own time.

Taking a deep breath, he whispers, "I broke up with Lewis."

Damn. "Jay honey, I'm so sorry. I don't want to sound like a bitch, but you knew you had to do it at some point. I mean, you're seeing another man."

"You're right, you sound like a total bitch." He managed a weak smile, and I know he's going to be okay. "It wasn't because I broke up with him. You're right, I knew I had to do it. It's what he said."

"You know you don't have to tell me right now Jay." I can see he's struggling with this and right now he needs to take the lead.

The way he looks at me, he's contemplating what to say, as if what he is going to say will hurt *me*. "He told me I was your little lap dog, a lost puppy and that I followed you where ever you go. That you're just using me until you find someone to spend your life with. That it's the reason people keep leaving me and why I'll end up a lonely old man. That-" He starts sobbing into his pillow.

I grab the antiseptic cream and start rubbing it into his back, giving him a moment to grieve his lost relationship. James has been abandoned by everyone he ever loved, one of those people being me. He spent five years on the street when his drug-addled mother kicked him out on his sixteenth birthday. I will never forgive myself and carry the guilt every day for leaving and not being there for him. After I escaped Grant and found James again, he moved in with us, and we've taken care of each other ever since.

"Well, he never really liked me anyway," I say and see James silently laughing as he calms his shuddering breath and wipes his swollen eyes. "You know none of what he said is true, right?"

He nods. "Yeah, but it doesn't hurt any less. He used my insecurities to deliberately hurt me because I unintentionally hurt him." He shakes his head and sits up, looking at me with that gorgeous smile of his, any bloke would be lucky to have him. "Thank you for everything, Dana." I smile, so he knows it's okay, but it doesn't make beating the crap out of him any easier. "Right, enough of this. Why are you here and not at work?"

"I was trying to call you, to tell you about my morning and my first assignment but you didn't answer, and I panicked." Tears prick my stinging eyes. The build up of emotions this morning from the panic attack in the lift, the supercharged atmosphere and weird conversation with Mr. Day, and now this with James has started to take its toll.

"Hey you, no crying. Okay?" He looks at me

with such sympathetic eyes. "It's done, everything's fine now. So tell me how your morning was and what's the first job?"

"Sightseeing in New York." He arches his brows. "I know very cliché." We both have a little laugh. "Are you up for walking around and taking some pictures with me?"

He gives me one of his big grins as if half-an-hour ago never happened. "Hell yeah, sweetie."

We arrive back at the Daylight tower at ten to five, laughing and going through some of the pictures I took today. "I think the ones you photo bombed are the best, but I don't think my boss will think the same as me." I smile at his full belly laugh.

"That's only because I look totally sexy in them, maybe he'll dish out a few of his *consequences* to me," James says with a wink and wraps his arm around my shoulder.

I told James all about what happened this morning with Mr. Day, he tried to make me see the funny side, but his words still kept niggling away at me.

"Dana, if he ever says anything to you like that again, I'll personally go see him myself. You shouldn't be nervous about going to work."

"Thanks, Jay."

We enter the lobby, and I tell James to wait for me, while I run upstairs. The quicker I let them know I'm back, the quicker James and I can celebrate with a drink.

"Hey Vanessa, I'm back." With three attempts at the lift, I'm standing in the doorway to her office.

She looks up at me. "Hey, how did you get on?"

"Yeah, really well. Got most of what I needed today, going to get the last few tomorrow and possibly retake some of today's ones." I feel pretty proud of myself, I can't believe everything I've managed to accomplish today.

She stands from her office chair and comes towards me. She smiles at me, placing her hand on my upper arm. "You've done really well today, now get yourself off home, and I'll see you in the morning."

"See you tomorrow." I smile and wave as I press the call button for the lift, determined to make it all the way down without having to get out. The car doors open and I push the ground floor. I step out after twelve levels, half way there. I manage to make it all the way down by the second time.

Walking towards the turnstiles, I wave to get James' attention. "Dana." A deep throaty voice to my right stops me in my tracks. Turning to the familiar sound I come face to face with Edward. All of this morning's conversation starts to ricochet around in my head, and I just want to get out of here. "How was your first day?"

"Mr. Day, hello. It was great thanks." James must have seen my discomfort because he picked that moment to call out my name. We both turn to him. "I'll see you tomorrow Mr. Day."

"I can see you're in a rush, anything nice

planned for tonight?" Stepping closer to me, I take a step back. He frowns but doesn't attempt to close the gap anymore.

"Just off to the pub." Starting to turn, I feel him watching me.

"Pub?"

"For a drink."

A look of recognition crosses his face with a suppressed grin he says, "Oh you mean a bar."

"No, I mean a pub." He gives me another knowing smile, and this time I know he's doing it deliberately.

He laughs, and it makes my stomach flutter. "They're called bars here. You should learn to speak proper English. Have a good time." He turns towards the lifts.

Just then I realize what he said. "I do speak proper English, I'm from England!" I shout after him. The sound of his laugh vibrating around the lobby ignited something inside me. This can only be a bad thing, yet I find myself looking forward to seeing him in the morning.

"Yep he's hot, I'll accept his consequences any day," James cooed as he slipped his arm in mine. We both laughed hard. Feeling like my back is burning I turn around to see Edward staring at me, with narrowed eyes, he looks extremely pissed off. "Forget about him sweetie, let's go get drunk." Kissing James on the cheek, I grab his hand and set off in search of the nearest bar.

"What is this one called?" I ask James letting the liquid slide down my throat.

"This would be a Cosmo," he replies looking like he'd just sucked on a lemon.

"It's not that bad, Jay." I manage, laughing at the face he is pulling. "I'm going to pop to the ladies." Just as I stand my legs turn to jelly. "When did I get this drunk?"

"About three cocktails ago." We both burst out laughing.

"That's rather irresponsible." We turn to the

familiar voice that interrupted us. "Get up, we're leaving."

Looking at Edward, I'm too stunned to even reply, James isn't though. "I'm sorry, who are you? And who the hell do you think you are?" James continues before he can be stopped. James knows exactly who Edward is but I leave him to it, he's in the zone. "And I am not irresponsible enough to let Dana leave with a complete stranger."

"I'm her boss. I would have thought you would have taken better care of your girlfriend instead of continuing to pour alcohol into her," Edward counters just a little too calmly. Turning to me he snarls, "You have to work tomorrow, Dana, I don't appreciate my employees being intoxicated."

Coming to my senses, I realize I'm getting angry. "That's right, you're my boss, not my babysitter. I am an adult, if I want to drink and get drunk, I will. My boyfriend always makes sure I'm safe." I argue, throwing my hands up in exasperation. "Come on Jay, the nights ruined now anyway.

Goodnight Mr. Day, see you in the morning." I grab my bag, while James is still chuckling away next to me at my referring to him as my boyfriend.

Trying to get past Edward without looking at or touching him was difficult, he's standing so close to me like he's drawing me into him. Stumbling past him he grabs my arm at the elbow. "Let me give you a ride home at least, you're not in a fit state to walk that far." I search his sparkling green eyes for some sort of hint as to what he's thinking. "Please Dana, I need to know you're safe." His eyes pleading with me, I nod.

"Saves me trying to hail a cab, I suppose."

Placing his hand on the small of my back, I jump slightly. "Relax," he whispers in my ear. Relaxing is very hard with that soft, sensual voice cooing at me.

We walk out of the bar and onto the pavement, the fresh air hits me, and I start to sway. Edward pulls his hands to my hips to steady me. James pulls me away from Edward and to his side. "I've got her Mr. Day," he says, following behind me into the back of a black car parked outside, once seated he wraps his arms around me. Edward climbs in after James looking like a five-year-old having a strop. What's his problem?

"Peter, we need to make a stop off on the way home at Miss Spencer's apartment."

"Yes, sir." Peter nods.

While James gives Peter our address, I turn to Edward. "Does everyone jump when you tell them to?"

Edward tries not to smile, but his eyes are giving him away. "I don't like being told no, especially when I'm paying them."

How can someone be so arrogant? "What happens if someone says no?"

"I try harder to convince them to say yes, or I fire them." His face is so serious, I can't work out if he's joking or not.

"Well, how convenient that is for you. Why would anyone want to say no?" I say with as much sarcasm as I can muster.

Edward doesn't say much more the rest of the

journey home. Pulling up outside the apartment, Peter comes round and opens the door. Edward climbs out, followed by James. As I'm climbing out Edward steps in between James and me. "I'd like to talk to you alone." He states trying to stop me getting out of the car.

"Get off her," I hear James say behind him.

"I just want to have a quick word with her. It will only take a moment." Still trying to push me back in the car, I try to reach out for James who grabs my hand and pulls me out.

"Don't touch her, look at what you've done." James continues, noticing my breathing has become erratic he begins to rub my back. I'm bent over with my hands on my knees while trying to curb the beginnings of a panic attack. Feeling Edward's eyes on me, I look up.

He must see the fear in my eyes. "I'm sorry if I scared you," he says sheepishly, his brow furrowing. He gets in the car and turns back to me. "I'm really sorry, I don't know what came over me." He sounds confused. He closes the car door, and it drives off.

I stand up straight, and James puts his arm around me. "I think this calls for a glass of wine and a Google search," he says leading me inside.

I had to laugh. "You know what Jay, that's not a bad idea."


"Right, what have you come up with?" I ask, flopping down next to James on the sofa and handing him a glass of white wine.

He takes a sip of his drink. "After I typed in his name, I got a lot of news articles. He's on Forbes list of the top fifty richest men in the world, owns several properties and vehicles, he's involved in a lot of businesses and supports a lot of charities. He inherited his business from his Uncle Nicolas Day when he died aged thirty-eight in a tragic accident, all the usual billionaire stuff. It also brought up a lot of pictures with him and other women. Very rarely is he seen with the same woman twice, except about six years ago, he was in a committed relationship with a woman called Payton-"

"What happened?" I enquire.

"Now that's the funny part, I can't find anything on why they broke up. Since then he hasn't been in any sort of relationship, although I did find these."

James turns the laptop towards me and shows me two articles. The first is about a public argument he had with his older brother Andrew which ended in him literally knocking his brother out, the picture has been removed for legal reasons. The second is of a woman called Sarah, claiming he beat her up and forced her into having sex with him after she told him she wasn't interested and again the picture has been removed.

"So basically, he has a raging temper, and he raped a woman because she said no?" I ask completely disgusted, remembering what Edward said, in the car about not liking it when people say no.

"Yes it looks bad, but the charges were dropped after no evidence of rape was found," he confirms.

"Do you think he paid her off?"

"I don't know, it all looks a bit suspicious. I mean look how he treated you tonight. You'd be wise to stay away from him sweetie."

"My brain is hurting Jay. He really didn't seem the type. But you're right, after tonight and the way he tried to put me back in the car... What would have happened?"

James hugs me tight to him, and I bury my head in the crook of his neck, thinking about what might have happened tonight if James hadn't of been there.

"Dana, don't even think about it, it never would have happened. Besides, I would never have left you on your own. Come on, let's get to bed it's late."

James walks me to my room, passing by the black room I try to ignore it. James just looks at me and shakes his head, it's amazing how he reads me so well. We say goodnight, and I watch James walk back to his room.

Closing my door, I start to undress and climb into my king sized four poster bed. I lie down and close my eyes, pulling the cover up and over my shoulders. Sleep is evading me, my brain is overworking and the events of the day with Edward just play over and over. Why does he affect me so much? The man abuses women, he beat up his brother and probably used his money to get out of a rape charge. He goes through women like clean underwear, except Payton... What did he do to her? What would have happened if I had left with him in the bar? What If I had got back in the car? What did he mean when he said there would be consequences? I have to stop thinking, I have to get this out of my system.

Sitting upright, I turn on the bedside lamp and pull a razor blade out of the drawer. Holding it, staring at it, I know I don't want to do it and that I should just put it back but my head is telling me otherwise. I'm at the point of no return, the point when all I can feel is something crawling beneath my skin, and I need to get it out. You'll feel so much better once it's done Dana, you know you will. Just a little cut, that's all you need to do. Lightly rubbing the sharp object over my wrists, I take a few deep breaths and start to push down, slicing across my skin. As the blood drips onto my quilt, I realize I've gone too deep. Throwing the blade to the floor I run to the bathroom, to grab a clean towel and antiseptic cream. James must hear me fussing around because he comes flying into the bathroom and starts shouting at me.

"What did you do, you stupid woman?" He grabs my arm and holds the towel down firmly, then the floodgates open.

Sobbing, I try to talk. "I'm so sorry Jay, I don't know what came over me. I'm sorry, I'm sorry, I'm sorry."

James pulls me to him, his t-shirt soaking up my tears. "It's okay honey, shhh now. I knew something was wrong I should have checked you were okay before I left you. I'm the one who should

53

be sorry." James holds the towel tighter on my arm after checking the wound. We silently cry together.

Sitting at the kitchen table, James has cleaned my arm up, applied antiseptic cream and is now wrapping a bandage around it. "Why didn't you come and get me, Dana? We could have dealt with this together."

"I don't know, really I don't. It all happened so quickly I wasn't thinking." I feel the tears pricking my sore eyes, and a lump in my throat starts to form.

James wipes the stray tear that runs down my cheek. "None of that now, what's done is done, we move forward."

Instead of going to my room, I jump in bed with James. Sometimes I wish he wasn't gay, he truly is my soul mate. With my head on his chest, I drift off into a dreamless sleep.

# Chapter 3

The next morning brings a hangover from hell and a sore arm. I can smell bacon and coffee. I get up and go to the bathroom, James has already been in here and cleaned up the mess. Turning on the shower, I take off my pajamas and unwrap the bandage from my wrist. The water is just a bit hotter than I would like, but it feels amazing. I stare down at my arm wondering what the hell I was thinking, I really am stupid. I must have been in the shower some time because James comes looking for me just as I'm getting out.

"Good morning beautiful. I was just about to send out a search party." After last night I didn't expect him to be so cheery with me. "How are you feeling?"

"I'm fine, feeling stupid and embarrassed but

other than that I'm all good." Hoping my smile will convince him.

"Show me your arm." I turn my wrist to him as he examines it. "This is really deep Dana, it could have been dangerous, but it's scabbing up nicely. Grab the cream and a bandage, and I'll give it another clean before you go to work."

After drying my hair and putting some lotion on, I search in my wardrobe for long sleeve tops. It's a good thing it's October, or it might look a bit weird. Finally settling on a cream cashmere top and black suit trousers I head to the living room. James has a cup of coffee and a bacon sandwich waiting for me at the table.

"Sit," he says and gestures to a chair. Rolling up the sleeve of my left arm he starts his attentive cleaning of the wound.

"Thank you, Jay," I say feeling so much love for the man sitting in front of me.

"It's just a bacon sandwich, don't go all gooey eyed on me." He brushes off my thanks just like he always does, he knows it wasn't the breakfast I was thanking him for.

"Have you got plans for today?" Clingy as it might be, I could use his company today.

"I've got a job interview for Reuters on Wall Street at ten but then nothing after that."

"Do you fancy lunch, and a walk around some tourist attractions with me later?"

"Girl, I'm always up for spending time with you. I'll meet you in the lobby of Daylight at noon."

"Sounds like a plan." I smile at him knowing that yesterday is in the past, for both of us.


I get to work ten minutes early, time to face the lifts. The vestibules are quite packed this morning, so I decide to break up the journey into three trips, stopping at the eighth, sixteenth and twenty-fourth floors getting to my desk with three minutes to spare.

"Morning, are you ready for another day?" Vanessa must be taking something, no one is this happy at nine in the morning. Her skin glowing with a slight tan, her legs look even better in her paisley green skirt.

"Yeah, I'm all set. Just going to spend the morning uploading the photos I took yesterday and go back out this afternoon." Starting up the computer, I get everything I need out of my bag.

"You know you have all day tomorrow to upload the photos, they don't need to be in till five." She sits on the edge of my desk.

"I know, but the weather forecast doesn't look too good today. Just in case I can't get the right photo, I'd like to know I have tomorrow to get them."

"Good thinking. Well, I'll leave you to it. If you need me, I'll be in my office." Getting up, she gives me a smile that flashes all of her Hollywood white teeth.

"Thanks, Vanessa."

I'm working for a matter of minutes before my desk phone rings, I really don't know if I want to answer it. "Hello, Dana Spencer speaking."

"Sometimes I wonder if you forget about me, not even calling me to tell me how your first day went, and then having to track you down myself."

"Hey Mum, I'm sorry. Jay and I went for drinks after work and didn't get in till late. I was going to call you later. My first day was great, how are you and Richard?" I love my Mum, but she can get a bit much sometimes. I think it's just fear that I'm going to disappear again, but she can't go two days without speaking to me, or she panics.

"We were just talking about having you and James over for dinner Saturday, what do you think? I'm glad everything's going well darling."

She sounds so happy it makes me burst out into a huge grin. "Saturday sounds great Mum. Listen I'm at work, so I've got to go, but I will call you tonight, I promise."

"Ok darling, I love you."

"I love you too Mum."

I put the phone down only for it to ring a second later, *seriously Mother,* I say to myself. I pick it up. "What did you forget?"

"I don't think that is the most professional way

to answer your work phone."

Oh crap! "Mr. Day, I'm sorry. What can I do for you?"

"Nothing Dana, I was calling about last night. I feel I might have overstepped some boundaries. Please call me Edward."

His voice is so sexy it makes the hairs on the back of my neck stand up. How does he do this to me? "I'd rather not Mr. Day, we have a professional relationship that is all. Yes, you crossed the line last night but what's done is done, everything is fine. Are you sure I can't do anything for you?

"No, thank you. I'm sorry you feel that way. I really hope I can make it up to you sometime. It was nice talking to you. If I need anything, I'll call."

"Goodbye, sir." I hear a sharp intake of breath before putting the phone down. I can barely believe my own brashness. The man gives me goosebumps in a good and bad way. Just as I put the phone down, I hear the chime of the lift. A young looking woman comes out with a large bouquet of flowers.

She walks over to the *Mode* receptionist, they talk for a moment and then the receptionist points to me. Huh?

"Delivery for Dana Spencer?" she asks me.

"Yeah that's me," I say signing for the large arrangement of orange and white calla lilies. "Thank you." She walks back to the lift. *They're probably from my Mum*, I think to myself as I open the card that accompanied the flowers.

*Forgive me, please.*
*I'm truly sorry for my behavior.*
*Edward.*

His mobile number is written under his name, I grab my phone and type out a quick response.

**You're forgiven.**
**Thank you for the flowers, they're beautiful.**
**Dana x**

After working at my desk all morning with no more interruptions, it's finally noon and time for lunch. Packing up my things I go into Vanessa's office. "I'm heading out to lunch and then going to head on to some sights, I'll-" I come to an abrupt halt at the sight of Edward. "Sorry, is Vanessa around?"

He looks at me, a bit nervous. "She should be back in a moment but if you're in a rush you can go, I'll let her know."

"Cheers." Edward is running his hands through his hair as if deciding to say something but chooses not to, so I turn and leave.

In the lobby, James is already waiting. "How did the interview go?" I ask as I reach him and pull him into a hug.

"Pretty well, yeah. Where do you want to go to lunch?" He's so happy, it makes me feel warm.

Linking my arm in his. "I think we should try the new Mexican place just round the corner." He nods, and just as we're walking out, I hear the familiar sound of Edward's voice calling after me. Ignoring the boss could get me in trouble, I'll just pretend I didn't hear him and talk to him later.

"You did not say that to your boss," James says after I tell him about the call from Edward this morning.

"Well, he shouldn't have done what he did last night. Although I do feel a little guilty now after he sent the flowers," I say and change the subject to dinner Saturday. "I think Mum just wants to check up on us."

"Can't wait, we can all go for a drink after to that private member's bar that Richard invited us to before," James says with excitement.

"I'll let Mum know later, I promised I'd call her. Maybe you can have a bit of a chat with her too, so she doesn't keep fussing over me," I plead with my roommate, who seems to think it's funny that I'm feeling harassed.

"Fine, but you owe me one." He smiles. "I need a shirt ironed for dinner Saturday, especially if we go out."

"You know if you wanted a favor, you could have just asked. You didn't need to use my Mum against me." Throwing a handful of tortilla chips at him across the table, I hit him straight in the head. We both start laughing so loud that people start to stare. "Are we hitting the mats tonight?" James and I took up a kickboxing class at the gym and found it's a necessary stress release.

"Yes, I think I need it. How's your arm? Are you feeling better today?" he asks with caution.

"Fine and yes," I say after a thoughtful moment. "Can we not talk about it, I just want to forget about it." James nods his agreement, and we spend the rest of lunch deciding what other sights I should photograph.

"Get out of the way you idiot." I couldn't stop laughing at James. I can't get any work done when he's around. "Let me get this last photo, and we can go."

"Fine, what do you want to do after the gym?" he says moving out of the way of the Chrysler building.

"That really is a stupid question, Jay."

I see the concern in his eyes before he starts to speak. "You can't drink away your problems, Dana."

"It's not problems Jay, it's reality, and there is nothing I can do about it. Not even Richard has had any luck finding Nathan or Grant. So if I want to drink to numb the pain, I will."

"But if they do find them-"

"They haven't, now drop it *please!*" I blink back the tears threatening to fall and compose myself, it's been weeks since I've cried over what Grant has done to me and I refuse to let him break me again.

"Come on, let's get you back to work. Then we can head to the gym, and you can kick the shit out of me for opening my big mouth." He gives me his biggest, cheesiest grin. I look up at him with my tear filled eyes, he sees the pain and the fear. "I love you, Dana, I'm sorry."

"Just hug me, will you?" We walk back to the Daylight tower, and James hangs around in the lobby as usual. I go to my desk, drop everything off and then head over to Vanessa's office to let her know I'm back.

"Dana?" A deep, husky voice comes up behind me.

"Mr. Day, you startled me. Is everything ok?"

He's looking at me like he's trying to figure something out. "I think I should be asking you that question. Have you been crying, what's wrong?"

"Nothing," I say, casually trying to brush him off. Who does he think he is, my therapist?

"Don't lie to me, please. Clearly, something has upset you, and I'd like to help."

I start to feel the anger rising now. Why does everyone think I need their help? "There is nothing you can do to help me. Excuse me, I have a kickboxing class at the gym that I must attend. Then I'm heading

66

home to a bottle of wine that has my name on it."

He glares at me, opening his mouth to say something and closing it again. Then he just steps to the side. Relieved, I run past him and out of the building as quick as possible. How does he make me feel like that, like I can't breathe when he's around?

"Dana, chill out!" James shouts at me while curled up and protecting his head.

I know I shouldn't take my anger out on James, but things just aren't sitting right. "Sorry Jay, I think I'm going to have to leave my job."

"Why?" He looks just as confused as me.

"Mr. Day, the way he is and his behavior, something isn't right." Maybe I'm over thinking this but why would my boss of two days be so interested in a photographer.

"Just see what happens. Maybe you affect him as much as he affects you. Ouch!" he says curling back up into a ball.

I couldn't help it I didn't mean to take James

down that hard, I just needed him to shut up. "I'm being stupid, I know. Right, I need a glass of wine."

"You want to go home or to a bar?" he asks.

"A bar sounds good. I'm going to have a shower, and I'll meet you out in front of the changing rooms."


Sitting in a wine bar two hours later and I'm drunk. "Dana, can I please take you home now?" I hear James' voice, but I don't answer. Instead, I down the rest of my glass and make my way to the exit.

"It's cold." James takes off his jacket and puts it around me. Just then I feel someone watching me. As I turn around, I watch as a familiar silhouette moves behind a building. "James, did you see that?"

"See what?" he replies slightly baffled, but I don't really hear him. Instead, I walk towards where the shadowy figure was standing. "Dana, what are you doing?" I look around the corner, and no one is there.

"Nothing, I must be seeing things." I smile at

him and grab his hand. "Let's go."

# Chapter 4

I wake up Friday morning, and I just want the world to swallow me whole. Today is the worst day of my life. Today I just want to stay in bed and shut everything out, but I can't, I have to work. The last couple of days have been easy, and Vanessa has been happy with my work. As for Edward, things have been great between us, and we really seem to be settling into our boss and employee roles.

*Knock, knock.*

"Hey sweetie, you awake?" James pops his head around the door.

"I'm up, you okay?" I manage a smile, but it doesn't convince James. He puts a coffee and a muffin on my bedside table and climbs into my bed, wrapping me up in his arms. He leans over and lights the candle in the muffin. "Happy birthday to Nathan.

Make a wish and blow out the candle."

I close my eyes and then blow out the flame. "Thanks, James." Where are you, Nathan?

He takes my arm. "Your wrist is looking better, only that big chunk of scab left." I nod and smile. "Come on, we need to get dressed and get you to work. This is the last day we can hang out before I start my new job."


An hour later we head out the front door. "Oh crap," I say just as the door slams shut. "Jay, please tell me you have your key?"

"No. Just a minute ago you told me you had yours." He gives me a murderous look.

"Yeah, but you see, my bag with the keys in are on the other side of that door." I look at him apologetically.

His face softens. "It's okay we will tell the doorman when we get downstairs, surely the building manager has a master key, or they can call a locksmith." He can tell how sorry I am because he puts his arm around me and says, "Hey don't worry about it, it's not the end of the world. You've got a lot on your mind today."

I had a feeling today would just be one big disaster, and I was right. Not only did I break my heel on the way to work, but I also got soaked when a passing taxi drove through a puddle. At Starbucks, the lid wasn't on my coffee properly, and I managed to spill scalding hot liquid down the front of my shirt. I take a seat at one of the tables, while James orders his coffee and wonder what else could go wrong.

"Ready for work," James asks with raised eyebrows at my coffee stained top.

"As I'll ever be." We walk in silence to the Daylight tower, I can feel James taking a breath every few minutes as if in preparation to say something, but he remains silent. "I'll be right down," I say to him as we reach the lobby. Making my way to the lifts, I press the call button.

"Miss Spencer, how are you today?" Edward's voice warms me inside.

"Fine, thanks. You?" I ask more to be polite.

"Better now that you're here," he says with a sly smile, then his face turns to a frown as he eyes my top.

"The lid wasn't on my coffee properly, a taxi soaked me, I've broken my shoe, and I've locked myself out of my apartment," I explain quickly, blushing crimson. The lift doors open and we step inside. "Please don't put your key thing in."

He looks at me and then nods his head in understanding. "Okay. So, are you enjoying it here?" he asks me, and I think he's just trying to distract me.

"Yeah, it's great." I smile genuinely. "I'm excited about my current assignment, it needs some-" Just then the lift car stops. "What's going on?" I walk up to the buttons and press the door open button, but nothing happens. I slowly feel the panic rising in me. "Edward, what's going on?" I start banging on the doors screaming, calling for anybody to help. I'm not sure what happens next but I'm pushed up against the side of the lift, and Edward's lips are on mine so hard, it feels like he's bruising them. I try to step away but he pulls me closer, and I feel his hand on my shirt, unbuttoning it. What the hell?

I'm gasping for air from panic and lust, when Edward grabs my bandaged wrist to get my attention, trying to get me to focus on him. I wince from the pain of his fingers digging into my healing wound. "What happened to your arm?"

I struggle to think of a good lie, the lack of oxygen to my brain is making it hard to think. "I sprained it, at the gym."

He narrows his eyes at me, and I know he's trying to tell if I'm lying. I start to feel dizzy and stumble, and he's suddenly reminded of why he wanted to get my attention in the first place. "Okay breathe. Calm down. Just let me take control. Don't think about it Dana, just feel me." I nod and let him carry on kissing me, working his way along my jaw and to the space behind my ear, I could pass out at any moment from lack of oxygen. He holds me up as he pulls my shirt apart and off my shoulders as he starts to kiss down my neck and across my collarbone. Just as my shirt falls to the floor, Edward has his lips on the tops of my breasts. He starts moving up my right collar bone and up to my ear. He nips the lobe and whispers, "Dana, What happened to your arm?"

Taking slow, shallow breaths, I'm so turned on, and he wants me to repeat myself. "I sprained it," I whisper as I kiss his neck and begin undoing his shirt, slowly moving my lips down towards his pecs and his nipple. Next to my five-foot-four frame this six-foot-two giant towers above me.

"Then why is it bleeding?" his voice growls at me with anger, holding my bandaged wrist up to show me. He must have caught the scab when he grabbed it the first time. "What did I say would happen if you did this again?" I stand there in silence my cheeks coloring with embarrassment. I'm half naked and incredibly turned on. "Answer me!" he asks in a raised voice.

"You said there would be consequences," I gushed the words out as quickly as I could.

"Good girl, now turn around. Bend over at a ninety-degree angle and hold on to the handrail in front of you."

Visibly shaking, I wonder if he is completely mad. "Excuse me? Are you serious?"

"Yes. Now do it!" His voice is commanding.

"What are you going to do?" My voice is quiet, he just glares at me with narrowed eyes. I do as he says because I'm curious and then I feel his hands on my hips pulling me back, so my arms are stretched in front of my head.

"Do not let go of that rail. Do you understand?" I nod because right now I'm just too shocked. "Answer me, Dana."

"Yes, sir." Sir? Where did that come from?

I hear a sharp intake of breath. "You just made me rock hard and very excited young lady." I feel him stand behind me and rub his hand over my covered slit causing me to get damp between my thighs. He lifts up my skirt and pulls my panties down, I couldn't be more exposed if I were completely naked. He stills,

76

and I feel him undo my bra and trace line after line with his finger, and I know he's tracing the scars that James left with the whip. "What happened to your back?" I stay quiet because I can't think of a suitable answer that wouldn't make me and James sound completely insane. "Fine." I feel his fingers circling the devil tattoo that I got done impulsively when I was seventeen. That's when I felt the first sting on my left bum cheek, in the exact spot of the little design.

"Oh god. You actually hit me." My cheeks were flaming with shame, yet I feel myself heating down below. If this is a punishment, why am I enjoying it?

"I didn't hit you, I spanked you. How did it feel?" he asks me this while rubbing the hot spot that his palm had just left. I couldn't do much more than make a moaning sound. "It sounds like you liked it."

*Smack, smack, smack.*

Three more times he spanks me on my rear. "What happened to your back, Dana?"

"An ex-boyfriend happened." I bend the truth, gasping through the pain that's gradually turning to pleasure the more he soothes it. Grant may not have inflicted the markings left by the whip, but he is definitely the reason for needing them. Just then the lift starts to move again, Edward helps me to dress quickly. As we reach the twenty-fourth floor, we step out. I feel like I'm on fire, and I realize I'm highly aroused. Why did spanking and pain make me horny? It never has before.

"Let me take you out to dinner, I can try to explain some of what you are feeling." As if reading my mind he knows I need answers, but I'm still too flustered to answer, so I just nod.

"Seriously Jay, I feel like I'm becoming a nodding dog," I confess to my best friend all that happened with Edward. After I had got back downstairs, James and I went to a diner for a well-deserved brunch, it's a shame it's too early for wine. "It's so frustrating, I've never been reduced to a driveling mess. Why does he affect me so much?"

"I think someone has a crush on their boss."

James gives me a lopsided smile, I know he's just trying to press my buttons. "Now tell me, Dana, do you *love* him?"

"You know I only have two loves in my life. You and Nathan," I try to say convincingly, but who am I trying to convince? James or myself?

"I know honey, I'm just playing. So you're going out to dinner with Edward, to find out why you enjoyed a spanking that was meant to be punishment," James says, summarizing everything I just said.

"Yes, basically." I need to understand this. Pain is pain, and what Edward did today was physical abuse and sexual misconduct in the workplace. Yet I find myself very excited about dinner with him tonight. "Come on, let's pay the bill. I have to get to Broadway and get pictures of the cast of this new play before they go on stage." As I call the waitress over, I spot someone in the corner of my eye. "James, look to your left do you see that person lurking near the lamppost across the road?" I whisper.

James gives me a confused look but casually looks to his left as if looking for something. "Yeah there is definitely someone over there, and they are staring right at you. Who is it?"

"I have no idea." But I have my suspicions.

"You're wearing that on a date with your boss?" James looks at me as if I'm one of the casts of Oliver Twist.

"Why does it matter what I'm wearing, I'm not naked. I'm in regular clothes. It's not a date, just dinner. So what if he's my boss, he's also just a guy, who happens to be a billionaire and I get butterflies every time I see him. Oh god! I can't wear this, help me!"

"You know talking to yourself is the first sign of insanity." James laughs, following me to my bedroom.

"Please help me find something to wear, then you can make all the jokes you want." I'm pleading now. What was I thinking, this isn't just dinner? This man does things to me, ignites a fire inside me like no one ever has before.

"You can never go wrong with the little black dress. Perfect for any situation you find yourself in. Like I don't know, being bent over a table and spanked." James starts laughing hysterically. I glare at him for taking the piss out of me, but he is right, when all else fails, wear the little black dress. I am worrying now, though, this isn't normal behavior for an employer and employee, what will this mean for our working relationship?

"You look beautiful," Edward says as he helps me into the back of his town car. "Peter, can you take us to the restaurant please."

"Thank you." I start to fidget with my hands not knowing what else to say. We spend most of the drive in silence, but I can feel Edwards burning gaze on me several times throughout the journey.

When we arrive at the restaurant, Edward takes my hand and helps me out of the car. Not letting go he pulls me straight inside where we are greeted by the maitre d'. "Good evening Mr. Day, your table is ready for you. This way please."

We take our seats and look at the drinks menu. "I'm not good with posh wines, can you suggest a good one?" I ask Edward, as my knowledge is limited to ten dollar bottles or less.

"How about a glass of water or soda? I think alcohol would be a bad idea for what we need to discuss tonight."

"Okay, I'll have a coke with no ice please," I reply, curiously wondering what we will be talking about.

"I'll have a soda water, please. We'll order our food shortly." Edward excuses the waiter.

"What's the deal?" I say before I realize what I've said. Edward looks at me puzzled. "You, you're so protective of me. I've known you for only a few days, but you treat me like you've known me a lifetime."

Edward takes a moment to think while the waiter brings our drinks. "We'll both have the steak, medium rare thank you," he says to the waiter, to move him along as quickly as possible. "Dana, when I first saw you I felt something. Something that I believe I've never felt before. This is hard for me to explain, it's like you're a magnet and you're pulling me in. That's why I had Vanessa set up a morning meeting for your first day. I needed to see you face to face and talk to you, to see if the feeling was the same then."

I'm stunned but manage to answer. "So when I first met you, you already knew who I was?" He nods. "So you knew who I was in the lift the first day when you helped me?" He nods again, and I think for a moment. "So what's with all this protectiveness? Why try dragging me out of a bar and manhandling me in the lift?"

"It wasn't manhandling," he says curtly, "it was a bit of light spanking. I can read body language well, Dana. When I saw you the first time you came to the Daylight for your interview, I could instantly tell that something was wrong. After I saw you, I followed you around a bit, and I did notice you were drinking every night. When you went to the gym, I could tell you were fighting some demons with how hard you were hitting your poor friend. Now I've seen the scars on your arms and back, it just confirmed things for me. I have this overwhelming urge to help you and protect you."

"So you're the one that's been lurking in the shadows the last few days?" I could have sworn it was someone else.

"No, I followed you a few days last week." He must see the panicked look on my face. "Is someone following you?"

"I'm sorry Edward I have to leave." I get up and start running, running as fast as my feet will take me. Panic takes over, why is he here? Why is he following me? Is Nathan with him?

"Dana, wait!" I hear Edward shouting behind me. I can't wait, I have to get home. My eyes are filling with tears and blurring my vision.

Nearly home I tell myself I've spent most of

the walk crying, trying to understand what is going on. I feel it before I see or hear anything, the knife at my throat. "Hey, there you sexy little thing." Bile rises from my stomach. "Maybe you can help me by getting on your knees and using that pretty little mouth of yours to make me come."

The man's voice is sleazy and is making me feel physically sick. "Please don't hurt me, here take my bag. Just please don't hurt me."

"I don't want to hurt you, and I don't want your bag. I want your pussy wrapped around my cock." His words are like cat claws on a blackboard. He starts to pull me towards a side alley and pushes me to the ground. I crawl on my hands and knees trying to get away. He grabs my hair and yanks on it pulling me back, almost ripping it from my scalp.

"Don't do this. Please, someone, help me!" His hand comes down heavy on my cheek, as he slaps me.

"Shut the fuck up, bitch. Open your legs, or I'll really make it hurt." Tears are falling out of the corner of my eyes, down my temples. He's trying to part my legs with his knees.

"If I were you, I'd get the fuck off her." I hear the familiar sound of Edward's voice and relief floods over me.

"This is my whore man, get your own," the man spits. Edward's eyes go dark and soulless right before he loses it. Running at the man he flattens him with one punch but Edward doesn't stop there. He continues to hit the masked man over, and over, and over.

"Edward, no. Please stop it, please take me home." I think he hears the urgency in my voice and the protectiveness I have for him because he stops. He walks towards me, picks me up and puts me in the back of the car. I fall into his arms, too shocked to say or do anything. "I should call nine-nine-nine," I say to no-one in particular.

"You mean nine-one-one, and please don't," Edward says, not making eye contact with me.

"That vile man almost raped me," I say, confusion and anger lacing my voice.

"But he didn't. I, on the other hand, just beat him to a pulp. Please don't call the police." The angst in his eyes is what persuades me in the end.

"Okay," I answer, cuddling back into his comforting embrace.

As we pull up outside my apartment, I jump out of the car. "Thank you for saving me and getting me home I dread to think what would have happened if you hadn't of turned up," I say to him rushing to get inside.

"Was that the person you thought was following you?" He grabs my elbow to stop me walking away, I shake my head. "Let me walk you up." He looks at me, sad and confused.

I shake my head again trying to hold back the tears. "Go home, I'll be okay. I've had the day from hell, and that arse has just made it so much worse. So I would appreciate it if you can just leave me to deal with this." I run to the lift and climb in.

When I reach the front door, I fly through it and straight into James' arms. "Hey, what's going on?"

he asks, his voice laced with concern while running his fingers over my burning red cheek and drying my tears. "What happened?"

"James, help me, please." He nods, knowing exactly what I'm saying. I head to the black room, removing my dress and bra as I go. "Use the whip." I walk in the room, fall to my knees and bow my head with my hands in my lap.

James knows better than to say anything to me right now. I hear the whooshing sound of the whip going through the air, it feels like forever before it lands on my back.

"Oh god!" I scream at the first hit. With the second and third lashing, I scream the pain away. Then the hairs on the nape of my neck stand up and I know he's in the room.

"Dana, what the fuck is this?" Edward stares at me with a look of anguish on his face. Not the emotion I expected to see.

# Chapter 5

"You need to leave," I hear James say as he walks towards Edward. "You can't be in this room."

Edward continues staring at me as my eyes fill with salty tears. He turns his head to James, narrowing his eyes. "You're meant to be her friend, what are you doing?"

"I'm helping her, now leave and close the door on the way out," James practically spits the words from his mouth.

"Helping her? You've ruined everything, you stupid man." James looks taken aback by Edwards words. "Dana this is wrong on so many levels, please tell me you see that?"

I'm momentarily speechless as I gather myself and think carefully about my answer, remembering that this man is my boss and I need to appear sane, but instead I crack. "Who the hell do you think you are judging me? You don't know me or anything about me. How did you even get in here?"

"I know more about you than you realize, and you left your front door open in your rush to get yourself whipped." he says with no emotion present on his face or in his voice.

Suddenly everything that's been stated in the last few minutes filters into my brain. "What do you mean, James has ruined everything? Why do you know so much about me? What the hell is going on here?"

"I can't answer all your questions right now, you just need to trust me." I can tell by the look in his eyes that his reply is genuine, but I hate being kept in the dark and I will not be led into something I know nothing about. Trust is built on honesty and truth, and Edward is giving me none of that. He realizes I'm not going to answer him and his frustration kicks in. "Fine, act like a child. When you decide you want to deal with this appropriately and face your problems head on, come find me. There is nothing more I can do here." He turns and walks out, I turn to James, and he shrugs his shoulders. There's a loud bang as the front door slams shut, my session was nowhere near as long as it needed to be and I can't deal with this. Emotions flooding from me, I make to leave. James is on me before I can make my escape.

"What are you going to do?" he questions me as he pins me to the floor.

I can't even answer him as I cry and the realization of what we do crushes me. Edward's right, this is all wrong. Why can't I just be normal?

James finally climbed off me, and we've been on the sofa eating junk food and watching *Friends* reruns since. Now James is snoring his head off next to me. James asked me over and over again what happened, but I brushed him off and told him we can have a proper chat tomorrow, after a good night sleep. I don't know what to think right now. So much is going through my mind, I visualize Edward standing there holding his arms open to me. I'm pulled from my reverie by the sound of the phone ringing. Leaning over James, I pick up the handset. "Hello."

"Dana it's Mum." Mum's voice always cheers me up.

"Hey, Mum, what's up?"

"It's about tomorrow dear, we are going to have to cancel. We will rearrange for soon okay. I've been thinking of you today, I just wanted you to know. Got to go dear, Richard is calling. I love you." And that was it, she hung up the phone, I barely got to say anything. What is going on here? I'll deal with Mum later, right now I need to know the answer to some of my other question, and at the moment there is only one person who can answer them.

I leave James sleeping on the sofa and call Edward.

"Edward Day." Such a polite and welcoming answer

"Hey, it's Dana. I was wondering if I could see you, please. "

"Why?" That was unexpected, I'm not sure how to answer him.

"Um... I'm not sure. I've been thinking about what you said, and I would like to talk."

"When?" This is not at all how I planned this to go, but I don't think I deserve the one-word answers.

Pride gets in my way. "Look don't worry about it, I shouldn't have called-"

"Dana, wait. I'm sorry I can send a car to get you now if you like?"

"It's ten at night, isn't it a bit late?"

"You said you wanted to talk, no time like the present." I know he's right, if I don't talk about this now, it will just go back into the box at the back of my brain, until the next time I lose control.

"Okay," I reply quickly before I can change my mind.

"I'll see you soon." He hangs up.


The intercom alerts me that Edward's driver has arrived to pick me up. I haven't woken James to tell him where I'm going but I left him a note, so he doesn't panic too much. As I exit the lobby I'm relieved to see Peter, I feel safer with a familiar face. "Good evening Miss Spencer," he says opening the car door for me.

"Good evening and thank you, Peter. Please call me Dana." I smile my biggest smile and settle into the back seat of the car excited and anxious about my upcoming meeting with Edward.

We drive in silence, and I have to admit it's making me a little nervous, so I try to make small talk. "How long have you worked for Edward, Peter?"

"His whole life."

"Wow, so what's he like?"

"Unique."

Is that it? I take it our conversation is over, or maybe he's just too professional to discuss his boss. We drive the rest of the way in silence, thinking about all the things that Edward has said and done in the last five days. Nothing is making sense. He told me at dinner that he felt like he was protective of me was because of feelings he felt towards me. But when he interrupted my session with James, he didn't seem surprised at all, more pained and angry than anything at what he saw. And what's been ruined? I'm so wrapped up in my thoughts that I don't realize we've pulled into an underground garage. "Where are we?" I ask Peter.

"Jackson Square, Greenwich Avenue in West Village, Miss Spencer. He's in the penthouse," he answers. Of course, he has a penthouse I tell myself. What I didn't expect, was for it to be Downtown. I pictured him with a large bachelor pad on the Upper East Side overlooking Central Park. Peter comes around and opens the car door. "He's a nice man who's been through a lot. His heart is in the right place." He winks at me as he closes the door, the small smile that plays on his lips says that was between us. He maneuvers me towards the lift and puts a key in the panel before pressing the call button.

"No, I can't get in there. Sorry, you'll have to

show me the stairs." I say backing away from the doors.

"There are no stairs to the penthouse, Miss Spencer," he says. "I will ride up with you."

Edward must have had all this planned and ready for me, he knew I would freak out. The doors open and we step in, as they close I take a deep breath. For a moment it feels like my stomach drops, then we come to a stop. "That was quick," I say sounding astonished.

"There are only eleven floors Miss Spencer, and this is Mr. Day's private elevator," he tells me as a way of explanation. The doors open and there he is standing in front of me in all his glory, his beautiful green eyes piercing my soul. God this man does things to me with just a look.

"Good evening Dana, do you think you could stop staring at me and step out of the elevator to let Peter leave?" His smile is all knowing, can he tell what I was thinking?

I blink myself back to reality. "I'm sorry, yes of

course. Bye Peter." I pick my tongue up off the floor and step out of the lift straight into the vast expanse of his apartment. It's very modern and plain looking. I feel his hand on the small of my back as he leads me through the lounge and into the kitchen.

He pulls a chair out and gestures for me to sit, still saying nothing. I watch as he walks to the fridge and pulls out a bottle of wine and two glasses from the cupboard. "Don't get used to this, I don't usually keep alcohol in the house."

Not really knowing how to answer him I just nod, just like I always end up doing when I'm around Edward.

"So why do you have a bottle then?" I ask as he sits at the table opposite me.

He looks at me with a cheeky smile. "Well this evening didn't go exactly how I planned, but it is certainly ending how I planned."

I'm shocked. "Did you think I would have come home with you earlier?"

"It's what I was hoping."

"Well, you don't know me as well as you think you do Mr. Day. You may be able to get any woman you want into bed, but not me." I stand to leave I knew this was a mistake, what was I thinking?

"Sit down Dana," His voice booms as if daring me to defy him. I don't. I turn and sit back down waiting to hear what he has to say. "I don't want to get you into bed."

I suddenly feel quite insulted, very righteous of me. "Really?"

He lets out a small chuckle. "Yes, really. The reason we went to dinner was to talk, you never let me finish what I had to say before you ran away." I look down at the table, guilty about my premature exit from the restaurant. "I was going to explain to you about what happened in the elevator at the Daylight building, why you enjoyed it and to offer you a proposition.

"You've confused me now." I must look so stupid to him.

"Dana, why do you harm yourself?" His voice

is soft and concerned.

"I went through some things, and it was how I dealt with it." I can't bring all this up now it's not the right time.

"Tell me." He's not asking me.

"If you know me so well then you'll already know." I counter him.

"I think I know. I know all about Grant, Nathan, and James, but I want to hear it from you." I must look like I'm about to pass out because he comes around to my side of the table and looks me straight in the eye. "You need to talk about this to start the process."

"Process? Wh-what pr-process?" I stutter. I can't believe this is happening, what is he talking about? How does he know about Grant?

"I probably know more than you do at this stage and I'm sorry about that. I'm also sorry that I can't tell you and that I know stuff that's private to you," he says.

"How do you know?" I ask, completely

stunned.

"This is really all for your benefit, I promise. You just need to trust me. I'm here to help you." He places his hands on my shoulders as if he is anchoring me to the chair so I can't run away.

"Then tell me what is going on, please. This is my life, I can't trust someone who keeps things from me." The emotions of the evening and this revelation collide, and I burst into tears, I just can't hold them back.

Edward pulls me into him and holds me tight against his chest as I sob until I have no more left in me. "Let it all out, Dana. It's all part of the process."

I raise my head to look at him, to search his eyes. "What process. Can you tell me that?"

"Yes I can, but we will wait till you are calmer and in a better state of mind to discuss it." Then he pulls me back to his chest, and we just sit there until I get my breath back.

For the next hour, we talk about nothing except TV, movies, and music. We have moved to the lounge, and I'm bundled up in his arms "My Dad was a big fan of Iron Maiden and Metallica, I preferred Journey." We are laughing and having fun, I'm always happy when I'm talking about my Dad.

"I have to agree with your Dad I'm afraid." I pull a funny face, and we both burst out laughing, the alcohol must be going to my head as I'm feeling a bit woozy.

"What happened to your Dad?" I know he already knows the answer to that question, but at least he's showing me some respect by asking me.

"He died of prostate cancer, when I was fourteen," I say quietly.

"I'm sorry." His sympathetic voice soothes me. "So tell me about Grant."

I stiffen, and he must feel it because he holds me tighter. "He's an ex-boyfriend." I'm short with him I know, but I don't think I'm ready for this.

"We can do this as slow as you like, Dana," he says rubbing the top of my arm. He turns me to face him. "How about I tell you some things about me, and

101

maybe that will help you open up."

I think about this, if he is willing to talk to me then surely I can do the same. I suppose it depends on what he has to say. Before that, I need to know one thing. "What is this process?"

He looks at me like he's trying to gauge my state of mind. "Okay, we'll start there. I know about you cutting yourself. I knew, when I asked you about the scars on your wrists, that they weren't done a long time ago. What I didn't know was how far it went, with the whipping and stuff. That did shock me because it will make things so much harder. I didn't realize how much you relied on the pain. It's no surprise that I'm attracted to you, but I didn't expect it to be this intense. I certainly didn't expect to feel this protective of you. When I saw the scars and how much you were drinking, I just knew I had to help you. I'm part of a foundation that raises money and awareness for children and young adults who have been a victim of any type of abuse. I want to help you through the process of healing so you don't keep hurting yourself and you accept what has happened to you and move on from it."

"Okay... well you got my attention. Seeing as you know so much about me, tell me something about you that you wouldn't normally tell anyone else."

He takes a deep breath, and I know that whatever he is about to tell me is a big deal for him. "I was abused as a teenager by my older brother. There wasn't much support back then for abused children, it wasn't really heard of or spoken about. The worst part was not being believed by my parents."

His eyes cloud over as if he's reliving the moment and I have a sudden urge to hold him, so I climb onto his lap and hold his face in the palms of my hands. I lean in and kiss him, he pulls back searching my eyes, and that is his undoing. He pulls me towards him and holds on to me like I'm a life raft stopping him from drowning. His lips pressed so hard against mine, his tongue parts my teeth as it enters my mouth and entwines with mine. I feel him shift beneath me and start to stand up picking me up with him. I wrap my legs around his lower torso and grip my arms around his neck as tight as I can as he carries me through the apartment. He kicks open a door, and a few seconds later I land on a bed with him on top of me. He continues his exploration of my mouth while lifting my top up, only parting our lips to remove my top over my head, and he's back on me again. He starts pulling my breast from my bra and playing with my nipple. They were erect from the moment his lips touched mine, but they seem to harden more. He moves his head to my nipple, and his tongue continues its assault there, I can feel the space between my legs becoming warm and wet, and my hips lift to grind against his groin to give myself some relief. As I try to remove his shirt he grabs both of my wrists and pins them to the bed beside my head, I try to remove them from his grasp, but he just holds them tighter and bites my nipple. I squeal but then the pain becomes something so much better, and I feel the heat travel all the way down to my clitoris.

"Don't move."

I still, his growled demand along with his restraining hands has my heart racing. I start to breathe heavily, trying to control the rising anxiety in me. "Relax," his sensual voice whispers in my ear.

"I-I can't, p-please stop." He does exactly that, but my breathing is still erratic. I can't seem to get it under control.

"Dana, look at me, please. You need to relax." Now I know I can trust him. I said stop, and he stopped. "I'm so sorry, really I am."

"It's okay. It's not your fault, it's another side effect of the ex-boyfriend." My breathing starts to settle.

"Another?" he asks, and I know he wants me to openly tell him.

"Yeah, the cutting, the claustrophobia, the panic attacks, all thanks to the ex-boyfriend. But you already knew that didn't you Mr. Day."

At least he has the decency this time to look a little guilty. "Not all of it, but yes I did. I'm sorry."

"How do you know all this stuff about me?" I'm starting to wonder if all the great things that have been happening recently aren't entirely what they appear to be.

"I told you there were things I couldn't tell you just yet, and this is one of them."

I look at his solemn expression, and with a sigh of realization, I know what he's trying to say. "You still want me to trust you?"

"Yes, that is what I'm hoping. You interrupted me earlier, while I was trying to explain some things to you." His lips half curl into a smile.

"Yeah, I know. I'm sorry. I just couldn't imagine what would have become of me if my Mum didn't believe me. I owe my life to her and Richard, I guess I just projected that onto you."

"Come here, and I'll tell you some more." I climb up the bed, tucking my breasts back in my bra as I go and lay into him with my arm across his chest and his arm under my head.

"This brother of yours, is he the one you

knocked out in public?"

His eyes narrow towards me. "How would you know about that?"

My cheeks flush with a little embarrassment "I may have done a Google search on you."

"I think the word hypocrite comes to mind, Miss Spencer. I may have to give you a spanking for that," he states seriously yet his face is anything but serious and I feel the twinges of pleasure starting to rise in my pubic area.

"That is something we do need to discuss, but we can do that later. You didn't answer my question."

He thinks for a moment, looking at me from the corner of his eye. Then in a resigned tone, he explains. "Yes the brother I knocked out was Andrew, he was provoking me at a business event, and I lost my temper. Not something that is done easily but when it comes to Drew, I can't control myself."

"How old are you?" I ask curiously.

"You mean you Googled me and didn't find out my age?" I shake my head. "I'm twenty-eight," he answers.

"How old is Drew?" I'm trying to work this all out.

"Thirty-one." Edward sees the cogs turning in my head. "Anyway after I told my parents what Drew was doing, they kicked me out. Well not kicked me out, I was only thirteen, but sent me to boarding school."

"So Drew was sixteen," I say.

He nods. "When I turned sixteen my Uncle Nick took me in. He did believe me, and he taught me all I needed to know about business. He pulled me from the depths of killing myself with alcohol and drugs, something I turned to, to get me through the pain. That's why I don't keep it in the house and rarely drink it. He died when I was twenty-two."

"There was only sixteen years between you?" I ask confused, remembering his uncle was thirty-eight when he died. He narrows his eyes at me. "Google," I answer simply.

"Yes, he's my Dad's youngest brother. Nick

was thirteen years younger," he confirms. "You like to work things out, don't you?"

I smile at his observation. "I don't like it when things don't make sense. Tell me about Nick," I say.

"He left everything to me. My family wasn't too happy about this as you can imagine, they wanted to turn it back into a family run business, but I refused to back down. My younger brother Matthew works with me, he's twenty-six and is the only real family I have now. Sometimes I'm required to attend an event that my parents and Drew will be at, but I try to avoid them at all costs. I later found out why my parents were so insistent on making it all a family run business again. I am the majority shareholder at my Father's publishing house thanks to Nick. He did it as revenge for me when my Father's company was in jeopardy, Nick came to the rescue. No one, not even me, knew that he did it because he was leaving everything to me. Otherwise, he would have let the publishing house go down the pan. Anyway, while Nick was alive, he founded a charity for abused children and young adults, which I was always grateful to him for. I trained to be a counselor before my uncle died so I could help people who have been through abuse and need help seeing the light at the end of the tunnel. One weekend Nick must not have been expecting me home from college because I walked in on him with a woman. It was not unusual for him but what he was doing was what fascinated me. Afterward, he explained what he was doing was spanking, he explained the pain and pleasure side of it and how arousing it can be. Kind of like when I spanked you and bit your nipple, you enjoyed it. The reason I'm telling you all this Dana is because I like to deliver pain, but only in a pleasurable way. It's my way of dealing with my past, I need to have that control. You like to receive it, as a way of dealing with your past. After seeing what damage the whip has done to your back, I'm more determined to intervene. So I propose this solution to you - as well as counseling you, let me be the one to give you the pain you require. I will help you to enjoy it, instead of you permanently marking your body. Instead of letting it be something you associate with fear and loss of control, I can help make it pleasurable until you don't need it anymore."

I sit in silence at this revelation. What this man has been through and has come out the other side. I open my mouth to say things several times, but nothing seems to be the right thing to say at this moment. Is it right or wrong that I'm very turned on by this proposition? Then another thought enters my mind, he wants to hurt me. I don't think I could cope with another man who wants to control me, who would take pleasure in beating me.

"Say something, please."

"Are you completely crazy?"

# Chapter 6

Right now all I know is that I need to get out of here. I jump off the bed, grab my top and walk towards the lift that brought me up here. "Dana. Please wait, can we just talk about this." I hear him moving after me, and as his legs are twice the length of mine, he's gaining on me, so I pick up the pace practically running now. "I think you misunderstood what I was saying."

"No, I'm pretty sure I understood perfectly," I shout behind me as I reach the lift and press the call button, nothing happens.

"You need to put the lift key in before the call button works." He looks at me with a knowing smile, I feel my anger rising.

"Could you please put the key in, so I can leave?"

He starts to shake his head and turns away calling over his shoulder to me "Not until you talk to me."

I'm shocked. "You can't do this, you can't keep me here because you're not getting what you want." There has to be a fire escape or something on a building like this.

"I can do what I like because I have the key. I'm the one with the power as you will soon find out." The grin on his face becomes so boyish, he looks like the cat that got the cream.

"Look whatever it is you're into, it doesn't do it for me." Trying to stay calm is becoming hard.

"Ah, but I think it does. You enjoyed being spanked, you became wet and hot. I felt it even through your panties. You need the pain, but I can help you enjoy it." The fact that he is managing to keep his composure during this means he is deadly serious.

"No wonder you didn't look shocked when you walked into the black room. You were probably turned on. Is that what James was ruining? You getting your hands on me, he was doing what you wanted to be doing, wasn't he?" I start to look around, there has to be an emergency exit somewhere.

"Actually I was both shocked and turned on. I was shocked as I said because I didn't realize how serious your need for pain was, that you were physically marking and scarring your body." His face looks angrier at this point. "But walking in and seeing you in such a submissive position, I just wanted to scoop you up and take you to bed."

"You're crazy, really, completely insane. So what did James ruin then? Come on spit it out." I must be starting to look like a crazy person myself.

A hint of something crosses his eyes "I can't tell you, I'm sorry. Come, it's time for bed." That's it he just starts walking towards the long hallway that houses the bedrooms.

"Did you not hear me? I'm going home, can I have the key please?"

"You are not leaving at this time of night, I will show you to your room." The calmness in him is becoming impatient.

"No, I'm going home now!"

"Dana! Follow me, or I will drag you kicking and screaming to the room, before restraining you to the bed to make sure you stay there until morning." The authority in his voice told me not to mess with him, but I've been bullied by one man before, and I'll be damned if I'm going to let it happen again.

"No." I dragged the word out sarcastically.

He starts towards me, so I turn and make a run for it. Heading through the open plan lounge and into the kitchen, I make my way to the other side of the island in the middle of the kitchen. As we dance around it I can't help but laugh, his face is so serious and frustrated.

"Don't laugh at me Dana, I'm not in the mood." This just makes me laugh more.

Mocking him, I say in a booming tone. "Me big boss man. I say. You do." I'm laughing so much I trip, and he's on me like a flash. Picking me up and hoisting me over his shoulder, he is soon carrying me through the apartment. "Put me down!" I'm screaming at him, kicking my legs and pounding my fist on his back. Throwing me off him and onto a bed, he drags my arm above my head and attaches it to a handcuff already in place on the headboard.

What the hell! I start to pull my arm to test the strength of the cuff. "You can't do this, it's illegal." He goes to leave. "What if I need the toilet?"

He turns and looks at me with a wicked grin. "Hold it! Soon you will realize it's easier to do as I say instead of defying me at every turn. Tomorrow you will receive your punishment. Goodnight." He starts to close the door.

"Are you not sleeping with me?" Confused and shocked at what is transpiring, that panic starts to rise.

"I don't share my bed, Dana." With that, he closes the door.

"Edward! Edward!" I'm shouting so loud I hear

my voice become hoarse. "Please don't leave me here."

The door opens. "Shut up and go to sleep or I will gag you too. You're going to need your energy in the morning."

This time I decide not to call his bluff. "I haven't agreed to your proposition yet."

"But we both know you will. Tell me you're not turned on right now. Tell me that your juices aren't flowing at this situation you've found yourself in." My body betrays me as my face becomes flushed. "I thought so." He walks towards me, and he undoes the cuff. "Get some sleep, I'll see you for breakfast at eight." He leaves the room, I hear him open another door and close it again. I wait to hear for any more movement, there's none.

Why am I not finding this more daunting or scary? *You know why* I hear the voice in my head tell me. *You are turned on, and you're curious.*

I get off the bed and tiptoe to the door, opening it and peering out to check if the coast is clear. Walking out into the hallway I make my way back to the living room where I dropped my handbag to retrieve my phone, I can't find it. I go to the kitchen and then retrace my steps to the bedroom. Realization dawns on me, that's what Edward went to get the first time he left the room when I was cuffed to the bed. I can't believe this, he actually has me imprisoned here. As I continue snooping around I come across a set of large double doors, I go to open it, but it's locked. Moving along I come across a big heavy metal door tucked away, it must be the fire escape, and I smile with relief. I consider opening it and running for my life, but would I actually be running for my life? Do I even want to? As this thought enters my mind I'm aware that I trust Edward, he's nothing like Grant, and I am curious to partake in this way of life he is offering me. It doesn't hurt to try it, does it? With my mind made up, I make my way back to my room and get out of my clothes. Settling into bed I wonder what tomorrow will bring, thinking of what sort of punishment I will receive and with a smile I drift off to sleep.

I'm woken with a start, it's still dark outside. I can hear muffled screaming, and panic rises in me. What the hell is going on? I get up and throw my top back on and walk in the direction of the sound. Standing outside Edward's room, I hear his painful screams as if he is being hurt in some way. I open the door quickly to find him writhing around on his sweat-drenched bed. Climbing in next to him I wrap my arms around him and pull him to me. I hold him tighter as his sweat covered body struggles against me. Tears spring to my eyes with every ear piercing cry he makes, he sounds terrified. "Edward," I whisper in his ear. "I'm here, you're dreaming, wake up."

His eyes spring open, and he rolls on top on me pinning my arms above my head before I even understand what is going on. His eyes still clouded by sleep start to clear, his angry, terrified face calming as he begins to recognize who I am. He stares me in the eye and then moves his hand down feeling my bare pussy with his hand. I gasp as he shoves two fingers inside me causing my arousal to spike. I don't say a word or struggle against his other hand that's restraining both of my wrists. Something about this moment tells me that he needs to do this, the pain and the plea in his eyes when he looks at me tells me he has to be in control again. When he thinks I'm ready and my sex is nice and lubricated he enters me. The thickness of his cock fills me completely as he thrusts straight into me. The head hitting straight on my cervix causing me to scream out but he doesn't ease up. He thrusts into me over and over again, each time the pain sparking off a warm tingling inside of me. I feel my climax rising, Edward feels it too. "Don't come, not yet, wait for me."

I feel the tingle move throughout me down to my toes making them curl, then back up to my sex, almost ready to explode. "Please, Edward. I need to come."

He speeds up, his thrusts becoming more determined. My head starts whipping from side to side as I struggle to control the orgasm that's trying to escape me, his hand moves up to my breast and pinches my nipple. A gasp comes out as I realize the pain is quickly becoming pleasurable. "Now Dana." That's all I need to hear. My orgasm comes quick and fast, I'm screaming his name as I fall apart beneath him. I ride out the last of the waves of pleasure as I feel the tightening of the muscles in the tops of his thighs, and know that his climax is on the way. He thrusts deeper as I feel his cock pulsate and welcome the warm liquid that fills me. He falls on top of me out of breath and exhausted, I lay under him with my arms wrapped around him till he is ready to move.

After a few minutes, he rolls off me and gets off the bed, putting a robe on he turns to me. "What are you doing in here? You shouldn't be here." His expression is one of disappointment, in himself or in me?

"I heard you scream, I thought you were hurt." He barely looks at me, just turns away and walks off into the bathroom, with nothing else to say.

At this moment I feel cheap and used, what was I thinking? I stand and pull my top down, leaving his room and walking back into my room. I decide to get in a quick shower before I flop back into bed feeling completely drained. I lay back with my head on the pillow staring at the ceiling. With tears falling silently from the corners of my eyes, I close them wondering what I did that was so wrong. Why had he treated me like that? Why didn't I leave through the fire escape when I had the chance?

I'm woken by someone banging on the door, momentarily disoriented as to where I am. Then I remember and hear the banging again. "Dana, I told you breakfast at eight, it's now quarter past. What's taking so long?" Is this guy for real?

I grunt as I roll over. "Well, it's not like I have a clock to tell me what the time is," I shout back. I am not in the mood for this man this morning.

The door flies open, and I grab the cover and pull it around me. "You are a guest in my house, I expect you to show me some respect." His voice is full of anger.

He has to be kidding me, I can't keep my temper in check any longer. "No, I'm a prisoner in your house and if someone hadn't of woke me up in the middle of the night, then shoved his dick in me, I probably would have been up sooner. I want my phone, a cup of coffee and to go home." I see his face flash a hint of guilt, but it is gone just as quickly. I stand up and start dressing, I go to walk out of the room, but he blocks my path. I take a few deep breaths. "Can you move please?" I ask as calmly as I can. I stare him in the eye, I need him to know he doesn't scare me. "Edward, move now!"

He looks down at me, my eyes burning with fury. He opens his mouth to speak and then closes it and walks off with an angry grunt back to his room. I make my way to the kitchen and find a fresh pot of coffee and two plates of cold pancakes on the table. Not really being in the mood for food I grab a mug and fill it with coffee adding a little milk and sugar.

Taking in the aroma, I realize this must be how the other half live. I'm lucky if I can afford a decent brand of instant, but nothing beats freshly ground Jamaican Blue Mountain. I sit on a stool at the island, the pancakes making my stomach turn. I sip my coffee appreciating the rich, fruity flavor, thinking about all that's happened in the last five days. When did life become so erratic? Maybe I should have stayed in England.

"You should eat." I'm snapped back by the sound of Edward's voice. "It's probably cold now, I can make you something else if you like?" He heads to the fridge and starts to pull items from the refrigerator.

"I'm not hungry, thank you," I snap.

"You have to eat." His face is expressionless.

Suddenly remembering I left my friend asleep on the sofa with only a note as an explanation, he'll be worried sick. "I would like my phone please, I need to call James and let him know I'm okay."

"He knows you're with me and that you're

safe," Edward says, his answer blunt and to the point.

"Why would he know that?" I'm aware that I'm starting to raise my voice but I'm also starting to become very concerned about James, and Edward is making me angry.

"Your phone has been ringing all morning. I answered it and simply explained to the foul-tempered young man on the other end that you were at my apartment and still asleep. I told him you would call back later," he says this so casually that I wonder if he even knows he's crossed the line.

"I need to call him now, and I need to go home. Please, Edward, don't make me beg." I'm pleading with him now, I know James will be frantic.

"Now I would love to see you beg." The first smile I've seen this morning is playing on his lips, but I'm going out of my head with worry.

"Is that what you want? You want me to beg? You want me to get down on my knees and beg you to let me have my personal belongings and my freedom back?" Tears start to form in my eyes as thoughts of James come to my head.

He sees the stray tears fall from my eyes and I quickly wipe them away defiantly. I will not let him see that he's getting to me. He saunters over to me and puts his hand under my chin, pushing it up, so I have to look at him. "I will compromise, you can call your friend if you sit down and talk to me like an adult."

"I'm not the one acting like a child Edward. You're the one that won't let me leave because you're not getting what you want." I throw my hands up in defeat and go back to my room. I lay on the bed for some time, I'm so angry, but I can't let it out. I need a release. Going into the en-suite I look for something, anything that will help me make just a small cut. I close my eyes and sit on the toilet, as realization dawns on me once again. This is what he wanted all along, he wanted me to need the pain. I refuse to bow down to him. He will not get the better of me.

I go back and sit on the bed, I'm so restless I can't stop fidgeting. I decide to close my eyes and try

126

to get a little more sleep. It takes a while, but I eventually succumb to my exhaustion.

I'm woken once again by knocking, does this man not understand boundaries. "Leave me alone!" I shout, hoping he will listen to me and just go away, of course, he doesn't.

"Dana, I've made you some lunch, can I come in?" Wow, he does have some manners.

"No. I'm not hungry, go away." I lay my head back on the pillow and listen to the sound of my own breathing, feeling sorry for myself.

"You need to eat." His voice sounds strained.

"Please just go away," I beg.

"Okay. I'll leave it out here in case you decide you want it. When you've become bored of being so stubborn and want to have some company, I'll be in my office or the library." Could his ego be any bigger?

"I wouldn't spend time with you if you were the last man on earth. I'd rather be on my own."

"Suit yourself."

I hear his footsteps as he walks to another

room. God, why does he have to be right? I know I'm stubborn, I hate backing down. I should stop letting my pride get in the way of everything, but I can't help myself. The craving for the pain is getting worse. I wish James were here, why didn't I stay with him last night?

I spend the afternoon pacing my room, over thinking and over analyzing everything. I realize the sun is going down which means it has to be at least early evening and my stomach is protesting against me not eating all day. I hear another knock on the door. "Dana, are you awake?"

I sit down on the bed and resign myself to defeat, I can't keep this up it's exhausting. "Yeah I'm up, come in."

I hear the door open, and he peers inside "Are you feeling better?" he asks, his tone emotionless.

"No, I'm tired and drained, and I give up." The craving for the pain has become almost too much to bear.

He looks at me and knows I'm not going to

fight him, I'm done. The expression on his face says this is a hollow victory for him. "Would you like to join me for dinner or I can bring you something?"

I stand and brush myself down. "No, I'd like to join you." He smiles, he looks so relieved. He presents me with his arm, and I wait for a beat. Giving him a small smile I take his arm, and he leads me to the dining room. I believe we have both waved our metaphorical white flags.

We sit to eat a meal that has been made by the housekeeper - she must have arrived while I was sulking - and we eat in silence. When we finish, and the table is cleared, I decide to try my luck. "When can I leave and have my phone back?"

He can tell the fight has gone from within me. "When we sit and talk like adults, I told you." I'm starting to shake now. "Are you okay?" he asks, his voice full of concern.

"Edward, I need a glass of wine, or I need pain. Please, can you give me one or the other?" I blurt out.

The concern in his eyes is worrying, he knows

as well as I do that this has gone too far. "Dana, I need you to look at me. You are responding like a drug addict having withdrawals right now."

"The pain is my drug, please give it to me." Just when I think I have no more tears left to cry more spring to my eyes.

"On one condition." I nod, knowing right now I will agree to anything. "You do things by my rules, am I clear?" I nod again. "Answer me, Dana, am I clear?"

"Yes."

"Yes, sir." His voice is so silky and smooth, it sends a shiver up my spine. "While we do this, you will address me as sir," he commands.

My breath catches in my throat. "Yes, sir."

"I am in control, and you do as I tell you."

"Yes, sir."

"No back talking. No questioning me or my authority."

"Yes, sir."

"What do you want Dana?"

"I need the pain, sir."

"So you want me to punish you?" Just hearing him say those words has me panting. "Dana!"

I jump. "Yes, sir."

"Then follow me." We stand and leave the dining room. He leads me to the double doors I came across last night that were locked. He pulls a key from his pocket and opens the door. I go in ahead of him and gasp at what I see in front of me. "Are you ready Dana?"

"Yes, sir."

# Chapter 7

The wall ahead of me is bright white, and I feel like I've entered into Heaven's waiting room. The walls on either side of me have floor to ceiling mirrors. I hear the door behind me close and lock. I turn and see Edward staring at me through hooded eyelids, he's assessing me, taking in my reaction. I decide to use this time to look around, there is a big chrome four-poster bed against the white wall with a white canopy all around. The bed linen is soft black cotton that quite nicely breaks up the sterile feel to the vast area. At the end of the bed, there is a black ottoman, just at waist height. Behind me is another white wall with a lot of black items hung up on it, making my way over to the wall I go to touch one of them, the leather looks so soft and inviting. Edward grabs my wrist before I get a chance and silently he pulls me towards the mirrors. He raises my arms above me and with his hands, finds the hem of my top, slowly pulling it over my head. Next, he brings his arms around my waist undoing the button of my jeans and pulls them down, tapping my ankle so I lift my foot out and then repeating with the other. I'm left wearing my matching black lace bra and panties.

"Tell me what you see?" His voice is a powerful entity in the room, full of such darkness in this room full of light.

I'm confused by the question, so I state the obvious. "You and me."

His eyes lock with mine in the mirror. "Look at yourself and tell me what you see, what you see every time you look in the mirror."

My breathing becomes heavy at his close proximity to me, his musky masculine smell and his warm breath on my neck. "I see small breasts, a fat arse, and a saggy belly. Someone not in proportion, someone ugly."

"Now tell me what you see when you look into

your own eyes," he says.

Tears fill my eyes. "I see someone who is so angry and upset with the world. Someone who will regret making the wrong decision every day of their life. Someone who lost everything, because they were too scared to stand up for themselves," I answer.

"Would you like to know what I see?" he asks, lifting my chin, so I'm forced to look at myself, I nod. "Answer me, Dana!"

"Y-Yes sir." My voice is wobbly, tears threaten to spill out, and this is not the sort of punishment I was thinking of.

"I see someone who pities herself." My mouth drops open in shock.

"That's not-" I begin to stutter.

"Dana I am talking, and I didn't interrupt you, so please don't interrupt me." His voice is tight and impatient.

"Yes, sir," I reply quietly.

"I see someone who believes the world owes them something for the crap hand they were dealt in life. Someone who has given up on fixing things and has accepted that this is it. That nothing will change. Someone who refuses to let go of the past and move on. Someone who wants to continuously punish themselves, for the wrong decisions they made, because they think that's all they're worth." Tears fall silently down my cheeks as I lower my head and look at my feet. "Look at yourself Dana." My head snaps back up, and I look into my own eyes. Is that really what people see when they look at me? "But I also see a breathtaking woman who has had her self-esteem shattered. Someone who is incredibly stubborn and stands up for what she believes in, even if she doesn't realize her past has made her stronger. Someone who uses physical pain to cover up the emotional pain that she has to live with on a day to day basis."

My head is spinning from all that it's trying to process. "Please stop."

He walks off and leaves me standing in silence, looking at my half naked form. When he returns he hands me a sharp shiny object. "Go on, cut yourself," he says casually, daring me. My brow furrows. "But watch yourself doing it."

"What the hell! What sort of game are you playing?" This has to be some kind of test.

"You need the pain, I've given you a way to get it. On the condition that when you do it, you look at yourself when you do."

I take a deep breath and with a shaky hand lower the blade to my wrist just as I do, Edward grabs my hand. "What do you see Dana?"

"I see someone who is scared and alone. Someone who doesn't know who to turn to because nobody else knows what she's going through," I answer so quietly I'm not sure he has heard me.

"Why can't you keep eye contact with yourself?"

"I don't like what I see. It's so hard to see myself like this, to see what other people must see."

"What makes you think no one else would understand what you're going through?" he queries. I stay quiet not really knowing how to answer. Am I really that self-absorbed? That I would think I am the only person to feel this way. "Are you starving to death Dana? Are you living on the streets trying to stay alive in the below-freezing temperatures? Do you live in a third world country, where the water you drink could kill you?" I shake my head. "Speak!" his voice bellows.

"No sir."

"So what makes you think that what you've been through should influence the rest of your life?" I drop my head, and he lifts my chin, our eyes meeting again in the mirror. "You *can* move past it. You have friends and family to support you." His grip on my wrist tightens. "Imagine the person in the mirror is not you. If you saw this person in this exact position, what would you do?"

The tears leaving my eyes are uncontrollable now, through sobs I manage to answer. "I'd go to her, take the blade from her and hug her. Tell her that there is another way of dealing with this."

At that moment Edward takes the blade from me, wraps his arms around me and says my words back to me. I sink to my knees with him still holding me, crying hysterically. He turns me around, so my head is on his chest. He grabs a handful of my hair and pulls my head backward. "Do you understand why I did this?" he says forcefully, willing me to understand.

"Yes, I think so." I feel so confused at the moment.

"What you saw when you looked in the mirror, is what I see when I look at you. It hurts me, and I want to help you like you wanted to help the girl in the mirror. There will be conditions, though. First, you have to stop drinking and second you are going to have to start working on the emotional side of things."

"I understand," I whisper.

"I didn't realize how much you relied on the physical pain so we will need to wean you off it like you would wean a drug addict off drugs, but we will do it in a controlled environment, and I will be locking your black room and keeping the key. Okay?"

"Okay." I smile at him for what is probably the first time today, because for the first time since Grant I can finally see the light at the end of the tunnel.

"We will talk more about this tomorrow, but right now I'm happy that we have made some progress. Please know that you are never alone, I will always be here and that I do understand what you're going through." I chuckle, and he pulls my head back again, his face deadly serious. "And I swear to god Dana, if you ever hurt yourself again I will personally bend you over my knee and spank your arse till it is red and raw and you won't be able to sit down for a week. Am I making myself clear?"

"Yes," I yelp as I feel his hand connect with my buttocks. "Yes, sir." He gives me such a big grin I can tell he's just as happy as I am that the tension between us has dissolved.

He nuzzles into my neck. "Promise me," he asks, needing extra reassurance.

"I promise." And I know I mean it.


We left the room, and Edward led me to his room, I did wonder what would happen now. Was he going to fuck me like he did last night? He walked over to his drawers and pulled out a pair of boxer shorts and a t-shirt. "Here, put these on I'll get your clothes washed for you." Well, I obviously wasn't going home tonight.

As I go over toward the clothes, I picked them up and thanked him, moving to the bathroom to change. We then settled down on the sofa, and he turned the TV on, but I couldn't concentrate I needed to know where I stood now.

"Where does this leave us, Edward?" I ask nervously.

"What do you mean?" he asks a little perplexed.

"What are we now?" I ask, blushing.

"Nothing has changed, I'm still your boss." His tone is clipped.

"I know." I sigh, I'll have to spell this out. "I mean are we together? Will we be having sex?"

"No." I wait for him to continue but he doesn't.

I'm confused, and this seems to be happening a lot with Edward, he's so cryptic. "What was last night about then?" I'm pretty sure I didn't imagine that.

"Last night shouldn't have happened, you shouldn't have been there. I'm sorry if that is not what you wanted to hear, but I don't have relationships, and I don't have casual sex. This is not about sex Dana, it's about healing."

I don't know why but this upsets me, I feel so stupid to think he would like me. I rise from the sofa and give a fake yawn. "I'm tired, I'm going to go to bed."

I start to leave, but he grabs me by the elbow, he watches me for a moment then lets me go. "Okay, goodnight."

"Yeah, night," I reply turning my back on him,

disappearing down the hallway to my room. I lie on my bed and reflect on the events of the day. Can I really keep this promise? Even with James and the black room, the urge to cut is still there. As I close my eyes and start to drift, I think maybe this is one promise I shouldn't continue making, I'll only break it like I always do.

I'm woken again by the terrified screams coming from Edward's room. I can't listen to this but I know I have to, he won't appreciate me going in there. I put my pillow over my head and start humming to drown out the sound. Eventually, it stops, I hear his door open and close and footsteps that come to a stop outside my door. It opens, and I lay still hoping he thinks I'm asleep. I hear his footsteps getting closer to me and then I feel the mattress dip. He strokes some hair off my face and leans down, kissing me on the cheek.

"Thank you for saving me last night sweetheart. I wish I hadn't of pushed you away so you would have come and saved me tonight," I hear him whisper, and I try not to react, as my heart constricts for him. I feel him stand and go to the door, he waits for a beat before closing it and continuing down the hallway to another room. I decide to try and get a bit more sleep, in the morning I'll ask him about his dreams.

When I wake again the sun is high in the sky, I decide to get up and get some coffee. The apartment is quiet, Edward must still be asleep after his broken night. When I go into the kitchen, I see my phone on the counter, and I smile to myself. I make coffee, shocked that the time on the coffee machine says it's eleven. Unashamedly I decide to catch up on Facebook and the daily news, I must have missed out on a lot yesterday. Suddenly I regret that decision as when I load up MSN news, there are pictures of Edward and me at the restaurant Friday night.

**Is New York's most eligible bachelor finally taken?**

This caption is above a picture of Edward with his hands on mine, did Edward know about this? I read through the texts that are all from James, asking where I am and what the hell I think I'm playing at. I also have several missed calls from both James and my Mum, great just what I need.

While Edward is asleep I decide to snoop around a bit, I find the library and the billiards room, and then I find his office next door to his bedroom. Curiosity gets the better of me, I decide to take a look around. Nothing out of the ordinary jumps out at me, the usual business stuff. It's actually quite impressive I can't help but be proud of him. Then something catches my eye, a cheque for one hundred thousand dollars made out to Edward's foundation. It's the sender that makes the hairs on my neck stand up, Richard Dalton. Why is my stepfather sending large cheques to Edward? Something is not right with all this I just can't put my finger on it.

I hear the toilet flush in the next room, so I put everything back where I found it and make a hasty retreat back to the kitchen. I start to pour another cup of coffee for us both when he comes up behind me and leans over my shoulder.

"Good morning, how did you sleep?" he asks. He's wearing only a pair of jogging bottoms his chest bare with just a smattering of hair. His hair is all tousled from sleep, he looks so sexy. I can't let him distract me, he is hiding something from me, and I want to know what.

"Great thanks." I offer a smile. "Thank you for my phone."

He can tell I'm a little on edge. "I was going to give it to you last night, but you went to bed early. Are you okay?" His voice is full of concern.

"Not really, apart from the fact that I now have to deal with an irate best friend and psycho Mother, neither of who will believe why I have ignored them for the last thirty-six hours, I've just checked the news, and we are all over it."

"Don't worry about James and your Mom I took care of that already. I don't want you having to deal with more shit than you already have to." He pulls me to him holding me in his embrace. "As for the picture, there isn't much I can do about that, and I'm sorry." He seems genuine when he says this, or maybe it's the sound of regret I hear.

We drink our coffee in almost silence. I want to ask him about the cheque but I can't, then he will know I was in his office. What is the connection between these two men, which as far as I'm aware have never met? "Can I go home now?"

The worry in his eyes, when they meet mine, is apparent. "Yes, of course, give me a moment to get myself together, and I'll drive you."

"It's okay I can just get a taxi, I just need you to use your key on the lift," I answer him quickly.

He shakes his head at me "Your clean clothes are there on the table. I'll be ready in five to taking you home."

Obviously, I'm not meant to argue with him. I snatch my clothes off the table and stomp back to my room, slamming the door. I'm aware I'm acting like a child, but he is treating me like one. I go into the bathroom to brush my teeth and have a quick wash, I can shower when I'm home.

I'm dressed and waiting by the lift doors. I need to get out of here, to see James and have a glass of wine. When Edward enters the vast living space, he eyes me suspiciously. "Eager are we? Anyone would think you want to get away from me."

"What makes you think that?" I roll my eyes and gesture my hands as if to say come on, hurry up.

He gathers the last things he needs and is finally at my side, giving me my bag, he puts the key in the panel and presses the call button. I let out a long breath that I didn't realize I had been holding. I practically run into the lift and then the doors close, I don't think I've ever been this happy to be inside one. The doors open to the underground garage, and with his hand on my back he leads me to his car. Now I'm impressed, the things you can buy when money is no object. In front of me is a Bugatti Veyron Vitesse. "Can I drive?" The words are out of my mouth before I realize.

"Do you have a driver's license?" he asks wearing a playful smile.

I must look like a kid on Christmas morning. "Yes!" I answer, jumping up and down.

"Have you driven in New York yet?" I stop dancing around and shake my head. "Then no, you may not drive." He then opens the passenger door for me to climb in. He leans over me to put my seatbelt on, I don't bother to argue. "Don't look so glum, maybe one day I'll let you take it out for a spin." He really does know how to put a smile on my face.

We travel in silence for a while, listening to the radio then he turns it down. "I have been meaning to ask you, on Friday why did you leave the restaurant so abruptly?"

Oh, I had forgotten about that. "Twice last week I noticed someone following me when you said you had also been following me I just thought it must have been you, but then you told me you weren't following me last week but the week before."

148

He thinks for a moment. "Who do you think is following you?"

"I have no idea." I have my suspicions, but Edward doesn't need to know this. It's a crazy idea, I know I'm just being paranoid. He's in England, and I'm in the States, he doesn't know where I am. I stare out the window the rest of the way home, I really don't want to discuss this with Edward, and I want to talk it through with James.

We pull up to my building, Edward comes around to open the door and helps me out. "Thanks for the ride, I'll see you tomorrow," I say trying not to sound rude or awkward.

I'm about to leave him on the side of the road when he grabs me. "I'm coming up with you. I'm locking that room of yours, remember?"

I take in a deep breath and let out a loud exasperated sigh. "Fine."

His grip on me tightens. "What's wrong?"

I'm starting to feel anxious, I'm so close to being in my own apartment, what is his problem?

"Nothing is wrong, I just want to see James and be in my own home." I can't keep the angered tone from my voice.

I open my front door and am relieved to be home. James comes flying out of the kitchen. "I'm sorry, I'm so sorry. I should have called, but that arsehole stole my phone," I start shouting as I point at Edward standing in the doorway. He just rolls his eyes at me.

"It's okay, he called to say you were adamant you wanted to leave his place in the early hours of the morning, and I agreed with him that you shouldn't be walking the street of New York at that time." I frown at him, my brow knotting in the middle of my forehead. "Last night he called to say you went to bed early before he could give you your phone, he told me you looked tired, and he didn't want to disturb you."

I hear Edward cough behind me, I turn on my heels looking at him my face aghast. "The key Dana, then I can leave you in peace."

"I'm sorry Mr. Day I don't feel like

accommodating you right now, please leave."

He grabs my upper arm and drags me through the apartment to my room, literally throwing me inside. "What do you think you are playing at?" he practically hisses. "You made me a promise."

"Oh I'm sorry, so you can lie and make me look stupid and let's not forget you treating me like a whore." I'm so angry at him now I'm shouting.

His jaw clenches as he walks towards me, grabbing my upper arms with his hands so tightly it starts to hurt. Lowering his face to within inches of mine, he growls at me, "Don't ever refer to yourself like that again."

"Sorry but I don't plan on being one of the many conquests you've had in your bed. Did you treat them all like this?"

"Be careful what you say Dana, a statement like that belittles you and disrespects me." I don't answer him, I just want him to leave. "I haven't lied Dana, twisted the truth a little, maybe. Now you will keep your promise, give me the key," he repeats himself sounding out each syllable.

I leave the room, and he is quick on my tail. I lock the black room door and take the key out, he puts his hand out to receive it. "You're an arse," I say.

He smiles as he takes the key from me, moving around me and out the front door without another word.

In the kitchen I'm relieved to find two glasses of wine already poured, it's midday, why not? "James, you read my mind."

I go to pick up a glass when he moves in to stop me. "Um... Wait-"

He's interrupted by a male voice behind me. "Hey, are you coming back to bed?" I turn to see the six-foot-four muscular vision of masculinity stood behind me, with dark brown floppy hair and eyes so dark they're almost black. I turn back to James who is blushing.

He bites his bottom lip and then answers my unasked question. "Dana this is Andy, Andy this is Dana."

152

I turn back to the man that has James' attention and find there is something eerily familiar about him.

# Chapter 8

I'm momentarily startled before my manners kick in. "Hi, lovely to meet you finally. This must be your drink."

Andy steps forward to take the drink. "Thank you, it's lovely to meet you too, all Jimmy does is talk about you," he replies, moving next to James. Both men are the same height, and now I just feel really short.

"Wow, Jimmy, I haven't heard you be called that in years," I say to James. "Why are you still in bed? It's lunch time, get some clothes on. We are going for lunch, I have so much to tell you." I turn back to Andy. "Will you be joining us?"

The heart-stopping smile he gives me makes me melt. "That would be great, thank you." He turns on his heels and heads back to James' room.

"So, Jimmy?" I question him sarcastically. "You brought him home to meet the family?"

James blushes a deep crimson. "I told him about you wanting to meet him, and he suggested he come stay. He seems to be really interested in getting to know you, so hopefully, this means it's getting serious. We'll just have to see how it goes."

"If you're happy, I'm happy." I give him a smile and let him go get dressed. I must just be paranoid at the moment, there has to be a reasonable explanation for why Andy looks so familiar.

We make our way downtown to a little Italian place that Andy recommends. Andy seems so laid back and down to earth it's impossible not to like the guy, not to mention he is easy on the eye. I stop this train of thought immediately. I cannot crush on my best friend's man. As we sit down to eat, Andy leaves to use the restroom. "Okay, I like him," I tell James with a huge grin that he returns instantly.

"Thank you for inviting him, I know you wanted to talk," he says warily.

"Jay, talk is an understatement. This has been the craziest weekend of my life, I just need to discuss it with someone." I'm beginning to feel out of control, and I just need to feel like my friend is anchoring me.

"Shoot, what's going on? And why does he have the key to our black room?" he questions.

At this moment Andy comes back to the table, James and I go quiet. "What are we talking about?"

James looks at me, and I nod with half closed eyes to say it's okay. "Dana had a pretty fucked up weekend and needed to talk about it."

Andy smiles. "Is this about the guy I heard you shouting with back at the apartment?" I start to blush but nod. "Okay I'm all ears, I've been told I'm a good listener and give good advice."

James and I both smile, this man puts me at such ease I could really get to like him. "Right, tell me what happened Friday after you left the apartment. Why did you come back in such a mess?" James starts.

Suddenly my head starts to spin. With

everything that has happened, I hadn't really had a chance to focus on all the events of Friday evening. "Oh god, Jay." My breathing is erratic, and Andy is next to me like a shot.

"Calm down and breathe," he says rubbing my back. What is it with this man? I start to calm instantly. I realize then that he reminds me of Edward, but so much more down to earth.

"Okay, I'm good thanks," I stammer slightly embarrassed, I take a few deep breaths. "Right, after leaving the apartment, we went to dinner at this beautiful little restaurant-"

"The one where the pictures were taken?" James interrupts.

"Yes that one, can I finish now?" He nods giving me a tight-lipped smile. "Anyway, we were talking, and he said that he had been following me-"

"So he was the one you saw lurking in the shadows?" James stops me again.

"If you let me finish I'll tell you."

He holds his hands up. "Okay, continue."

"Well that's what I thought, but he said he had followed me the previous week before he had even met me." I can see James wants to say something, so I raise my eyebrows, silently giving him permission to interrupt.

"You know that's really weird right. All the stuff he's been saying and doing to you at work, and now following you." James sounds genuinely concerned.

"What has this man been doing?" Andy asks, I forgot he was sitting there.

"It's a long story babe I'll tell you later. Sorry girl, carry on with what you were saying." James addresses us both.

"Anyway I kind of freaked out and left, and I started running Jay, I mean really running. Then out of nowhere, this prick with a knife tried to drag me down an alley." My eyes start to fill with tears, and the sudden urge for pain has returned.

"Oh my god! Why didn't you tell me you silly cow? What happened? Have you spoken to the police?" James pours me a glass of wine and I down half of it.

"I'm sorry." I'm stammering as my brain remembers what went on. "Edward happened, that's why I can't go to the police. I'm just lucky Edward was there, he beat the guy nearly half to death. I got home and headed straight for the black room, and the rest you know."

James comes round the table and pulls me into a massive bear hug, he's not slim or muscular but lean and big built. He gives the best hugs. "Okay, so what happened after I went to sleep?"

"Well, I needed answers. Why was he so determined to help me? What had you ruined? That sort of thing." James stays quiet, so I continue, telling him about everything that happened after I arrived at Jackson Square. He listens intently and nods in the right places, then I take another sip of wine. "Oh shit, I'm not supposed to be drinking. Edward said I'm not allowed to drink."

I think at this point James loses it and Andy

has to help me calm him down. "He's a fucking arsehole Dana. He called your Mum and me and said you were being irrational and that you were drunk and he put you to bed." I don't think I've seen James' face this angry before. "Drink the wine!" he practically shouts at me.

"Jimmy come on, calm down. You don't want to be like that Edward guy." Andy sounds like he has the voice of an angel right now. It works, and we all manage to sit and have a nice meal, laughing more than I have in a long while. Andy is really good for James, I don't know why I was ever worried.

Back at the apartment, I take a long awaited shower, just feeling the need to get the weekend off my skin. We still never discussed what we initially went to dinner for in the first place, why did I enjoy the spanking he gave me in the lift? Why does my womb tighten every time he says the words? Isn't he contradicting himself, saying I can't harm myself but he can deliver pain to me? Oh god, why is this all so confusing? I need to get out of my head. I climb out of the shower and put on my slob clothes and go into the living room to join James and Andy on the sofa. We catch up on the Saturday night TV that we missed last night and order pizza for dinner. Back to my normal life with my best friend, this has been the weirdest weekend of my life, and I'm not looking forward to going to work tomorrow. After dinner, I decide to turn in early, with no sign of Andy going home I don't want to be a gooseberry. "I'll see you in the morning nice and early for your first day at your new job." I smile excitedly at James.

"Night night sweetie, see you in the morning," James answers me.

Not long after going into my room I hear James' bedroom door shut, and I can't help but breathe a sigh of relief for him. Andy seems like he's a keeper.

Monday morning arrives too quickly for my liking, I hardly feel like I've slept. I drag myself out of bed and across the hallway to the bathroom, just as

Andy is exiting. I nearly jump out of my skin. "Good morning Dana. Sorry if I startled you."

"Morning Andy, don't worry about it." I close the bathroom door behind me and almost instantly hear a knock. "Yeah?"

"Would you like some coffee?" Andy's smooth voice carries through the door.

"I would love one thanks." He leaves me in peace to continue getting ready for work. When I'm done, I hurriedly head back to my room to get dressed when I realize the time.

"Jay, where are you?" I call through the apartment, running to the kitchen to pick up the coffee that Andy so kindly made me.

"In here girl!" he shouts from his room.

I enter and stop in my stride. "Wow, Mr. Ward you do scrub up nicely."

"Do I look okay?" he asks rather shyly.

"You look amazing." I give him a huge hug and kiss on the cheek. "Listen I've got to get going I'm late, just wanted to wish you good luck."

162

James lowers his head, I can't help but wonder what he is thinking. "Do you think that maybe things are too great right now?"

"Don't you dare, don't do that. Things are great so enjoy it, don't start thinking something's going to go wrong."

"Thanks, Dee," he says with a wide grin using his nickname for me that he hasn't used since we were twelve.

I manage to hail a taxi to work for the first time since being in Manhattan - Andy taught me yesterday - so I end up being five minutes early, although today I wish I wasn't. Just as I get to my desk, Vanessa comes bouncing out of her office. "Hey did you have a good weekend?"

"Fantastic," I answer trying to keep the sarcasm from my tone.

"Okay, well Mr. Day called down and asked if you could pop up to his office he has an important assignment for you. I think it means it involves a celebrity."

I roll my eyes and shake my head with a small smile on my lips, some people get star struck so easily. "Does he want me to go up now?"

"Yeah if you wouldn't mind, it'll get him off my back. The man must think I can make you appear out of thin air judging by the number of times he's called me in the last half an hour."

"I'm not late, am I?" I check my watch and the office clock.

"No, you're not." She laughs. "That's what I can't understand, why he didn't just wait till nine and ask for you?" She's interrupted by the phone on her desk. "Hello." She holds up her index finger to indicate she will be one minute. "Yes, Mr. Day. She's just arrived. I'll send her straight up." Then she holds the phone away from her ear. "Impatient asshole."

"I better get up there," I say.

"Dana, I saw the pictures of you and Edward in the news-"

I stop her there. "It's not what it looks like, we

164

were just having dinner."

"Hey, I'm not judging you. Just be careful with Edward, he's had a lot of bad press when it comes to women," she says with caution.

"Yeah, oddly enough that's all Google had to say about him too." I'm laughing as I walk back towards the lift bank and press the call button. As the doors open I shout back. "I'll let him know you said hi!" I hear a loud cackle come from her office as the doors close.

I let Edward's receptionist Rachael know I'm here and take a seat in the waiting area. I must be sitting there for at least ten minutes, not only have I not been offered a drink but if Edward so urgently needed to see me, why am I still sitting here? "Miss Spencer, Mr. Day will see you now."

I stand up feeling the anger rise in me. "Oh, will he now?" I mutter under my breath. How dare he demand to see me from half-past eight, but leave me sitting in his reception for as long as he pleases. Outside his office, I take a few deep breaths and then knock.

"Come in." I hear the smooth voice of the man that makes my entire body obey his every command.

I open the door and peer round it. "You wanted to see me Mr. Day?"

He shows his brilliant white-toothed smile, god he's sexy. "Take a seat. How are you?"

What's his game? I keep my expression passive. "Great thanks, is there something I can help you with?"

He frowns at me looking confused and worried. "Is something wrong Dana?"

"Not that I'm aware of." My inner-self does a little victory dance. Don't treat me like a fool.

He rounds his desk and heads to the sofa I'm sitting on, I sit up straight and keep a professional distance. "Good. I have a really special assignment for you. We have just interviewed film star Cain Cunningham, and now we need to do the photo shoot. I know you don't usually do this type of photography but, I was wondering if you would like

166

the opportunity."

"Did you say, Cain Cunningham?" He nods "Are you serious? You're not kidding around?" I swear my grin makes the Cheshire cat look like it's frowning.

"I'm not joking. I love your work, and I really think you're the best person for the job."

I can't hold back anymore, I literally jump at him throwing myself on top of him with my arms wrapped around his neck. "Thank you, thank you, thank you. You have no idea what this means to me."

"I'm glad you're pleased, and I'm happy that you're not in a mood anymore." He raises his eyebrows at me, and I look away sheepishly. Wrapping his arm around me and uses the other to lift my chin to look at him. "What was wrong?"

I know I'm blushing, "It's stupid don't worry about it." His face is disbelieving. "Fine, I was annoyed that you had been eager to see me and then when I got up here you made me wait."

He smiles and lets out a snigger. "I had an important phone call that I had to deal with, that came at the most unfortunate time. I'm sorry."

"I'm sorry I shouldn't have jumped to conclusions," I say. He's rubbing his hand up and down my spine, sending a shiver right through me.

"Were you eager to see me?" he asks looking so arrogant but still extremely good looking.

"No." I look away from him. "Maybe." I look back at him with a lopsided smile.

"Well if it's any consolation, I've missed you too." Now it's his turn to look sheepish.

"Why?" I ask wrinkling my nose in confusion.

"I can't answer that just yet, not because I don't want to tell you, but because I don't really know myself. Right now I know I have to keep my emotions in check so I can help you." He seems rather sad about this fact.

"You make me sound like a client that you're doing business with." I sound offended.

"Well in a way you sort of are," he answers quickly. "I'm not boyfriend material Dana, I need you to know that."

168

I don't know why but I feel like I've had my heart broken. Did I expect more from Edward or did my feelings for him just grow without me realizing? "I understand," I say plastering on a fake smile and perking myself up as if I'm unaffected by his words. "We still need to discuss the whole spanking scenario," I say gesturing my hands in a roundabout way. "I mean that was the reason we went to dinner Friday."

"Would you like to talk about it now or maybe at dinner tonight?" A second date with Manhattan's most eligible bachelor?

"Dinner sounds great," I answer.

"I'll pick you up at seven." I nod. "Ok let's talk about Cain Cunningham. You need to fly out to his home in California-"

"What!" This man can't be serious.

"He's in California. You'll catch the red eye tomorrow at ten."

"Until when?" The panic on my face must be apparent because Edward looks extremely concerned.

"Thursday," he says slowly. "With no delays, you'll be back in New York, Friday morning."

"Ok, do I have an itinerary?" I ask with a shaky voice. I can't believe he's giving me so much responsibility, I'm just not sure about the 'going solo' bit.

"Yes you will, and you'll be taking an assistant with you. You'll start at his home in San Francisco and then head down to his second home in Beverly Hills, where he will be residing while filming his next movie." He must see me breathe a sigh of relief. "Are you feeling better?"

"I am now I know I'm not going alone." I let out a little giggle. "Thank you for giving me this responsibility, I promise you won't regret it."

"I know I won't." His eyes are full of confidence. In me?

"Who is coming with me?" I suddenly realize I may not know them.

"Simon will be accompanying you," he answers. Simon works in my department, and I get on

170

really well with him, he's one of the girls really. "I thought that might make you happy."

"I don't know what to say, Edward. Thank you," I gush. Then he leans in and kisses me. I pull back. "I don't think that's such a good idea."

"Maybe, but it doesn't stop me from wanting to do it." He leans in again, and I jump off him.

"We still have so much to discuss let's not confuse things." He nods his understanding but looks disappointed. Oddly this kind of cheers me up, I'm under his skin as much as he is under mine. "What do you want me doing for the next couple of days?"

"I would like you to read the interview and use it to set the scene for the photo shoot." He says, back behind the businessman mask.

"Well, that won't take me two days, anything else?" I ask, maybe I should be using my initiative.

"Research him, find out all you can. That way you won't slip up talking about anything that will make him feel uncomfortable," he answers. His phone rings and I see concerned lines appear on his face. "I have to take this, if you need anything just call Rachael."

This is his polite way of telling me to get out. "Thanks and I will, see you tonight." I lean in and give him a peck on the cheek. I turn and saunter out. I know his gaze is on me I can feel the heat on my back.

I'm back on the twenty-fourth floor, looking through the interview. I can't believe in forty-eight hours I'm going to be taking photos of *the* Cain Cunningham. I can't help but start daydreaming.

"Sleeping on the job?" I'm snapped out of my reverie by Simon, my new assistant, well for the week anyway.

"No just letting my mind wander. Wow is it mid day already?" I stutter, as my cheeks flush.

"Mm-hmm, I believe you. Are you doing anything for lunch? I thought maybe we could go to the deli and start planning our trip." He seems so excited, I hope he knows this is work and not a holiday.

"Yeah that sounds great, I didn't have time for

breakfast." We reach the lobby and my mobile rings, I see James' name flashing up. "Hey dude," I answer, and I hear him laugh down the phone. "How's the first day going?"

"Yeah it's brilliant, everyone is such a laugh. They want to take me out for welcome drinks tonight, and I wondered if you wanted to join us?" His cheerful voice brings a smile to my face.

"I'm having dinner with Edward tonight, and I don't think it's a good idea that I go to places serving alcohol," I say, disappointed.

"Tell me you're joking, and that you're not blowing me off for that douche bag?" He seems angry, what is his problem? "He tells you to stop drinking, and you do it, just like that. If he tells you to jump off a cliff, would you do that too?"

I try to stay calm but my voice betrays me, I start shouting at him. "Firstly, you have been asking me to cut back on the alcohol for ages, I do it, and now you're having a go at me. Secondly, I'm going to dinner with Edward because he is sending me to

California tomorrow evening to do a photo shoot with Cain Cunningham and we have a few details to iron out. And thirdly, he is not the douche bag Jay, you are." I hang up, feeling like a part of me has been torn out. I hate arguing with him. I probably overreacted, he just wanted to share this exciting time with me, and I threw it back in his face. If anything I'm the bloody douche bag.

"Is everything okay?" I turn and see Simon beside me. I forgot about him, and at some point, during my phone call, we entered the deli.

"Yeah sorry, my roommate," I say pointing to my phone. "What are you having?"

We order and take a seat, we eat while talking about all the things we can go see and visit while we're in California. Simon starts to look a bit shifty, his eyes darting back and forth between me and something behind me.

"What's the matter?" I ask a little concerned.

"A guy is looking through the window at us," he answers. As I turn around so does the man at the window, then he walks off. I stand and run out of the deli, but he's gone. Simon joins me on the pavement. "Someone you know?"

I shake my head. "I really hope not."

# Chapter 9

I find it hard to concentrate the rest of the day. I really wish I hadn't of shouted at James now. I decide to send him a quick text.

**Hey, just wanted to say sorry for earlier.**
**Also, I'm still being followed xx**

I must have waited at least half an hour and then finally there is a reply.

**Ask Edward.**
**He probably knows who it is.**

What the hell?

**Do you know who it is? Xx**

This is getting ridiculous now. I don't know what to do.

**No. Sorry Dana I'm being a dick, I doubt Edward knows.**
**You know me I'm just being a jealous idiot. Love ya girl xxx**

I'm smiling now, we never argue for long, but why would he say something like that unless there is some truth in it. I think it might be best just to let it go, for now at least, I'll bring it up when things between us are less fragile.

**After dinner, I'll come meet you for that drink.**
**So proud of you. Love ya too xxx**

When the clock strikes five, I close everything down and leave. I rush home to jump in the shower and get ready. With Edward picking me up at seven it doesn't give me much time. Just as I arrive back at our apartment building, Andy is leaving the lobby. "Hey, have you been here all day?"

"No." He chuckles and pulls me into a hug. "I was looking for Jimmy."

It's still weird hearing someone call him that again. "He's going out with some of his colleagues, a sort of welcome to the office drinks."

His face seems to convey recognition. "Yeah he asked me to join him, I thought he wanted me to meet him here." He's fidgeting, I can't help but feel like he's not being entirely truthful. "Well, I better go, he'll be wondering where I am." He gives another chuckle.

"Cool, Edward and I will see you later on then," I say.

"Are you both coming too?" he asks, I thought I saw panic cross his face.

"I'm going to dinner with him first then we'll both be joining you later."

"Both of you?" he asks again.

"Yeah," I say trying not to sound worried. Why is he being so cagey, does he know Edward?

"That's a shame I would have liked to meet him, but I can only go for a little while. I have a lot of work to do." He's back to smiling.

"Hopefully we will get there before you leave, if not we will have to arrange a night out when I get back," I say remembering I'm not going to be here for the next few days.

"You off somewhere?" he says frowning. "James didn't say."

"I only found out today. I'm off to California for a photo shoot tomorrow night. I'll be back Friday morning so we can do something Friday night if you like?"

"I can't do Friday night, I have a business function. How does Saturday sound?"

"Perfect." I look at my watch and realize the time. "Listen I've got to go, or I'll be late, see you later yeah?"

He nods "Most definitely, if not tonight it will be tomorrow before you leave." We hug each other, and I make a quick dash up to the apartment.

Edward arrives dead on at seven. He's wearing a black suit and crisp white shirt, with black shoes. He isn't wearing a tie, and his top button is undone. How does he make looking casual so sexy?

"Hi there sweetheart, you look beautiful." He gives me his Hollywood smile, making me blush. I'm wearing a knee-length leaf green dress, that matches the green in my hazel eyes and have left my red hair loose around my shoulders.

"You don't look too bad yourself," I counter.

As we make our way out of the building, I instantly notice the Bugatti. "No Peter tonight?" I ask.

"No I thought you might like tonight to be a little more private," he says.

"Can I drive?" I ask with so much hope in my voice.

"No, I love my car too much," he says with a playful grin.

"Spoil sport." I give him a smarmy look and get in the car, he leans in to put my seat belt on. "I'm not five," I say snatching the belt from his hands.

"Could have fooled me." He counters slamming the door. How does he bring out my stubborn side so much?

We pull up outside Park Avenue Tower. Edward passes his keys to the valet as we head inside. "Are we eating here?" I ask.

"Yes, at Aquavit. They serve the most amazing Nordic cuisine. I'll bring you for lunch one day when they serve an a la carte menu of Scandinavian classics. Their Swedish meatballs are magnificent. I didn't know what your preferences were so I decided on the eight-course chef's tasting menu of their more modern Nordic selection. I hope that's okay?" He speaks with such passion.

I'm a bit perplexed. "I have no idea what you just said, but it sounds lovely. Thank you for going to such a great effort for me, you didn't have to."

"I know but I love this place, and I wanted to

share it with you." He goes silent like he's suddenly said too much.

I hook my hand around his arm, and he escorts me in. The place is stunning with modern and rustic elements. We have just taken our seats when a waiter approaches us. "Will you have the wine pairing with your courses?"

Edward answers straight away. "No thank you, can we have two bottles of still water."

"Of course sir," the waiter says before scurrying off.

"It would have been nice if you had asked me if I would like the wine," I say snappily.

Edward gives me a stern look. "I would appreciate you sober for this conversation. Besides I thought we agreed, no alcohol."

I stare back at him aghast. "I'm not an alcoholic, Edward. Please don't treat me like one."

"I'm sorry, I just think for now we should stick to water," he says not making eye contact with me. What is he hiding?

"Fine, whatever." I sulk.

"Stop acting like a child Dana, seriously." He actually looks angry with me.

"Then stop treating me like one." The waiter comes back with our water. "Excuse me, I'm sorry to be a pain, but I would like the wine pairing with my courses," I say seeing Edwards jaw clench.

"Yes ma'am, of course," the waiter says looking a little flustered.

"No, she won't" Edward chimes in.

"Yes I will, evidence to the contrary, this man is not my father, and I'm of legal drinking age. So please bring the wine," I argue back.

"Dana." It's a warning, but I've had enough of this man and his stupid rules.

"Thank you," I say to the awkward looking waiter, who looks to me, then Edward and then turns and leaves as quick as his feet will allow. I turn to Edward with victory evident in my expression.

"You're not drinking it, so you can wipe that look off your face," he states with his eyes trained on his water bottle.

"I will do as I please." I give him a polite smile, why the hell did I come for dinner with him?

"You will not disobey me," he says through gritted teeth, anger rising in his face.

"Screw you." I stand from the table.

"Sit down!" he shouts slamming his fist on the table top, causing everyone to go quiet and stare at us. I continue making my way to the exit. I hear Edward's chair scrape on the floor as he stands up. "Dana, come back here."

I scurry out the door and manage to hail the first taxi to go past - thank you, Andy - and head to the bar James is at. I start wondering what happened to Edward, did he follow me out? Then I do a mental check trying to remember if I told him which bar we were going to after dinner, I'm relieved to remember I didn't. He is going to be so pissed off at me, I have a stupid grin plastered on my face.

We pull up outside the bar, and I hand the driver a twenty dollar bill, telling him to keep the change. I duck inside the bar as quickly as possible.

I spot James and come up behind him, startling him. "Hey girl, so glad you could make it. Glass of wine for M'lady?"

I chuckle at him, I can tell he is a little tipsy. "Yes please, kind sir. I obviously have some catching up to do." We both laugh and head to the bar. "Is Andy still around?" I ask him after we give our order to the barman.

"You just missed him, he was disappointed that he couldn't wait around any longer for you. It's hard to believe I've only known him five weeks, I feel like I've known him forever. I'm acting like a giddy teenager," he says with a smile the size of the Joker's.

"He seems like a great guy, I'm glad you're happy Jay. He doesn't come across as a game player either, spending as much time with you as he can." Let's hope he doesn't prove me wrong.

"He's coming over later, once he's finished dealing with a difficult client. Are you okay with him spending so much time at the apartment?" He sounds worried about my answer.

"I told you before that I'm happy if you're happy. I get on well with Andy, so it's fine," I tell him taking a large sip of wine. Ahh, that's nice.

James takes me back to his group of co-workers and introduces me. They are a really friendly bunch and seem to like James. We all have a good laugh and the night begins to draw to a close. Feeling a little drunk I think back to Edward and start laughing hysterically. James asks what's so funny and between gasping for air I tell him what happened before I got to the bar, he then joins me in my fits of laughter. We stumble the fifteen blocks home singing all the nineties British classics when the Bugatti I love so much pulls up beside us.

"Get in the car now!" Edward commands but I'm too drunk to care.

"No, go away. We're having fun, and you're a spoilsport." I make sure I pronounce the words as clearly as possible in my drunken state, but James and I just end up laughing again. Edward opens his door and gets out. "What are you going to do caveman?" This really doesn't help the matter, because Edward bends down and picks me up, placing me in the car in one swoop. "You can't do this, it's kidnapping."

"Shut the fuck up Dana, you have no idea how pissed I am at you and right now. It would be in your best interest for you to stay quiet." He doesn't sound angry, more disappointed.

We drive in silence for a while, and then I turn to him. "You're such a douche bag," I say.

His brow creases and I see his lips twitch as he tries to suppress a smile. "If you're going to start name calling, at least think of something original."

"Where are we going?" I ask knowing we are not going back to my apartment.

"Back to my place," he answers casually.

"I want to go home please, all my work stuff is there." I'm starting to become really irritated with this man that I've known only a week.

"You're not going to work tomorrow, so it doesn't matter." He sees the confusion on my face.

"You'll need to sleep tomorrow, with the time difference in California the last thing you want is jetlag." Does he really think this is normal?

"Don't you think that maybe, you should have asked me first." My temper flaring due to the alcohol consumption and this impossible man.

"You're not capable of making a sensible decision," he answers with such disdain.

I'm just about to argue back when I feel my stomach roll which reminds me that I haven't eaten anything but have had several drinks on an empty stomach. I heave trying to hold it back, but it doesn't work. Feeling the bile rise in my throat I am scrambling for the window button when Edward calls my name. I turn to him and unable to hold it back anymore, I throw up in his lap managing to avoid getting any on my dress. Once I'm finished, he opens the windows not saying a word, but I can see in his face that he would kill me if he could.

I didn't make matters any better when I turn to him in my drunken, giggling state. "Karma's a bitch."

We pull into the garage of his building, and he still hasn't said a word to me. I go to get out of the car when he's on me like a shot, dragging me forcefully from the car. "Chill out will you. Sorry about your car, but seeing as I wasn't meant to be in it in the first place, I'm blaming you."

"When are you going to grow up Dana? When will you start taking responsibility for your actions?" He sounds exasperated.

It hurts when he treats me like an errant teenager. "I don't see what problem it is of yours. I want to go home, you can't keep me here," I say turning my back on him.

He walks in front of me and puts his key in the lift panel. "Come up and have a cup of coffee and sober up. If you still want to go home in an hour then I'll take you," he replies.

I give a tired sigh, I can't fight anymore. "Fine."

We step into the lift car and start our ascent. I

feel him staring at me, but I don't turn to him. I really have had enough and can't wait to get on the plane tomorrow, I need to get away from him. Maybe some distance between us will help me figure out what it is I'm feeling. We step off the lift into his apartment, the vast space always seems to amaze me, but still as impersonal as before. "You go brush your teeth and change if you want, I'm going to jump in a quick shower then I'll make us both some coffee," he says to me watching my cheeks go bright red with embarrassment.

"I'm really sorry, you know, about the car and the vomit all over you and stuff," I manage to stammer.

"It's okay, it's not the first time I've been thrown up on." He raises one eyebrow with a mock expression, but I see an amused smile playing on his lips, my heart jumps out of my chest. I know I'm very attracted to this man, but I need to keep my emotions under control.

I head to the room that I stayed in before, it

seems a little more welcoming this time. On the bed is a new silk nightdress and robe. I pick it up, it feels exquisite, so soft between my fingers. There is also a new chest of drawers and wardrobe in the room that wasn't there before, I open the drawer and find several new bra and knickers set. Why has he done this? Another drawer is full of toiletries with a new toothbrush and even a razor. I'll give him credit, though, he thought of everything. In the wardrobe, there are a couple of pairs of jeans and tops and a beautiful evening gown. I hear a knock on the door. "I see you found everything." He looks a little worried.

"Yeah, how long do you think I'm staying here?" I ask trying to keep the hostility from my voice, as my anxiety rises.

"Well, I just thought... I thought because last time, you had no clothes and now you do," he stutters and stammers his way through the sentence.

"I want to say that it's thoughtful of you, but it's a little creepy," I respond bluntly.

"I'm sorry. I'm not used to feeling like this and

I'm not sure how I'm supposed to act," he states wryly like it's difficult for him to admit.

"Feeling like what?" I question him.

"It doesn't matter, why don't you get yourself comfortable and meet me in the kitchen." When he closes the door, I gather the toiletries I need and make my way to the bathroom. After I get out of my dress and take a shower, I put on my new nightdress and robe.

I find Edward in the kitchen. "Hey sweetheart, are you staying?" His voice sounds hopeful.

"It's late. If it's still okay, I'll go home in the morning," I say.

His smile is one of relief. "Of course, here's your coffee. Do you know how to play pool?" he says casually drinking his coffee after placing mine in front of me.

"Yeah I'm great, me and James spent a lot of time on the pool table growing up."

"I have a pool table if you want to play?" he asks.

"Yeah, I'm up for a game. Are you any good?" I question him.

"I haven't played for a long time. I've had no one to play with," he answers quietly.

"Don't you just go out to a bar and have a few games with some mates?" I ask.

"All my 'mates' are in the business world," he says in a terrible English cockney accent, making us both laugh. "We're so busy that we only really socialize at business functions and events."

"Sounds kind of lonely. I don't think I could spend half of my life isolated or locked up in an office." I try to sound casual.

"It's no big deal. I speak to people all day. I still have a laugh and joke with people, but by the end of the day, I'm too tired to socialize. Which reminds me, did you like the dress in your wardrobe?" he asks.

"I did, but I don't know when I will ever wear such a beautiful garment," I answer honestly.

He opens the door to the billiards room, and we go in, placing our drinks on a side table, he starts to set up the balls. "I was wondering if you would attend a business event with me on Friday evening as my plus one?"

"Really? Wow, thank you. What is the function?" I ask a little worried.

"A dinner and dance, wear the dress in your closet, it will look nice on you." I narrow my eyes at him, and he gives me a knowing smile, all tension in the air gone. He knew I would say yes. I look at his happy face, his eyes glisten with joy, and his smile melts me. At that moment I know I'm screwed. I'm falling in love with him, and there is nothing I can do to stop it. This can only end in disaster and a broken heart. He must see the pain contort my face because he suddenly looks concerned. "You okay over there?" he asks.

I shake the worry off and smile. "Always, just trying to decide if I should go easy on you or not." I lie.

"Fighting talk, give me all you got." We both laugh, and he breaks.

We're playing for at least ten minutes when I feel comfortable enough to ask. "So come on, tell me why I liked the spanking?"

He looks at me thoughtfully. "Do you know that every single person in the world, whether they admit it or not, has at some point or another fantasized about spanking or being spanked. Yet only about ten percent of people will act on it because the rest believe it's a taboo subject, that it is not correct behavior. Those people are never truly free. You like the pain, but the sort of pain you inflict upon yourself is just pain. You knew when I said I would punish you, that there would be pleasure involved as well, I saw the way your body reacted. That is what you have been craving, that's why you became wet."

"So what does that mean, what does it make me?" I ask lining up to take my shot.

"You sweetheart are submissive," he says this as my cue hits the white ball startling me sending the white ball off into the pocket. "You should concentrate more, you're distracted too easily." He

195

laughs.

"I'm not a submissive," I growl.

"Don't get defensive Dana, it's nothing to be ashamed of. Some people become submissive, it's a life choice. But some people are born submissive, it's in their DNA. No matter how hard they try to hide from it, it will always be there, and they will never be fully satisfied in life or sexually. You were born submissive, it's in your blood. The way you yield to my every command, even when you're being stubborn and disobeying me. You know in your heart that you should do as you are told. After I saw the pose you were in when I saw you in your black room, I knew then you were a true submissive. You shouldn't be scared of who you are, in fact, if embraced properly, it can bring you so much pleasure," he says with such confidence.

I'm stunned and angry all at once, I'm not thinking straight. "I've heard all that before, and it was a lie. I will never submit to another man again." Just then I realize what I've said.

"Again?" he questions me.

"Just drop it please Edward, I want to go home now," I say to him.

"No, you aren't going to keep running away from this. When things get tough you run, no more running," he states firmly.

"Please don't do this." I'm practically begging.

"Talk to me Dana," he commands quietly but assertively.

I know that this is it, I was going to have to face the memories sooner or later, and so I take a deep breath. "Grant," I start.

"Tell me about him, from the start. I want to hear it from you." So we sit on a sofa in the corner of the billiards room, and I begin.

"When we first started dating he was fantastic. I thought I was so in love with him. My mum and I were arguing like mad and her boyfriend at the time, Clay, was horrible. I was angry at my mum, my dad had been dead only eighteen months, and she had moved on. I ended up running away about a month before my sixteenth birthday. Grant let me move in with him, he kept telling me I did the right thing and that I was welcome to stay with him as long as I wanted. Even his parents welcomed me with open arms." I'm starting to struggle now, and Edward moves closer placing his hand over mine, giving me the support to continue. "About three years later Grant was doing some work on his parent's car, he messed up, and there was an accident killing both of his parents. It was heartbreaking for both of us, but Grant was carrying the guilt. At first, he just withdrew from me, then he started drinking and then he started hitting me. After a while, he told me all that stuff you did about being submissive. He told me I was a pain slut and that I loved it when he stuck his cock so far down my throat I gagged." I take a minute to calm myself before I continue, Edward is rubbing his thumb soothingly over my knuckles. "He told me that I was his willing whore to do what he wants with, even forcing sex on me. He was always telling me he knew I wanted it even though I said no. He told me I was his

198

submissive and I would be his forever. That no one else would have me, he would make sure of that. One thing led to another, and I knew I had to get away, but when I tried to leave him, he locked me in a cupboard under the stairs for over two weeks. He gave me food and water, and I had to thank him with sexual favors. Then he disappeared. I was found by Richards private detectives a day or two later. I'm not sure how long it really was, every minute in there seemed like an hour. He had apparently become aware of people looking for me and knew that they were getting close." I'm sobbing now, and my voice is barely audible.

"I take it that's why you're claustrophobic." I nod trying to stop any more tears from falling. "Listen to me, Dana that was not a typical dominant and submissive relationship. A submissive should not be scared of her Dom. She should trust him, and he should know her limits and obey her when she uses her safe word. Did you have a safe word?" I shake my head, knowing where he is going with this. "He used your willingness against you as an excuse to justify what he was doing because he knew it was wrong. What he did, was domestic abuse. I would never discipline you in anger, it should be fun and exciting, and you should want to be punished because you know the pleasure that will come afterward. Did the police ever catch him?" he asks with compassion in his voice.

"No, I was twenty-one by the time I was rescued and moved back home. The police had no luck tracking him down. I reconnected with James, he had gone through a lot of crap too, and that's when we decided to help each other. Six months ago I was asleep when I felt James waking me up and dragging me out of my house because it was on fire. The fire investigation officer ruled it an arson attack. So Richard moved us in with him, as he had his suspicions about who was behind the fire, and now we're here in New York," I say trying to end this horrific ordeal on a light note.

"And they still haven't found him?" he asks

again.

"Nope, the police and Richards private detectives are still out there hunting him down," I answer.

"Why are there private detectives looking for him too?" He tries to ask without prying.

"Because Grant has something of mine," I snarl, all tears gone, "and I want it back."

# Chapter 10

I get up off the sofa and walk towards the pool table. "I do believe it's two shots to you, sir." Right now I need to get off this topic of conversation.

"Dana," he says, his voice deep but full of desire, happy to move off the subject of Grant. "Are you mocking me?" He gets up and walks towards the table as I carry on walking around it.

"No, sir," I answer innocuously.

"Are you teasing me?" he asks, his strides closing the gap between us.

I pause at the edge of the table. "Maybe, sir." I give him a provoking smile.

"It's not very nice to tease people, young lady." Edward moves his leg between mine effectively pinning me to the side on the table.

I place my hands on the top of the table and

lift myself up, so I'm sitting on it. At this point, he moves his whole body between my legs. "What are you going to do about it?" I ask as angelically as I can. His bright green eyes look full of conflict like he's trying to decide something.

He opens my robe and tucks his arms inside wrapping them around my waist, pulling himself closer to me. I can't help it, I wrap my legs around his lower body, and my hands fly into his hair. His face is in my neck kissing and licking the sensitive skin of my clavicle, and then I feel his teeth sink into the muscle of my neck. Just when I think he's about to draw blood, he lets go. The pain that was there a moment ago has turned into something warm that travels through my body to the pit of my womb, then I feel it ignite my clit. Wow, he was right, you can get pleasure from pain. "I shouldn't be doing this," he mumbles into my hair then starts nipping along my jaw.

"Why not? Don't you think it's time you gave me some answers?" I ask.

"Not yet," he replies and continues what he was doing. I don't fight him, there is a time and place to discuss those matters and now is not it.

I pull on his hair as his mouth reaches my lips, searching his eyes for something, anything, but the only thing I can see is heated desire. That's good enough, I allow his lips to reach mine as he forcefully kisses me like he's wanted to do this for forever. His tongue enters my mouth, and I don't stop it, in fact, I welcome it. I lightly brush my teeth against it and suck on it. He tastes so good, with a hint of mint. He pulls back still holding me in place and looks at me. "What's wrong?" I ask.

He takes a deep, exasperated breath and then exhales. "Oh, fuck it," he says, lifting me further back onto the table as he climbs on, potting balls into their pockets as he goes. He's on top of me, and I'm not sure which one of us is panting faster, his hands are all over me, clumsy like he hasn't touched a woman in ages. His eyes divert to my arm, he lifts it and kisses the last part of the remaining scab. "It's healing nicely, please don't mark your beautiful body again," he says as he pulls the small spaghetti straps of my night dress off my shoulders exposing my breasts. His hand starts to massage my left breast, as he takes my right nipple in his mouth. I'm not sure what to do, so I run my hands up his back and into his hair. Gasping and panting as he bites down on my nipple, his hand moves down making slow circles on my belly and then down my thigh. Finding the hem of my nightie his fingers slip under it and works their way up my bare skin to the crease of my labia. I stiffen, and he looks at me for approval to which I nod unable to speak. His mouth is quickly back on my nipple. His finger and thumb massage my clit and the sensation is overwhelming as he alternates the pressure, I've never felt anything like this before.

"Stop!" I pant. "I think I'm going to pee." His eyes strain up to see me, and he gives a little chuckle with his teeth still clenched onto my nipple.

He lets go just briefly. "Trust me, you're not going to pee. Relax and let go."

I try to do as he tells me, I feel like I'm delirious. Is this a dream? Then I hear his deep voice somewhere in the never ending black space in front of me, telling me to let go and come for him. I'm really not sure what happens at this point, stars start to fly into my vision lighting up the darkness, I think I'm crying and laughing at the same time. I hear screams of pleasure and realize they're coming from me, I can't hold on any longer, everything in my abdomen hurts. With one final scream of pleasure, my body convulses as a lot of fluid leaves my pussy. I'm spent, I lay there for a long time just trying to catch my breath, tears rolling down my temples as I laugh. I feel Edwards hand just lightly and slowly rubbing my cheek, I know he's trying to slow my breathing. As I start to come back to the real world I try to sit up, I feel how soggy and wet the blue baize on the table is, and my cheeks redden with embarrassment.

Edward must see this because he is next to me in a second. "Don't you dare feel embarrassed, that's not urine," he says soothingly pulling me towards him. "I take it you've never had an orgasm like that."

I shake my still cloudy head. "Is that what happened?" I ask. He nods but doesn't say anything letting this all sink in. "No, that's never happened to me before," I say still astonished.

"Do you feel the satisfaction and fulfillment you experienced because you let yourself go, relieving yourself of your inhibition?" he asks his eyes so full of wisdom like he's trying to get through to me and make me understand.

I nod still speechless, there is silence between us for a few minutes. "Sorry if I ruined your table."

He laughs so hard, it's a beautiful sound to hear. Pulling me into him, he says, "Don't worry, I might have to play pool in here more often now." He's grinning at me, and I can't help but smile back as my heart beats just that little bit faster. Our moment is over when we hear a phone ringing from his pocket, he pulls it out and looks at the screen. "I have to take this," he says jumping off the table. "Hello." I hear a woman's frantic voice but can't make out what she's saying. "Payton, slow down. Is Caroline conscious?" Payton is his ex-girlfriend, I remember the article James showed me. "Ok let me know when the ambulance gets there and I'll meet you at the emergency room. I just have to drop an employee off at home." He's still talking away on the phone but I block it out now, I'm hurting. How did I ever believe that something could happen between us? "Dana?" I hear Edward call me. "I need to go out-"

I stop him mid-sentence. "That's fine, I'll get my stuff. I hope everything is okay?" I say in a clipped tone.

"I'm sure it will be." That's all he says, no explanation, nothing. *He doesn't owe you an explanation*, I tell myself, *he's just your boss.*

Back in my room, I decide to put my dress back on, as it managed to stay vomit free. I think about putting on jeans and a t-shirt, but stubbornness gets the better of me. I grab my bag and walk back to the living room. "I'm ready," I say trying to act nonchalant.

He looks at me confused. "It's freezing out there, why don't you put on something a little warmer?"

"No thanks, let's go." He eyes me suspiciously but chooses not to say anything.

We exit the lift into the underground garage and Edward leads me to a black town car, I smile behind him remembering what I did to his other car. "Jump in," he calls across the bonnet.

"Who's Caroline?" The words are out of my mouth before I can stop them.

He takes a deep breath and is looking anywhere but at me. "Just a friend, get in the car please."

"I'm good, I'll get a taxi." I begin to walk off, but by the sounds of the heavy footsteps approaching me quickly from behind, I know that it's futile.

He picks me up and walks me hurriedly back to the car, placing me in the seat. Where he then does the seat belt. I don't say anything I know I'm being stubborn and childish. He looks at me with such discontent, he shakes his head as he starts the car and I feel so foolish.

We pull up outside my apartment, we haven't spoken a word since I got in the car. As I go to get out, he stops me. "Please think before you do things, stop behaving like a child." Then he lets me go. This just annoys me more, I can't speak to him right now. He's hurt me so much tonight. "Don't worry about work tomorrow, make sure you get some rest. I'll pick you up just after five on Friday, you can get ready at my place."

Sometimes I really need to keep my mouth shut, now is one of those times, but I don't. "Oh shoot, I forgot I'm going for drinks with James and his boyfriend on Friday. Sorry to let you down, lucky for you I'm no one important, just an employee," I say slamming the car door.

"Really?" I hear him shout from the vehicle, his voice angry and frustrated. The door opens and then slams closed. "No wonder Nathan isn't in your life anymore, you make no attempt to even act like an adult."

I freeze at the sound of Nathan's name. How does he even know about Nathan? How dare he judge me, if he really knows about me then he should be aware that Nathan not being here was not my choice. I turn to him with disgust in my eyes and can see that he instantly regrets his outburst.

"Dana I'm so sorry, I don't know why-"

I can't listen to him anymore. "Fuck you, Edward," I spit the vile words from my mouth, turning on my heels and heading into my building. I hear what sounds like a window smash, but I just keep walking.

I'm not even worried about the lift ride up to my apartment, I'm too devastated. How dare he bring Nathan into this. Tonight I've realized I don't mean anything to him, whatever he says. I can't behave like a child, but he can act like a bully. I pull my key from my bag and open the front door, startled by the figure sitting on the sofa in almost darkness. "Sorry if I scared you," Andy says, closing the lid of the laptop.

"It's okay, I didn't think anyone would be up," I say turning on the lights. "James told me you were meeting a client or something, how did it go?" I ask trying to make conversation. I really don't know why as I'm so tired and want to go to sleep, but something tells me I won't be sleeping well tonight.

"It went okay, I wasn't fully prepared because of the amount of time I spent with James this weekend. So I was just burning the midnight oil, hoping to catch up." I smile and nod my acknowledgment. He takes a moment to look at his watch then back to me. "It's two in the morning, you're either home really late or really early."

I rub my hand along my forehead. "Honestly, I have no idea which," I answer.

"You want to tell me about it?" he queries. "James filled me in on what happened up until you were whisked away by Prince Charming."

I eye him suspiciously, but he seems genuinely worried. "The short version is, he wouldn't let me go home till I was sober. We drank coffee, played pool, he forced information out of me and made me come all over the pool table. Then he gets a call from his ex-girlfriend Payton, about another girl named Caroline, called me his employee and brought me home." I see Andy's face grimace, and I realize I may have gone into too much detail. My phone starts ringing in my bag, I see Edward's name on the screen, so I ignore it, I really can't be bothered with him tonight. I'll deal with him tomorrow, he can stew for a while. I put my phone on silent and turn back to Andy. "Sorry." I give him an embarrassed smile.

"Don't be, you've got it off your chest. Did he actually call you his employee after the thing on the pool table?" It's Andy's turn to look a bit embarrassed and awkward now.

I laugh and nod. "Then I acted like a stroppy fifteen-year-old and said I wouldn't attend this dinner and dance event he invited me to on Friday. I lied a little and said I was going for drinks with you and James. Then he said something that really hurt me and I told him where to go," I say with a sad smile.

"What did he say?" he asks.

"It doesn't matter, I just want to forget about it. What I don't get is why Payton's calling him if they broke up years ago and why he wouldn't tell me who Caroline was," I reply.

"Listen, Dana, I didn't want to mention this before because I thought this thing with you and Edward was just a weekend thing." I can hear the nervousness in his voice, and his hands have become fidgety. "I mix in some of the same circles he does, he really isn't a good man. Did he tell you why he broke up with Payton?" I shake my head feeling a little nervous myself now. "She was pregnant, and he didn't want a baby. Caroline is his five-year-old daughter." He stays silent for a moment letting me take it all in and make sense of it.

"Are you sure about this?" I ask, knowing the answer already.

He nods, his eyes look so sad. "I'm so sorry Dana." He wraps his arms around me as silent tears fall down my cheek.

I wipe them away defiantly. "I know the truth now." I give Andy a tight-lipped smile. "I'm going to get some sleep. Thanks, Andy I'll see you in the morning." I give him another squeeze and head to my room.

I'm so angry with myself after letting my feelings for Edward get out of control. I need to stop this, no more letting him bully me. I get under my bed covers and settle in for the night, I must have been tired because I was asleep as soon as my head hit the pillow.

I wake up the following morning with a pounding head. Stress really isn't good for me. I check the time on my bedside clock, It's only six in the morning. I decide to jump in the shower, I'll try to grab a couple of hours of sleep this afternoon before I leave this evening. At least I've got the day off and don't have to deal with Edward. I grab my towels and head to the bathroom, turn on the shower and wait for it to get to my required temperature. I turn around to hang my towels on the heated towel rail and come face to face with Andy.

He instantly jumps back out of the bathroom. "Sorry, God I'm sorry. The door was unlocked, and I didn't realize anyone was in here."

I wrap a towel around me and head out into the hallway. "Andy I'm sorry. James and I have this rule that we don't lock any doors, I thought he would have told you." He looks just as embarrassed as me.

"He did, I just forgot, I'm still half asleep. Can we pretend this didn't happen?" he asks a little sheepishly.

He looks so cute when he blushes. "Sounds good to me."

I head back into the bathroom and get in my waiting shower. When I'm finished I check the hallway thoroughly before running to my room, I don't want to get Andy all red-faced again. I put on a pair of jogging bottoms and one of James' old baggy t-shirts and go to the kitchen where I hear Andy pottering around trying to find things. "What are you looking for?" Andy jumps back from the cupboard. "Sorry didn't mean to scare you." I can't help smiling, his face was a picture.

"Just looking for things to make breakfast, do you want a coffee?" he asks.

"That sounds lovely. Is James up yet?" My question is answered when I hear the shower start running again. "I'll make us some bacon sandwiches."

Andy chuckles a little. "I haven't had a bacon sandwich in years."

I'm slightly shocked at this revelation. "Well you'll be having them a lot when you're here, that's more or less what we live on, and sausage sandwiches too."

By the time the bacon is cooked, James is sitting at the table. I put my arms around him from behind and kiss his cheek. "I'm sorry about last night."

He looks up at me, and I can tell I've already been forgiven. "It's cool, Andy caught me up on everything when he finally came to bed last night."

"I love you, you know that right?" I say heading back to finish the sandwiches.

"I know, I love you too girl." I place breakfast in front of us all and refill the mugs with coffee.

I listen to Andy telling a story about his meeting the night before, and how disastrous it was, we're all laughing. I feel so much more relaxed today, I wish life could be this laid back all the time.

I decide to clear up while James and Andy get their stuff ready for work. I'm just procrastinating now, I know I have to pack a bag and get all my stuff sorted. Looking out the window - I love looking at the city from up here - I remember that I need to call my Mum. I haven't spoken to her since she called Friday to cancel on me. Why hasn't she called? She calls me every day. Edward talked to her Saturday when he wouldn't give me my phone back, but I haven't heard from her. What is going on? Suddenly my eyes lock on to a figure standing across the street, and I jump back from the window. "James! James!" I'm screaming now.

218

James and Andy both come running in to see me with my back up against the wall next to the window. "What's wrong?" James says his brow furrowed and a concerned look crossing his face.

I point to the window. "The person who's following me, they're standing across the street."

James makes his way to the window and confirms the figure is still standing there. "He can't see us this high up Dana, take a look and see if you know him."

I slowly move back in front of the window. "I can't really make him out myself," I say turning to James. "I mean we're twenty-two floors up."

James runs off to his room. "Here try these," he says as he re-enters the room.

He hands me a pair of binoculars, I raise an eyebrow at him but decide not to comment. Looking back out the window, I can sort of see the man, but I can't tell if I know him. "His face is too concealed," I tell James as I pass back the binoculars.

Andy retrieves them. "No idea at all?" he asks.

I'm being paranoid, it can't be him. "No." I give them both a small smile, I don't want James to worry. "Anyway I'll be in California tonight, maybe I just need the break. Though I'm not looking forward to the time change, it took long enough for me to adjust when we moved here."

James puts his arm around me. "What time do you leave?"

"It's all in the itinerary. A car will pick me up here to take me to LaGuardia airport at seven tonight, my flight is at ten and will arrive in SFO at one am local time. After a day there we take another plane from San Francisco to LAX and then leave Los Angeles at nine pm local time and will arrive back at LGA at five am our time. I will hopefully be back and in my bed by seven Friday morning." I smile, feeling quite chuffed with myself that I memorized it all.

James and Andy are giving me such strange looks, anyone would think I've grown a second head. I'm pulled into a tight hug with my best friend. "I can't believe how grown up you are," he says mockingly.

I punch him on the arm. "Go to work. Can you let the front desk know not to let anyone up that isn't on the approved list? Also that I don't want to be disturbed if anyone should ask for me," I say. At least I'm safe up here, whoever it is following me they can't get to me here.

"Yeah not a problem, see you tonight and go pack your bag." James knows me so well, he knows I will leave it until about an hour before I'm due to go.

I wave them both off and close the door, double locking it just in case. I decide to call my Mum, I should really let her know I'm leaving the state. When I retrieve my mobile phone, I'm shocked to find fifty-eight missed calls, four voicemails, and ten text messages, all from Edward. What the hell? It won't hurt to keep him waiting a little longer. I will deal with him in a moment. I dial my Mum, and it rings twice the other end when she answers. "Dana, darling, how are you?"

Really? I haven't spoken to her for five days, why is she not frantic? "I'm okay Mum, I haven't spoken to you for a few days I thought I should get in touch."

"Well, it's lovely to hear from you. How's your job going?" she asks.

"Yeah, it's great. That's why I'm calling, to let you know I'm off to California for two days," I say as nonchalantly as possible.

"You're what? Dana, you can't go that far, you need to be close by where we can keep an eye on you," she says in the frantic voice I've been waiting for.

There's the Mum I know and love so much. "Sorry but I have to, my boss is sending me tonight."

"Who's going with you?"

"My assistant and me, that's all." I'm feeling tired now, I know where this is going.

"At least let us hire Carl again to accompany you," she states like it's no big deal.

"Mum I don't need a bodyguard-"

"Dana," she interrupts me. "Please, for me."

She really does know how to make me feel

guilty. "Fine, I don't care."

I hear a loud crash from my hallway, I jump out of my skin. "What was that?" she asks. I take a few tentative steps out of my bedroom towards the front door where I heard the bang. My heart is beating so hard. "Dana?" I hear my Mum through the handset.

I look to see the door hanging off its hinges, and then I see him. "Edward, what are you doing?" He looks really pissed off, and I suddenly feel scared. He marches towards me, his eyes bulging from his head. He looks tired like he's had no sleep, he takes the phone from me, tells my Mum I'll ring her back and puts the handset on the side. I'm not sure what I'm supposed to do, Edward just stands there staring at me. Maybe this time, I've pushed him too far.

# Chapter 11

I take a few steps back, but Edward is on my tail. I hit the wall, and he is practically on top of me. "When someone leaves you nearly sixty missed calls, you're supposed to call them back!" he screams in my face, he sounds scared. I can't deal with his close proximity, so I push him hard and move to the side.

"Jeeze, what is your problem?" I'm raising my voice now.

"You didn't answer your phone." His voice is slightly less manic now.

"So fucking what, it's a free country. If I don't want to answer my phone, I won't. Besides you only dropped me home six hours ago. In England, we'd call this stalking. You have also kidnapped me, held me against my will and now we can add breaking and entering to that list. I should be calling nine-nine-nine-

"

"Nine-one-one." He corrects me.

"Oh shut the fuck up! I didn't answer your call because it was gone two in the morning when you dropped me off, I was tired and wanted to sleep. I literally only just checked my phone because I forgot it was on silent and thought I would deal with my Mum first because it would have been a quicker conversation." I'm really losing it now, and he is just standing there taking it. "You're a psycho, do you know that?"

He stares at me for ages before replying, "I'm sorry, I just wanted to explain everything about last night, and when you weren't answering your phone I got worried. I told you I don't know how to deal with all this stuff, I need you to bear with me." His voice sounds strangled, and his eyes have diverted to the floor.

My head is really starting to hurt now. "What are you talking about? Why are you worried about me? You dropped me off at home and saw me go inside. Did you think you were special enough that I would hurt myself over you? Firstly I don't break promises, and secondly, you're not worth it." He winces, and I feel terrible for saying these things, but the guy just broke my door down because he hadn't heard from me for six hours. "And why do I have to bear with you? Nothing is going on between us, I'm just your employee, remember? I shouldn't have to put up with this crap Edward. Now, who's acting like a child?" I move to the sofa and sit down because if I don't, I will fall down. Edward is so controlling, I don't need people trying to control me.

"I'm sorry I just wanted to explain everything." He gestures with his hand, and I notice it has a bandage around it.

I grab hold of it. "What happened to your hand?" I ask, baffled.

He looks a little embarrassed. "I punched the back window of the car last night after I upset you."

I don't know whether to laugh or go mad. "Seems like I'm not the only one with problems." I look to his hand and then my front door. "I think you have some anger management issues."

"They only seem to have surfaced since I met you, you push me," he practically growls.

"I don't have time for this, don't blame me for your shit. I have packing to do, and you need to leave. Please send someone to replace the door, not all of us can afford to go breaking things every time we throw our toys out of our pram."

He has the decency to look a bit ashamed. He throws an envelope that he retrieved from his jacket pocket down on the table. "Your plane tickets," he says.

"Thank you. Now can you please leave?" I ask, not because I'm still mad but because I need some space.

"Of course. I'll have someone here to fix the door within the hour." He goes to walk out then stops. "I really am sorry," he says sombrely.

"I know, I'll call you later." I concede.

Once Edward leaves I watch out the window

for him. I see him leave the building, stop at his car and then walk across the street to the man that has been following me for the last week. He looks like he's talking to him, then Edward points to something up high, finishes his conversation and then he walks off, and Edward returns to his car. I feel utterly betrayed, James was right, Edward does know who's following me. I suddenly feel like I can't hold back my emotions, I find the first thing I can and throw it at the wall. Once I finish crying about the knife that has metaphorically been stabbed in my back, I realize I threw my coffee mug, and it's shattered across the floor. I crawl towards it like a starving person finding food, I pick up a piece and just stare at it. I don't know how long I am there, but I continuously bring the broken piece down to my already scarred wrist and then pull it back. Just when I think I'm about to slice it across the delicate skin, I'm interrupted.

"Dana?" I look up and see Andy. I smile my relief and throw the broken piece on the floor. "Are you okay?" I shake my head and tears start to move again. He leans down and picks me up with one arm under my back and one under my legs. I wrap my arms around his neck, and he puts me down on the sofa. He then goes over to all the broken fragments and starts to clear it up.

"Andy, don't worry about it, I'll do it," I say feeling guilty that he has come back to this.

"I'll do it, I don't want you to hurt yourself," he answers me. "I mean... you know, like when you pick it up you might cut your hand," he rambles on quickly.

"Thank you," Is pretty much all I can reply. "Why are you back, I thought you were going to the office?"

"James was worried about you when we left, so when I dropped him off at work, I told him I would come back here, so you weren't on your own." He smiles like it's no big deal.

"I'm sorry I know you have loads of work to do, please don't let me keep you." I feel so terrible, I can't believe he would do this for James. They've known each other only five weeks, and it's like they've been together for years.

"It's fine, I don't really need to be in the office to do the work I need to do today. What happened to the door?" His confused face is rather funny.

"Edward happened. The guy has real anger management issues," I say, and then I start to think. "Is that what you were trying to tell me last night? When you said he wasn't a good man?"

Andy gives me a half smile. "Yeah I'm just sorry I wasn't here to knock him out, he will never learn."

I'm a little taken aback by this statement. "What do you mean?" I can't help but ask the question.

"I don't want to gossip because I don't know how true it is. There was some bad press about him a few years ago. There was a girl he had been seeing, Sarah I think her name was, she accused him of doing some awful things to her," he says, but I can see in his face that he is struggling with telling me.

"I think I saw that article when I Googled him.

It said that no charges were pressed," I say carefully.

Knowing how James and I reacted to this, and that money was involved. Andy just confirms our theories. "He paid her off."

I nod and press my lips into a thin line. "That's what I thought."

Andy has been on his laptop all day, while I just dawdle around trying to pack my bag. Someone came to fix the door, but nothing else has happened, the apartment has been quiet. I can't help but think about what Andy told me and how I'm going to deal with Edward. I'm just going to have to cut him off completely, and that may include leaving my job. Andy appears in the doorway to my room. "I thought you might need a cup of coffee," he says, placing the cup on the side.

"Do you read minds? I swear I was just thinking about making a cup." I laugh.

"No, but I wanted one and thought you would too," he says and turns to leave.

"Andy, what do you do?" I ask feeling like I need to clear my head of Edward for a while.

"I'm an Inquiry Agent," he responds quickly.

"What does that entail?" Now I'm just being nosy.

"Clients hire me to find out information about their competitors, but I do take on some personal work too if the price is right," he answers.

"That sounds amazing, so what you working on at the moment?"

He eyes me suspiciously. "I shouldn't tell you, client confidentiality and all that but I suppose it won't hurt. I'm working for a Father, his ex-girlfriend killed one of their children and kidnapped the other, and my job is to find her."

I nod not really knowing what to say. "That's awful, but it sounds like it's a rewarding career if you get the required results."

He smiles. "It is." Andy goes back to his laptop, and I go back to packing.

James appears in my room at five-thirty. "I see

you haven't packed yet, but found time to get a new front door," he states with a smirk.

I'm so happy to see James. "Shut up," I say slapping his arm and pulling him into a hug.

"Andy filled me in on the Edward stuff. What are you going to do Dana?" he asks sombrely.

"I think I'm going to have to quit and look for a new job," I say.

"I'm sorry honey, I know you love working there," he responds. "Right let's get some food in and enjoy the next hour before you leave me."

We eat our Chinese and James helps me finish packing just in time for when a car pulls up outside. "Right, I'm off. I'll let you know when I arrive, though you probably won't see it till the morning." I'm starting to get nervous now.

James pulls me into a hug. "Come here. You're going to do great, I'll speak to you tomorrow, and I'll see you on Friday morning." He smiles at me and ruffles my hair.

I hug Andy next. "Take care of James for me

won't you," I say.

"Always, go have fun," he answers.

I exit the lift into the lobby and walk out the main doors to a limo. The driver is standing waiting for me, he takes my suitcase and opens the door for me. As I climb in, I feel the electricity on my skin, and I know before I see him that Edward is in the car too.

"Why are you here?" I ask as calmly as possible.

"I wanted to go with you to the airport and run through what you will be doing while you're away." He sounds casual enough.

"Okay, shoot," I say.

"I'm sorry about today I-"

I interrupt him. "You wanted to talk work, let's stick to that subject shall we?"

He recoils at my words. "I can see you're still upset with me, this was a mistake. I'm sorry."

"Can you stop apologizing please, I'm not mad anymore. I'm tired and a little overwhelmed by how controlling you can be. Let's just talk about work for now. I want a clear head, and we can talk properly when I get back," I say feeling a little deflated.

"I was wondering if you might reconsider attending the dinner with me on Friday. I really enjoy your company, and I have no doubt that you will make a very unpleasant evening more bearable." He looks down at his fingers resting in his lap. "My brother Drew will be in attendance along with my parents-"

I stop him there, what he is basically saying is that he needs me to go with him. "Of course I'll come, but as friends, no funny business," I smirk at him.

"Deal." I see the carefree smile I get to see so rarely on his face, and I can't help the small giggle that escapes. "Thank you," he says pulling my hand to his lips and kissing my knuckles. "You don't know what this means to me."

I need to ask him about Caroline and Payton, about his anger issues and why he was talking to my stalker. I can't do it now, it's not the time. I'll just have to send him an email when I get to San Francisco.

Cowardly maybe, but at least I can ask what I need to without him distracting me with his gleaming gemstone colored eyes and the fullness of his curved lips. I shake my head to get rid of the thought, I'm just distracting myself now.

We arrive at LaGuardia Airport just before eight, I start looking around for Simon. "Have fun, just because you're working it doesn't mean you can't relax a little too." Edward is standing behind me with such a boyish grin, it's hard not to get caught up in that face.

"I'll try, but I think I'll be too star struck to relax, I'll constantly be tripping over my words." He laughs, and I have to smile.

"Dana. Mr. Day." I hear Simon behind me and turn towards him. He pulls me into a hug, giving me a kiss on the cheek.

"Hey, you ready?" I ask.

"As I'll ever be, did you come to wave us off Mr. Day?" He laughs and holds his hand out to Edward.

Edward chuckles and takes his hand in a firm handshake. "No I rode over with Dana, just wanted to make sure she had everything under control and knows what she has to do," he says looking towards me out the corner of his eye, with his eyelids half closed.

"Cool, well we'd better go check in. See you in a couple of days Mr. Day," Simon says.

I turn to Edward and wave. "See you later!" I shout over my shoulder.

"Dana!" I hear Edward call from behind me, by the time I turn around he's almost touching me. He puts one hand on my back and one on my neck and pulls me towards him. Smashing his lips on to mine full force, I'm momentarily startled before I give myself over to the kiss. He eventually pulls back. "I just wanted to show you how I feel, I think we really need to talk when you get back."

I'm too shocked to answer. "Mm-hmm." Is the best I can do, so much for not letting him distract me. What am I meant to do now?

# Chapter 12

We've arrived! It's a lot warmer here than I was expecting, even for the middle of the night. There is a car waiting for us outside San Francisco International, just as I knew there would be. My Mum would never let me off that easily. "Thank you, Carl," I say to the driver holding open the door, who will also be my bodyguard for the next few days.

"Good to see you again Miss Spencer," he replies with a winning grin.

"Please call me Dana, I hate formalities. This is my assistant Simon." I introduce them, and they shake hands.

"Wow, Mr. Day went all out, didn't he?" Simon says as we settle into the back of the car.

"This isn't Edwards doing, it's my overbearing Mother's," I say as I press a button to lower the privacy screen. "I take it you know where we're going, Carl."

"I do Dana, don't worry I'll be as discreet as I can. There is no immediate threat so I wouldn't need to stick to you like glue." He starts to chuckle, and I laugh along with him. Carl knows as well as I do how much my Mother over exaggerates. Though I do wonder how he made it here before us.

We drive the majority of the way in silence, mostly due to tiredness, I can't wait to check in and sleep. As we pull up outside The St Regis, I couldn't be more relieved. Sometimes I really feel like I fit too much into one day. We check in, and I head straight to my room barely saying goodnight to the two men. I send a quick text to James and Edward letting them know I've arrived. Then leaving my suitcase in the middle of the suite I climb into bed fully clothed and sleep.

When morning arrives I'm feeling a little better, then I remember why I'm here and start to move in a frenzy to get myself ready to meet Cain

Cunningham. After showering and applying make-up, I straighten my hair, knowing full well that it will be frizzy again once I step outside. I pick out a knee length dress with three quarter length sleeves, perfect for a warm but breezy day and a pair of flat shoes. Armed with my sunglasses and camera equipment, I head down for breakfast. Simon is already there eating as much of the continental buffet as he can, I make a beeline for the coffee. Picking up a blueberry muffin, I go and sit at his table. "Morning," I say.

He looks up at me from the newspaper with a smile. "Morning, how did you sleep?" he asks.

"Like a log, you?" I question back.

"I was too excited to get any proper sleep, I was like a kid on Christmas Eve," he gushes. I have to laugh at him.

We finish up our coffee, and I notice Carl in the corner of the restaurant being discreet like he said. "Come on let's get going, we don't want to be late." We rise from our chairs and from the corner of my eye I see Carl stand too, he isn't even going to finish his coffee.

"I hope you don't mind, but when we finish, I was hoping to go catch up with some old college friends while we're here. You're welcome to come along if you want?" Simon tells me.

"That sounds great, let's hope we get what we need quickly," I say trying to feign hope.

"How long do these things usually take?" he asks.

"There is no real minimum timeframe, but depending how the model is behaving and how well the equipment is working, we could be here up to twelve hours if we are unlucky," I answer seeing the hope leave his eyes now.

"Well we better get to it then," he declares.

Cain Cunningham. What can I say? He is more stunning in person. His bald shiny head and dark brown eyes that remind me of Andy's, so dark they are almost black. He's incredibly toned, I don't think

I've ever seen muscles that big, well except on TV. *Don't say stupid stuff like that out loud*, I scald myself. I wonder if his tan is real or fake bake, maybe I should just keep my mind on the job. "Mr. Cunningham," I say approaching him with my hand out. "It's a pleasure to meet you."

He takes my hand but doesn't shake it. Instead, he gets down on one knee, takes my hand in his, lowers his lips to the knuckles and kisses them. He looks up at me through hooded eyelids. "Believe me the pleasure is all mine." His voice is so deep, it sounds mysterious, almost dangerous.

I can't help the involuntary shiver that creeps up my spine, and I'm sure he notices. I'm speechless, so I just stand there like an idiot, staring at him, my mouth gaping.

Simon taps me on the shoulder. "When you've finished playing Guinevere to his Lancelot, we have a job to do."

I narrow my eyes and stick my tongue out. "Spoil sport."

We spend most of the day laughing, but we do get a lot of work done. Cain is so laid back, but not the most graceful model.

We go down to the beach when we finish, cooling off the day with a cocktail. Simon headed off a little while ago when I told him to go meet his friends, he had done all he could. I told him I would meet him at the bar, I was having so much fun talking to Cain. "I hate having my picture taken," he says.

"But you're a movie star?" I ask slightly confused.

"I love being in front of a camera, but I don't like posing." He pouts mockingly as he says this, I lift my camera and snap a shot of his duck face. "You better delete that." His voice feigning seriousness.

"I was thinking of keeping it and blackmailing you, how much is it worth?" I ask nonchalantly.

Before I know it he pounces on me, pinning my arms with his knees and lifting my camera above his head. "Are you going to get rid of the picture?" he asks again. I can't answer because I'm laughing too much, I just manage to shake my head. The fingertips of his free hand start slowly walking up the side of my rib cage. "I wonder how ticklish you are?" he contemplates, and I know it's a threat.

"No please don't, I will get rid of the picture," I say hastily.

"Now I just don't know if I believe you or not." His fingers still slowly creeping up my side.

"I promise I will." I start to fidget and laugh as his fingers get close to my underarm.

With that, he starts to tickle me mercilessly, after writhing around and laughing hysterically he finally stops allowing me to get my breath back. "Are you okay?" he laughs climbing off me and helping me sit up.

"I made you a promise, didn't you believe me?" I ask feeling a little hurt.

"Of course I believed you, it was just too tempting, and I couldn't help myself." He gives me a lopsided smile, and I give him a mock look of disgust. "Let me take you to dinner, to make it up to you."

I have to do a quick mental recap of what was just said, yep that's definitely what he just said, and I didn't imagine it. Cain Cunningham just asked me out to dinner. Crap, I promised Simon I would meet him.

"Earth to Dana, come in Dana," Cain says shaking his hand in front of my face. "Is the idea of going to dinner with me so boring that you momentarily went into a coma?"

"What? No of course not, I just remembered I'm supposed to meet Simon," I say trying to hide my disappointment.

"He's with his friends, I'm sure he won't mind," he says.

"I made a promise, and I can't break it, I'm sorry." I shrug.

"You're a good friend. If it's not too rude to ask, maybe I can join you. I'd really like to spend a bit more time with you." He seems nervous.

"That would be great you'd be doing me a favor, I won't feel like such a gooseberry amongst his friends then." I can't stop smiling, can I class this as a date?

What is it with rich people having drivers? We're in the back of Cain's car being driven to the bar. "Is that car following us, Jesse?" Cain asks his driver.

I turn around to see which car he's referring to. "Don't worry about him, that's my bodyguard, Carl." He raises his eyebrows as if asking a silent question. "Don't ask, my mother is a little excessive," I say waving my hand dismissively.


God, I don't remember the last time I had this much carefree fun, drinking because I want to and not to numb the pain. We spend the majority of the evening playing drinking games and listening to Simon and his friends reminisce about their college days. Cain and I decide to leave the boys to it and head off in search of food. "How long have you been in America?" he asks me as we sit down to eat our cheeseburgers and chips.

"Just over a month now," I answer. "Wow, these chips are amazing."

"We call them fries," he says.

"Same thing, isn't it?" I ask.

"Well yeah but what we call chips, you would call crisps I think," he says a little uncertain.

"Ah yeah, it's strange you know, we both speak the same language, but yet it feels like I'm learning a whole new one," I reply.

"Do you think you could help me?" he asks tentatively.

"Depends on what with," I smirk back.

"The film I start working on next week, the lead female role is an English woman. I was wondering if you might run lines with me so I can get a feel for the authenticity." He smiles shyly.

"Wow Cain Cunningham wants me to help him with his script, how could I say no to such an honor?" I pretend to faint in my chair.

"It's a good job I'm not asking you to act, you'd be terrible," he says with a wicked grin.

My mouth gapes open, feigning insult. We both burst out laughing. "Yeah sure, why not? But seriously don't expect anything professional, I really can't act." We both continue laughing and make our way back to his car.

"Where would you like to go to practice?" he asks.

"Can we go back to the beach?" I ask. I love the beach and the feel of the damp sand between my toes, the wind has picked up a bit, but it's still warm.

"Whatever the lady wants," he replies.

We sit on the well-lit beach front, reading through the lines of Cain's script. I'm so nervous I just keep giggling. "You know this really isn't helping," he says, but he's just laughing at me too.

"I'm sorry." I take a few deep breaths. "I'll try to compose myself." I feel stupid doing this, I can't act and I know I'll just end up embarrassing myself. What was it Edward said about letting go of my inhibitions? "Okay, let's start again."

We read lines for a while, and I actually feel myself settle into the role, I feel like I'm really playing the part. Cain is giving it his all, as he comes to the end of his line he steps up close to me. I look down at the script to find out what I'm supposed to say next. "Oh that's it, you just have to kiss her and leave her at the train station," I say to him, he is still gazing at me intently.

He leans in, wraps his hand around my neck and plants his lips on mine. I'm shocked to start with but slowly ease into it, wrapping my arms around him till he finally lets me go. "I thought you said you couldn't act, that was one hell of a kiss," he tells me, desire filling his eyes.

That wasn't acting, but I won't be telling him that. His eyes are beckoning me, I need to put some distance between us before things go too far. "I should probably get back to the hotel, we have a plane to catch at seven in the morning to Los Angeles."

"Of course, well at least I get to spend one more day with you," he says.

I smile. "Hey if you're ever in New York you

can look me up," I tell him honestly, we got on so well, it will be nice to have another friend.

"I will definitely take you up on that offer." He smiles at me and walks me to the car where Carl is waiting.

"Good evening Dana, ready to go?" Carl asks, I nod and turn to give Cain a quick hug.

"See you tomorrow, Dana," Cain says as Carl closes the car door.

On the drive back to the hotel I pull my phone out and call James. "Hey girl, how's California?" It's good to hear his voice.

"It's great, I'm missing you, though," I say feeling a little sad that he is not here with me.

"So, is Cain Cunningham a real prima donna?" he asks.

"Actually, he is really down to earth and so nice. We hung out this evening, and he kissed me," I say. I hear James take a sharp intake of breath. "Don't get jealous he was just acting, I was helping him with his lines."

"You had Cain Cunningham's lips on yours?" he asks shakily.

"Yep," I answer acting uninterested. *I'm getting really good at this acting stuff*, I think to myself and smile.

"Do not wash your lips till you get home so I can lick them clean," he states slightly manically.

"Eww James, that's disgusting." We both start laughing. "I'll give you a call tomorrow, love you," I say blowing kisses down the phone.

"Okay, love you too, girl." He hangs up, and I decide to text Edward.

**Thank you again for sending me here.**
**It's been amazing.**
**I'm having the time of my life.**
**D xx**

I press the send button and throw my phone back in my bag just as we pull up at the hotel. "Is Simon back yet?" I ask Carl.

"I brought him back about an hour ago," he says.

"I didn't see you leave, did you break my Mum's rules and leave me unattended?" I ask, trying to be serious.

"Cain's driver, Jesse, was watching over you both otherwise I wouldn't have left you, I like my balls intact." He smiles with a raised eyebrow, and I have to let out a giggle. I hear my phone beep in my bag, I'll check it when I get upstairs.

I say goodnight to Carl and knock on Simon's door to see if he's still awake. "Hey, how was your evening?" he asks me with a slur.

"It was great, just wanted to say thanks for inviting me along to meet your college friends, it was so much fun," I gush.

"They loved you, and I'm under strict orders to tell you that you're now one of the gang." He smiles sleepily.

"I'm going to take that as a good thing." I lean in and hug him. "Get some sleep, we have to be on a plane at seven. Wake up call is set for five, sweet dreams." I run off laughing, he will have one hell of a hangover in the morning.

I decide to take a shower once I'm back in my room. I love the beach but not so much the sticky feeling of the salt from the air on my skin. As the hot water drips down onto my slightly sun-kissed skin, I can't help but think what a crazy day it's been and also about how much James will hurt me for washing my face. I wrap one of the hotels big, fluffy, white bath sheets around my body and pad my way over to the bed. I retrieve my phone from my bag to find the message from Edward waiting for me.

**You know how to make me smile,**
**You're welcome.**
**Edward**

I smile at my phone and place it on the bedside cabinet, deciding it would probably be best if I get some sleep as I have to be up in a few hours. I lay my head on my pillow and think of the moment Cain kissed me, but then I see Edward and that smile of his that melts my heart. That moment of weakness now consumes me with guilt, do I tell him or is ignorance really bliss?

I hear the sound of the hotel phone cutting through my peaceful dream and know that it's time to get up, but I don't want to. My dream is so much better than reality, Nathan and I are together again. My eyelids flutter open and I know I've been brought back to the real world, where Nathan is missing, and I'm all alone. I answer my wake-up call, and head to the bathroom for a quick freshen up. Getting dressed, I then throw everything in my suitcase ready for our early departure. Right now I need caffeine and to make sure Simon is up. I fling open my room door, and I'm frozen on the spot. The sight of three large and intimidating looking men standing right in front of it suddenly has me worried and on edge. What is going on?

# Chapter 13

"Miss Spencer, I'm afraid I can't let you leave the room," one of the big men steps forward and says.

"Dana!" I hear the familiar voice of Simon coming from the hallway.

"It's okay Dave, I'm here now," Carl says, arriving at my room. "Dana we need to step inside and talk," he says to me gesturing me back in the suite.

I do as I'm asked. "Carl, what's going on? Who are those men?"

Carl puts three newspapers on the table, I lean over to take a look and my hand flies to my mouth, there are pictures of Cain and I covering all of the front pages. I pick up one of them that also has pictures of Edward and I on it and scan it, the

headline reads *'What a difference a Day makes'*
bloody stupid play on words. I decide to read the
article.

*Has billionaire Edward Day been traded in for*
*movie star Cain Cunningham? The picture in the top*
*left shows Day eating dinner on Friday evening with a*
*woman confirmed by our sources to be Dana Spencer,*
*stepdaughter to British millionaire and entrepreneur*
*Richard Dalton. The pair was then spotted at Aquavit*
*arguing, when the fiery redhead walked out on him at*
*the restaurant, as seen in the above picture. Now*
*spotted in California with A-list action hero Cain*
*Cunningham (see photos below), laughing and holding*
*hands and spending a lot of time getting cozy on the*
*beach, The pair were even caught kissing towards the*
*end of the night. Who will win the heart of this fiery*
*redhead, Edward or Cain? We want to hear your*
*views.*

"I need to call Edward," I say lunging into my

bag for my phone. "I still don't understand why there are three huge men stationed outside my door."

Carl rests his hand on mine. "Edward will be busy right now, Dana. I need you to take a look at this picture for me." He pulls out what appears to be a snapshot taken from a CCTV recording. I look down and freeze instantly. "Do you know who this is?"

I nod still shocked at what I'm seeing. "That's Grant, why do you have a picture of Grant?" I'm starting to shake.

"I need you to calm down so I can explain," he says rubbing my back. "You were sent to California because Grant has been following you. Your Mother and Richard wanted to keep you safe and enlisted Edward to help."

I shake my head. "No, that can't be right. When I spoke to my Mum, she didn't want me to come to California, that's why you were hired," I say.

"Your Mother knew that pretending she didn't like the idea would be the only way you would agree with me coming along, I've been in California since yesterday," he explains.

"You told me there was no immediate threat," I say, repeating what he said when we arrived.

"There wasn't an immediate threat here in California. While you were here, they were removing Grant from New York," he answers.

"So why do we need the rat pack outside?" I ask.

"It was okay when Grant didn't know where you were but now thanks to smartphones and the internet, you're all over the national newspapers. Grant was on a plane back to England last night as far as I'm aware but now he probably knows you're in California. We didn't want to take any chances," he says in a calm voice.

"What about Nathan?" Carl just shakes his head at me. "I still need to call Edward." I can feel the emotion rising in me.

"Dana, I'd leave it for a bit. He's a little pissed off about the newspapers." Carl tries to be tactful, but I know what he really means, Edward thinks I've acted recklessly and betrayed him.

"That's why I need to call him, so let me do what I need to do," I say trying to stop my bottom lip from wobbling by biting it. Carl backs off, and I walk into the bedroom dialing Edward's number.

He answers on the second ring. "I'm not in the mood right now Dana, what is it?" He sounds so detached.

I can't hold back anymore, and I start to cry. "Please, believe me, those pictures are not what they look like. We were having fun, and they have been interpreted wrong." I'm pleading with him.

"How do they misinterpret a kiss, Dana? Explain to me, why you were kissing him." He's really not happy with me.

Now I'm angry. "What is your problem?"

"Thanks to your reckless behavior, I have been up half the night arranging extra security to keep you safe. God knows why, when all you do is think about yourself." His voice is so cold.

"I haven't lied, unlike you." My temper is rising

by the second.

"I have photographic evidence, Dana," he says while dodging my comment.

"Fine, believe what you want. The kiss was because I was helping him run lines before he starts filming. It was part of the script. Although I'm not sure why I'm explaining this to you. You are my boss who likes to blow hot and cold all the time, not my boyfriend. You, on the other hand, have been keeping a hell of a lot of secrets from me." I'm not even thinking about what I'm saying now. I really need to slow down and think, I can't let him know I found Richards cheque in his office.

"I'm sorry that I didn't tell you about Grant," he states in an authoritative tone.

"I'm not just talking about Grant, although James told me you probably knew who was following me and I didn't believe him until I saw you talking to my stalker outside my apartment Tuesday morning. I guess I owe James an apology," I say, irritated that he thinks he can treat me this way.

"Listen to me Dana, when I spoke to your Mom on Saturday evening after you went to bed, she said they had received an anonymous letter, threatening your life. She asked me to keep an eye on you because she had her suspicions that it was Grant. I told them that you mentioned someone was following you. We decided the best course of action was to get you out of the state, so you were out of danger, and we could deal with him. That is why I was so scared yesterday when you were ignoring my calls, I thought something bad had happened. So when you saw me approaching him outside your building, I was getting him to look up at the CCTV camera that watches the entrance to the building opposite yours. I managed to get a full face still image from the recording, and I showed it to Richard, who confirmed it was Grant. The same image Carl should have shown you this morning," he finishes explaining.

"Why didn't anyone tell me what was going on, I'm not a child," I answer, ultimately hurt and betrayed that no one trusted me enough to tell me this important piece of information.

"I thought it would be best, your safety is my top priority," he replies.

"So now I'm a liar and obviously too stupid to look after myself. When you think you can trust me, call me." With that, I hang up the phone.

It starts ringing again almost instantly but I ignore it, the man is a psycho and needs a time out. I walk back into the sitting area of the suite to find Carl on the phone, he turns to me. "Hold on a second, she's here." He hands the phone to me telling me it's Edward calling, I find the 'end call' button and press it. Carl looks at me shocked. "He was really pissed off Dana."

"Why are you even my bodyguard, you're such a wimp. The guy is a nut case, do your job and protect me from him." Carl tries really hard to suppress the grin forming on his face, which I don't help with when I burst out laughing.

"So what is all this about Dana?" Simon says gesturing to the newspapers.

"Simon we were just having a laugh as friends nothing more, look how they made it seem in the bar. You were there, you know it wasn't like that," I say pleading with my eyes that someone believes me.

"Oh yeah, this is when we were playing one of the games, and you tripped, Cain grabbed you and dipped you to make it look like it was a deliberate fall," he says.

I hear Carl's phone ringing behind me. "Hello... Mr. Day she doesn't want to talk to you right now. Yes, I know that but I'm her bodyguard, it is my job to protect her, and right now she has asked me to protect her from you." God, I would love to hear the other side of this conversation, I bet Edward is pulling his hair out. I listen as Carl continues, "Mr. Day if it's any help, I was there last night when the alleged kiss took place. It was nothing like the tabloids were making it out to be. They were just acting. Okay, I'll get her to call you when she's calmed down." With that Carl hangs up and gives me a cheeky smile. "Don't ever call me a wimp again." I burst out laughing.

Cain has arranged for us to take his private plane down to LA. At first, I wasn't sure it was the best idea, but after thinking about it, I realized I had nothing to hide, as nothing is going on. I am beyond relieved when we arrive at Cain's beach house in Santa Monica. Cain found the whole scenario amusing, even after I told him about Edward. "So let me get this straight, you're not with this guy, but he's acting like you've committed the biggest act of adultery," Cain says.

I have to laugh, he has such a way with words. "Yep, that's about it in a nutshell." I have to admit I'm starting to feel less tense now. When my phone rings for the billionth time this morning, I groan inwardly, until I see that it's James calling. "God are you a sound for sore ears," I gush at him.

"Are you drunk? You know that's not the right saying," he queries.

I chuckle slightly. "Well I can't see you, so that

264

was the next best way to express to you how happy I am to hear your voice," I say, running the sentence back through my head to make sure it makes sense.

"How sweet... and strange, tell me what's going on girl?" he demands.

I fill James in on everything from the three strange men outside the hotel suite to Carl's verbal abuse on Edward. "What do I do, Jay?"

"D, I've told you already how I feel about how Edward is acting. It's up to you to decide where to go from here," he says sympathetically.

"I think I'm in love with him," I quickly tell him before I lose my nerve. "I hate him so much at times, but when he's not stressing out, he really is amazing."

"Then I think you need to talk to him. The way he's acting, tells me he has some strong feelings for you too," he states logically.

"But he's a psycho, I'm so confused." I decide I really need to have a self-talking to before making any impulsive decisions.

"I've got to go back to work now. I'll speak to

you later, and I'll have a big hug waiting for you when you get home tomorrow morning. Love you," he says with so much fondness.

"Love you too, bye." I hang up and get back to the job at hand. "Are you ready for more posing Mr. Cunningham?"

"Such the professional, eh Miss Spencer?" Cain's reply has me laughing, and we get on with the shoot before we procrastinate anymore.


I decide to go back down to the beach before we head off home. The magnitude of everything that's happened since this morning finally hits me and I let the emotions flood out. I feel someone putting a jacket on my shoulders to protect my bare arms from the cold winds of the evening. "You okay?" Cain asks.

I nod. "Just everything has finally got on top of me. I can't be strong anymore," I answer honestly.

He wraps his arms around me, while I cry more tears. "I'm sure everything will work out, and as for your ex, it seems like you're safe now." He gives me a genuine smile. I don't say anything else, just continue leaning on Cain for support until I feel I can support myself again.

Waiting at LAX for our flight back to New York, we sit in a bar and enjoy a drink before we board. "Isn't that Cain?" Simon says pointing to the silenced TV screen.

I look up, he's completely surrounded by paparazzi and reporters. "Excuse me," I get the attention of the barman. "Could you turn this up please?" I ask. He does, and I listen to the report.

*"Movie star Cain Cunningham, today called the paparazzi and reporters 'lying scum'. After being seen together for the second time in two days, the action star was swarmed by the press and asked to comment on the nature of his relationship with Dana Spencer, who was also recently pictured out at dinner with Edward Day, owner of Day Publication. Cain tried to wade through the crowd but was struck in the face*

*with a microphone, which angered the already frustrated star. He spoke to the reporters briefly and then lashed out and broke several news cameras. Here's what happened.*

The screen then switches to Cain trying to work his way through the press while they take his picture, the flash most likely blinding him and all asking questions at once. The microphone hits his cheek bone, and I think he swears, as there is a bleep. Then he turns and addresses them.

*"Dana and I are just friends, that is the real truth. I just hope you're all happy with yourselves, by fabricating this lie you have severely complicated the lives of everyone involved. The picture of us on the beach earlier this evening wasn't a 'lover's embrace' as it was put, but was me comforting a friend who was crying because of all this. Is it still funny and entertaining now? Are you going to go home tonight and laugh about your (bleep) up, while everyone tries*

*to fix what your (beep) has broken? You're lying scum all of you, go to hell. Now get out of my (bleep)-ing face."*

With that, he snatches the camera from the cameraman and throws it on the floor.

"I can't believe he did that," I hear Simon's voice from beside me.

"Me neither. Right, lets' go catch that plane. Time to go home," I muse as we stand and gather our bags together.

We arrive back in New York just before six in the morning, surprisingly the airport is really busy. Simon and I wait for our bags, still under the watchful eye of the rat pack. All I can think about now is getting home, giving James a massive hug and then getting into bed. As we exit into the arrivals lounge, I'm shocked to see Edward standing there with a dozen red roses. I walk towards him with tears in my eyes. "Forgive me, I was such an idiot," he says sheepishly.

"Of course, but next time maybe you could

hear me out first before assuming I'm guilty?" I ask warily.

"I hope there won't be a next time, I've learned my lesson." He gives me a boyish grin.

"Edward?" He turns to me with what still looks like worry in his eyes. "What does this mean for us?" I ask.

"That is a conversation that is going to take far too long to discuss right now. You need to get home and get some sleep. Will you still attend the dinner tonight?" he asks.

I have to smile at him, sometimes he reminds me of a little boy looking for reassurance. "Yeah, I'm still coming. I mean I have a dress and everything, I wouldn't want it to go to waste," I reply teasingly.

"I better let you get home. I'll pick you up at five this evening, and you can get ready at my place," he states.

"Actually I was wondering if you might give me a lift home, I'd like to spend a little more time with you," I ask diverting my eyes to my feet.

He wraps his arms around me and pulls me to him, kissing my head. "I would love to." With that, I look up at him, and his lips come down and meet mine. The lips I've been waiting for since all the drama in California started.

I say goodbye to Simon and Carl, and we drive back to my apartment without saying a word to each other, the sound of the music filling the silence. With his hand in mine, I feel content and happy, and I wonder how long I've wanted this. Probably from the day he put his hands on my shoulder in the lift, and I felt that first spark of electricity. Edward's voice interrupts my train of thought. "I'll see you later, please try and get some sleep."

I laugh. "I really can't see that being a problem." With that answer, he leans over and kisses me hard.

"Now get out, before I take you back to my place," he says with a salacious grin.

"Promises, promises," I counter as I get out of the car, and hear the sound of his deep throaty laugh.

I love that sound, I love that man. "Yep," I tell myself out loud as I reach the lobby. "I'm screwed."

# Chapter 14

"Hey honey, I'm home," I call out to James as I enter the apartment. James comes running at me from the kitchen and practically squeezes the life out of me. "I've missed you too," I gasp when he finally lets me go.

"You are never leaving me again," he says determinedly.

"That's a little overdramatic, Jay." I laugh.

I hear Andy laugh as he comes out of James' room. "No, seriously, you're not leaving him again. All he did was mope around and talk about you for the last forty-eight hours."

"Ah did my poor Jamesy Wamesy miss me?" I stick out my bottom lip, mocking him.

He pokes his tongue at me and heads back to the kitchen. "Coffee?" he calls over his shoulder.

"Yes please, sweetie," I say in my innocuous voice, I'm rewarded with one of his brilliant white Hollywood smiles.

"Dana." Andy approaches from behind and hugs me. "Apart from all the press stuff, how was your trip?"

I have to smile. "All in all, it was unbelievable. It was so much fun, I really wish it wasn't over so soon. But Edward was waiting for me at the airport with flowers when we came through arrivals, so that made coming home a bit sweeter." James hands Andy and me a coffee. "I'm going to drink this, and then I'm going to bed. I may not be here when you get back tonight." I turn to James. "Edward is picking me up at five for this dinner thing this evening."

"You're going then?" Andy asks.

"Yeah, Edward has some issues with his parents and one of his brothers. He wants me to go to hold his hand, I suppose," I say with a chuckle.

Both Andy and James laugh with me. "In that case," Andy interrupts, "James and I shall see you there."

"What! You're both coming?" Relief floods through me. "That makes me feel a lot better about going, at least I'll know people. We get to have our drinks together after all." A big smile plays on my lips. I look at Andy and James and then think of Edward, I can't believe how much life has changed and how happy we are. I don't think things could get any better.

I see James and Andy off to work, I can't help checking out the window, no weirdo stalker standing across the street. I smile to myself and head to my bed, exhaustion taking over. I'll shower when I wake up. As I'm setting the alarm on my phone, a familiar sound alerts me of an incoming message from Edward.

**Sleep well sweetheart,**
**Looking forward to seeing you later.**
**Edward.**

My heart melts, how can he be so Dr. Jekyll and Mr. Hyde?

**Have a good day at work,**

**Don't sack anyone.**

**See you tonight.**

**D xx**

I hug my phone and settle under my covers to sleep, I'm so excited about tonight. Me and Edward, James and Andy, it's going to be so much fun.

"Dance with me?" Edward asks.

I offer my hand as we start to waltz around the ballroom, but why are we dancing to the sound of my alarm?

My eyes flutter open, and I sigh as I'm woken rudely from my pleasant dream, one which I hope becomes a reality really soon. It's four o'clock, I have an hour till Edward gets here. I jump in a quick shower and change. Feeling semi-human I turn on the kettle, needing a caffeine fix. I start to pack things I will probably need to get ready, then I remember that Edward already got me a lot of the stuff I use. I haven't really had a chance to think about how I feel about that, or what it means. Why would someone go to all the effort to find out what toiletries I use or what dress size I am? Then a sudden thought occurs to me, how did he know all that stuff? Do I really want to know? Probably not. James was wrong, talking to yourself isn't the first sign of insanity, answering yourself is. I spend the next half hour pottering around the apartment trying to make myself busy, each minute feeling like an hour. Five o'clock comes and goes, where is he? Then my phone pings the message tone.

**So sorry, got held up.**
**Forgive me, on my way.**
**Edward.**

How could I not forgive him? He's so sweet.

Besides he does have to run a multi-billion dollar company, I would be surprised if he was on time.

The buzzing intercom pulls me from my reverie, he's here, and I'm more nervous than I thought I would be. "I love your front door," he says with a slight smile as I open it.

"Yeah, this nut case decided to kick the last one in, but I like this one too," I say raising my eyebrows and give him a side smile.

"Well at least he replaced it," he counters.

"It wouldn't have needed replacing-"

He interrupts me by slamming his lips onto mine. "He isn't going to do it again," he says pulling away from my mouth. "Unless you leave him worrying again, then he has every right to."

"Maybe this time he could wait a little more than six hours, though," I smirk.

"In all fairness, his brain was over-thinking, and at the time he thought every second counted," he says his face wincing.

"Well then maybe he could knock first to

check I'm not answering," I counter futilely.

"I stand by my previous statement," he says lifting his chin in a no-nonsense way.

"Have I got any hope of winning this argument?" I ask.

"This is not an argument, it's a disagreement. And no, you don't," he finally answers. His lips twist into a smirk, and all I can think about is how I can't wait for those lips to be on me again. "Shall we get going?"

"Yeah." We head down to the lobby and onto the street, I see the Bugatti and smile. "You had it cleaned then?" I can't help my cheeks burning bright red.

"Yeah, it no longer smells like vomit," he answers sarcastically.

"Can I drive?" I ask knowing the answer, but I'm always hopeful.

"Yeah, sure," he answers.

Oh my god. "Really?" I reply, my grin splitting my face in two.

"No." And with that he unlocks the car and climbs in the driver's side, shaking his head and laughing as he goes.

"You are so mean," I say pouting at him. "You will regret messing with me."

He turns to me narrowing his eyes but with the biggest grin playing on his lips. "Is that a threat?" he asks feigning seriousness.

"It's a promise." I try to mirror his expression but fail when I burst out laughing, and he joins me.

He puts the car in drive, and we head back to his apartment, he grabs my hand and doesn't let it go until we are parked in his space and have to exit the vehicle. As he helps me out of the car, he places both his hands on my waist and looks me straight in the eyes, as if he wants to say something. He just shakes his head. "Stay tonight, I have so much I want to say to you, but right now I don't have enough time," he says nervously. I smile at him and nod my response.

In my room, I start to relax a little. Edward has hired a woman called Sienna to style my hair and do my make-up, I'm not sure if I should be happy or insulted. Either way, it's two less things for me to worry about as I hate both of those jobs. When I'm all made up I step into my dress, it's the same color green as Edward's eyes. The dress is a floor length halter neck, which is completely backless and barely covers the top of my bum. I'm relieved to find enhanced support for the chest since there's no way I could wear a bra with it. And with a slit all the way up the side I'm glad I shaved my legs because tights or stockings are not an option. I finish off getting ready, putting my black heels on and spray my favorite Jimmy Choo Flash perfume all over me. I'm singing along to "Wake Me Up" by Avicii and literally jump out of my skin when I'm tapped on the shoulder. "Oh God you scared the life out of me," I say blushing furiously. "I didn't hear you come in."

"I knocked and everything," he says holding his hands up as if pleading his innocence. "You have a beautiful voice."

"Thank you, is everything ok?" I ask.

"Yeah, why wouldn't it be?" He smiles.

"Because you're staring," I reply.

"I can't help it, you look stunning."

My lips purse together. "It's amazing what you can do with a bit of make-up and some hairspray."

"Although I do hope I didn't get charged full price for that dress," he says frowning.

"Why? What's wrong with it?" I ask

Touching the bare skin on my back and then on my right leg. "Half of it appears to be missing, and there is a big rip up the side," he says with a smirk on his lips.

We laugh in unison, but his laughter seems more nervous. "You've had your scars covered up? he asks.

"Sienna noticed them and said she could use some of her products to mask them slightly," I reply. "Just because I caused them, it doesn't mean I'm proud of them."

"I'm just a little surprised that's all," he says as he lightly runs a finger over one of the more prominent marks. "Please don't mark your body again."

"I already told you I wouldn't," I say softly, he gives me a small smile of relief, but he's still tense. "What's wrong?"

"Here goes. The reason I was late earlier was because I had to pick up a package. I have something for you, I hope you don't mind."

I eye him suspiciously. "That depends on what it is."

He leads me to the kitchen. On the island, I see a black velvet box. He picks it up and opens it without saying a word. Inside there is a white gold necklace with a pear shaped Columbian emerald pendant and matching earrings, they're so exquisite. "I thought they would go with the dress," he says. I'm speechless, all I can do is lightly run my fingers over the bright green gem. "May I?" He gestures to the necklace.

"Please." I pull my hair out of the way as he secures the chain around my neck.

"This is a very unique piece of jewelry, I hope you won't freak out when I tell you why." He seems apprehensive, I stay silent and listen to what he has to say. He takes the pendant in his hand and opens it. "Inside here is a GPS tracker, I would like you to keep this necklace on so that I can always find you *if* you need me."

I'm shocked. "What the hell, you want me to wear a tracking device so you can keep an eye on me. This is taking it to a whole new level of psycho, do you know that?" I'm shouting manically while trying to remove the offending piece.

"Dana, stop and listen please." I do as he asks. "If you look here, there is a button so you can turn it on and off as you please." Now I'm just confused. "After finding out Grant was here and he was stalking you, we don't know what his motives were. This is for your safety. If you ever find yourself in danger or a situation where you need me but for some reason can't use a phone, you can just turn it on and I will receive an alert and will know where to find you instantly." He lowers his eyes now waiting for my reply.

"Wow, I'm sorry." He looks at me, and I know I can see the worry in his eyes. "This is a really thoughtful gift, thank you," I say smiling, I lean forward and place a kiss on his lips. "So do the earrings do the same?"

"No, they're just accessories," he replies.

Very beautiful and expensive accessories. I can't believe he did this for me, who knew he cared about me so much. "Thank you," I say again, and he knows I'm not just thanking him for the necklace.

"You're very welcome, your safety is so important to me," he says softly.

"Hello Dr. Jekyll," I murmur.

"What?" he asks with a raised eyebrow.

"Nothing." I smile.

He smiles back, and his eyes are full of joy. "Shall we?" he says, picking up my wrap and places it around my shoulders. He offers his arm and slipping mine through his, we head down to the lobby.

"I've never been in here, I've always been taken to the underground garage." He laughs at me.

"You make it sound like I'm keeping a dirty little secret." He whispers in my ear, and we both chuckle. "Peter is waiting for us outside, and I just need to have a quick chat with the front desk." I follow him as he walks to reception.

"Mr. Day, how can I help you today?" the happy lady with way too much make-up on asks. She seriously needs to stop smiling at Edward like that or I may have to jump the desk and pummel her.

"I would like the spare key to the penthouse lift and to add Dana here to my list of approved visitors please," Edward states without batting an eyelid.

I look at him from the corner of my eye. *He's giving me a key*, I think to myself, and a slight smile rests on my lips. "Certainly sir," the receptionist says in a sexy voice. I wait to hear Edward's reaction, there is nothing. It seems it's only when I call him sir, that he is affected. He signs all the papers and accepts the key, nodding his thanks, he takes my arm, and we head outside.

"I hope you won't think this is too forward of me, but I would like you to be able to come over and *leave* when you like." I can't help but laugh at his emphasis on the word 'leave.'

"Thank you I really appreciate the gesture," I say faintly.

"I do trust you, Dana, that's what this represents. All the stuff that happened in California was because I was stupid. It's been a long time since I've felt anything for a woman and I've never felt anything like this. It's scary, and I'm sorry I let you down." Wow, the guy can give a speech.

"Hey don't sweat, we're all good. You can show me how sorry you are later, sir," I say with a wink. With his sharp intake of breath and the sudden throbbing between my legs, I'm not sure either of us will make it till the end of the night.

We climb into the car. "The London NYC please, Peter."

Peter starts the car, and we head out into the traffic. "Is that where the event is being held?" I ask, and he nods in response. "You're aware that we could take the E train and be there in ten minutes and it will probably be quicker than driving with this traffic."

"I am aware, yes. The subway is too much hassle and at this time of day is occupied by too many people," he replies.

I gasp at him. "It's people like you who are killing this planet. Can't be bothered to share public transport with people for a bit, but instead pollute the air with your gas guzzlers, just so you can be comfy. You should be ashamed of yourself, how do you sleep at night?" I narrow my eyes at him as he looks at me wide-eyed. I have to turn my face away to stop myself from laughing.

"Dana, I'm... I'm sorry I didn't realize you cared so much about the environment," he stutters.

I burst out laughing, I can't help it. "I'm just joking, your face was a picture you were so shocked." I continue laughing, and I can feel my eyes watering and my stomach cramping.

"That was a really mean trick to play on someone," he says pouting and huffing a little. "I really thought I had offended you."

"You won't trick me about driving the Bugatti again now, will you?" I can't help but gloat.

"Remind me never to piss you off. If you can hold a grudge over that, who knows what you're capable of?" he says, his words dripping with sarcasm. I lean in to kiss him, and when I pull away, I burst out laughing again. Edward just shakes his head at me, and I laugh some more, even Peter chuckles a little in the driver's seat.

After I calm down, I think about tonight. "Oh, by the way, James and his boyfriend will be there tonight too," I say excitedly.

"Cool." Edward gives me a genuine smile. "I look forward to getting to know him."

"What as opposed to all the times you didn't talk to him because you were too busy harassing and kidnapping me?" I say casually.

"Sometimes I wonder if you deliberately wind me up, so I'll give you a spanking," he teases as we get out of the car.

I raise my hand to my mouth in a mock gasp. "I can't believe you'd think that, I would never do such a thing," I pause before adding, "Sir."

He narrows his eyes at me, they're full of such lust and desire. "That's it, get in the car we are going home."

I can't help laughing again. "You made me get all dressed up. I'm not letting it go to waste. You can wait till later, I'll try not to make it too difficult for you." I wink at him, and I swear I heard him growl.

He walks towards me and offers me his arm. "Shall we?" I smile, nod and hook my arm through his. As we walk towards the entrance, there are loads of paparazzi hanging around outside. Edward poses with me next to him but refuses to answer any of their questions about the nature of our relationship, something I'm happy about as certain things are just private. We make our way into the hotel, and I'm overwhelmed, the place is magnificent. We are escorted to the Hyde room that has been set up for the meal, nearly everyone is already seated. An older man walks up to Edward and slaps him on the back.

"Edward." The old man looks me up and down, then back to Edward. "Where did you find this one?" My mouth opens in shock at this rudeness. "Close your mouth dear, he won't need you to open it till later."

"Father," Edward's tone is clipped. "This is Dana, my girlfriend. Dana this is my Father, Michael."

Edward's Father laughs so loud everyone stops and stares. "Let's see how long this one lasts. You should be rushing Payton up the aisle son, having a child out of wedlock disgraces the family name."

"Good night Father." Edward grabs my hand, and we start to walk to our seats.

"Are you still refusing to dine with your family?" Michael shouts after us. "Should be a laugh tonight, your poof of a brother has brought his new boyfriend."

"We should take our seats," Edward whispers in my ear.

"Why didn't you tell me about your daughter?" I ask quickly.

"It's a long story, can we discuss it later please?" he replies, and I don't argue, there's a time and a place.

I nod and take a quick look around. "I can't see James," I say.

"Not everyone is in this room, there is another group of people in the St. James room," he answers pulling out my chair for me. "Whoever your roommate is seeing, is a very important person."

"So why aren't you in that room then?" I have to ask.

"There are people in that room I don't wish to socialize with over dinner. We will all come together in this room afterward, though," he replies. "Who did you say James' boyfriend was?"

"I didn't, his name is-" I'm interrupted by an elderly gentleman on stage with a microphone.

"Ladies and gentleman, if you would like to take your seats, dinner is ready to be served." He hands the microphone back to a waiter and takes his place. Edward's attention has been diverted to some of the other men at the table, I listen but don't understand most of what they are discussing. The atmosphere is so light, everyone is happy and laughing. Maybe tonight won't be as bad as I thought, I'll just try and keep Edward away from his family. I must remind him to point them out to me so I can avoid them too. We enjoyed a four-course meal, most of which I can't pronounce but was lovely all the same. The chocolate fondant dessert with almond ice cream was the best part.

Just when I think I can't eat anymore, the waiters serve coffee and petit fours, I mean it would be rude to say no. "You really like your food, don't you?" I hear Edward whisper to me.

"Is there something wrong with that?" I ask.

"Not at all, on the contrary, it's a breath of fresh air to see a woman eat real food and not just a salad." He chuckles as I look around the room and see so many women still looking hungry, turning their noses up at the petit fours, drinking water instead of coffee and I laugh along with him.

After letting our food settle, the elderly gentleman is on stage again. "Ladies and gentleman, if you would like to make your way to the bar and get a drink, we can start setting up for the band. Thank you."

"What would you like to drink?" Edward asks.

I'm shocked. "Are you actually asking me what I want to drink?" I can't help but tease him. He raises both his eyebrows at me, and I give him my most innocent smile. "Could I have a glass of white wine please?" He gives me a smile, and we head to the bar. As Edward is ordering, I see James and Andy come in. "I'll be right back, I've just spotted James."

He nods. "Okay, I'll come find you in a second." He kisses me, and I walk over to meet my roommate.

"Dana, you look way too sexy tonight girl. If I

wasn't in a committed relationship, you might actually have had a chance of converting me," James states adding a wolf whistle as I turn on the spot showing off all the dress, I lean in and give him a squeeze.

"I'm not sure if I should be worried or not, Dana you look magnificent," Andy says as he arrives next to James. I thank him as well and give him a kiss on the cheek. I turn around to see where Edward is and he's heading towards me with a face like thunder.

I try to walk towards him. "Hey what's-" He ignores me and pushes past me.

"Who do you think you are? Stay the hell away from her Drew, am I clear?" Edward shouts at Andy.

I grab Edward's arm. "Hey chill out, it was just a kiss on the cheek. This is James and his boyfriend, Andy." I gesture to the pair.

"This would also be my brother Andrew," he says with an eerie calm.

No, that can't be. I knew things were too good to be true.

# Chapter 15

Looking from one to the other, I realize why Andy looked so familiar to me. Although they don't look terribly alike, they have the same eye shape and nose and the same floppy hair.

"Why did you never tell me you were Edward's brother?" I have to ask Andy. I find my head and my heart conflicting now. I love Andy, and he's perfect for James, but I hate Drew for what he did to Edward. How can I be feeling these things when it's about the same person?

"I wanted you to get to know me for me before Eddie here started filling your mind with bullshit. With the way you're acting now, I'm assuming he already has." Andy squares his jaw, ready to defend himself.

"What bullshit?" James asks.

I turn to him with narrowed eyes. "Did you know?" I ask accusingly.

"No Dana, I didn't. What bullshit?" he asks again.

"Andy or Drew or whatever his name is, abused Edward when he was only a teenager," I hiss through gritted teeth.

James recoils at my words and detaches himself from Andy. "Still spreading those lies Eddie?" Andy says smarmily

"What's she talking about Andy?" James asks, he looks so scared.

"James let me take you home. You don't need this, you don't need men like him, come on," I say going to reach for his arm.

"Why don't you let Jimmy make his own decision? You're always telling him what to do, Dana. If you say jump, he asks how high. Even he's getting fed up with you and your possessiveness, not to mention how incredibly stupid you are." James tries to interrupt Andy's speech, but he continues, "He thinks you will never learn your lesson. He told me how you just abandoned him for your ex, the one that treated you like shit and how you were lucky to get away from that relationship alive. Then here you are, abandoning him again, back in the arms of another psycho." Andy stands between us as I go for James.

"Is that right?" I ask James, but he looks away. "I can't believe you have been bad mouthing me, yet you couldn't tell me yourself? You're supposed to be my friend, my brother. How dare you!" James has the decency to look guilty. "Don't worry James I won't be needing you anymore. Lewis was right, you will end up a lonely old man." I instantly regret saying this as James storms out of the hotel, I'll deal with him in a minute.

"Why would James think I'm a psycho?" Edward turns to me.

I open my mouth to speak when I hear Andy's voice again, has he not done enough?

"Let's see, shall we. You were following her around, dragged her out of a bar, held her prisoner for two days, handcuffed her to a bed, spanked her in an elevator, kidnapped her off the street and broke her door down. Is there anything I missed Dana?" He turns to me now. I feel my heart pounding in my chest, as he recites all the bad things that I told him in confidence.

"You are such a fucking arse." I can't keep the venom from my voice.

"You're kind of fucked up Eddie. I think the best part was when she came to comfort you while you had a nightmare and you practically forced yourself on her then treated her like a cheap whore. What was it you were screaming Eddie?" I literally feel the air leave me and tears welling up in my eyes because I know what's coming. I can't believe he is doing this to me, to his brother. "Oh yeah, that's it. Please don't hurt me, stop it. Mommy, please make him stop." Silent tears fall down my cheek as I watch Edward's jaw clench. "Mommy couldn't save poor little Edward though could she? Because Edward is a liar. What would Caroline think of you?" Edward is still not reacting, and that worries me, there is an eerie calm about him. "She does look good naked, though, doesn't she Eddie? Plus she's got that cute little tattoo of a horny devil on her left ass cheek, very apt." He turns and winks at me, and I can't hold my emotions in anymore. I think the biggest mistake Andy makes right now is laughing. Edward lunges at him and pummels his fists into his face, Andy doesn't even have a chance to defend himself.

I start to panic. "Edward, stop!" I scream at him. He looks at me and the expression on his face scares me, he hates me. "Edward, I'm sorry. Please take me home, and we can talk." Andy is out cold, his nose bleeding and his lip is split open. Edward stands up and walks to the bar, ignoring me and everyone in the crowd that's gathered. Standing there on my own with everyone staring at me, I turn and head to the ladies room and lock myself in a stall. Then I let it all go. I cry my heart out for Edward, and for James, and even a little for Andy. How do things go from being so good to so bad in the blink of an eye? After I calm myself down, I find my phone in my bag, a missed call, and voicemail from James. I listen to the voicemail before I call him back.

*"Hey, Dana I just wanted to tell you how sorry I am. I was just angry and jealous and was being stupid. I shouldn't have gone shooting my mouth off like that. I don't know if you will ever forgive me, but please know that you were my life. My heart is broken Dana, for Andy but mostly for you. It's too much pain to deal with-"*

I feel my heart rate rising as I start to panic, he's talking in the past tense and crying. I hear the cruel and destructive sound of the running water from the shower.

*"I will always love you, Dana. I am truly grateful to have had you as a friend. You saved my life more times than you will ever know, bye baby girl.*

That's it, the phone line goes dead. One of my worst nightmares is coming true, the world around me becomes distorted as my primary focus now is getting to James. With tears running down my face and my breathing erratic, I leave the ladies room and run outside. I hail a taxi. I don't even remember how I got from the toilets to outside the hotel. "West 67th Street!" I shout at the driver. "Please hurry."

"This isn't a movie, lady," the driver responds and slowly pulls out into traffic.

This feels like the longest journey of my life, thoughts of what I'm going to find when I get home are going through my head. We pull up outside my building, and I throw the driver a twenty dollar bill. I'm willing the lift to move quicker and pleading with all the gods and deities in the universe that James is okay. I run through my front door to the bathroom door, pulling the handle down and just as I knew it would be, the door was locked. "James, open the door!" I'm screaming at him and banging the door so hard. I knew we should have removed the lock, why didn't I listen to my instincts. "Please, please I'm begging you, please open the door!" My voice on the verge of hysteria. I try to kick the door down, but it doesn't budge. I hear my phone in the distance, and I run to it with one thing in mind, I don't even check who is calling so I can save a few seconds. "Help me!" I shout down the phone through my tears, I realize I'm shaking. I run to James' room and grab his quilt I'll need to warm him up once I get in there.

The voice I hear brings such joy and pain to my heart. "Dana?" Edward sounds concerned, and I'm not surprised.

"Help me please, he's locked the door, and I can't get in. He's not answering, please help me!" I cry out to him and drop the phone as I continue banging on the door. "James, James, I'm sorry. Oh god please, I'm sorry." I sink to the floor, bringing my knees up and wrapping my arms around them. I'm rocking back and forth, I'm so scared. "Please be okay, please be okay," I whisper to myself over and over again.

"Dana!" I hear Edward shout as he and

another man come flying through to the hallway. "What's going on?"

"It's James, he's in there, and I can't get in." Edward gestures for us to move out of the way, the door gives way after the first kick.

I run in and find James unconscious, I run into the shower and turn it off as Edward pulls him out. His lips are blue, and his skin is different shades of purple, red and blue. I throw the quilt down, and we move him on to it. Then I strip and pull the rest of the quilt over us both. I wrap myself around him, hoping to transfer my body heat. "We need to get him to A and E," I say.

"A and E?" the guy with Edward asks.

"She means the ER," Edward replies jumping into action, he pulls his phone out. "We need an ambulance please," I hear him ask.

"James open your eyes, please open your eyes and talk to me. You are not leaving me like this. I love you, and I need you. You're my family, my brother. You need to be here when Nathan comes back, please don't leave me." I'm pleading with his lifeless body.

A little while later the paramedics arrive, and Edward literally has to drag me from James' still unconscious form so they can do their job. "Come on, you need to get dressed, and I'll drive you to the hospital," he says, wrapping me in a towel.

I go into my room and start to rummage through my clothes. "I can't wear that or that, James would hate that," I mumble to myself throwing clothes out of my wardrobe.

"Dana, I don't think it matters what you wear," Edward says sympathetically, moving me out of the way and reaching in himself to pull out a top and jeans. "Matthew, can you get Dana a glass of water please?" he asks the strange man in my room, who oddly enough looks a lot like Edward and Andy.

"Is that your younger brother?" I ask.

"Yes, that's Matthew. I was with him when I called you, he said he saw you leave the hotel in a panic," he replies while helping me put my underwear on.

"Keep him away from James and me, the last thing I need is to deal with another one of you Day men causing havoc in our lives," I say in an angry tone.

"I'm sure that won't be a problem, Matthew has a girlfriend." He looks up at me with a small smile.

"Here you go Dana," Matthew says handing me a glass of water.

"Thank you, so are you an arse like your brothers?" I ask sincerely.

He laughs, and I notice it's the same as Edward's. "I'm worse than Edward," he replies with a smile playing on his lips, I feel the warmth in my heart from his admission, and I can't help the smile on my face in this dreadful time.

"Come on, let's go," Edward says, putting his arm around me as I stand. "Everything will be okay, I promise."

"Please don't make promises you can't keep." My voice is full of fear.

"This is one promise I can keep. Whatever

happens, I promise you everything will be okay."

"I'm so sorry Edward, for everything that has happened tonight. This is my entire fault. Thank you for coming even though you hate me right now," I say trying to hold back more tears that threaten to fall.

"I don't hate you, I could never hate you. I was angry, but not with you. Andrew has always known what buttons of mine to push, he knows how to provoke me. I don't blame you, this isn't your fault. Do you believe me?" he asks while pulling me into a tight embrace and kissing the top of my head, I nod holding on to him tightly. "Come on, let's get going," he says. With his arm still around me, we make our way out to the car.

We drive in silence, my brain elsewhere. I can't stop thinking about James, will he still be alive when I get to him. I did everything I was supposed to do, I wrapped him up and used my body heat to warm him. "We're here," Matthew says from the driver's seat.

I don't move, I don't think I even blink. "Hey,

you ready?" Edward says in a soothing voice next to me. I turn to him, my eyes are glassy with unshed tears and nod.

We head straight to reception. "Can I help you?" the lady behind the desk asks.

"I'm looking for James Ward, he was brought in by ambulance a little while ago," I say.

"Are you a relative?" she asks.

"He's my brother," I lie quickly, well he's the next best thing.

She taps away on her computer for what seems like hours. *Please be okay James.* "If you would like to take a seat in the waiting room, I'll have a doctor come and speak to you as soon as one is available."

"Is he okay? Please tell me he's still alive." The tears start to fall.

"I can't give you any information, I'm sorry. If you take a seat a doctor will be with you soon," she says softly.

Edward puts his arm around me, pulling me

away from the reception desk and guiding me to a chair. "He'll be okay," he states firmly.

"Why won't they tell me anything?" I'm so scared.

"A doctor will be here soon, just try and relax." He puts his arm around me, and I rest my head on his shoulder.

"What's going on? Where is he?" I hear a familiar booming voice and open my eyes.

"Andy?" I say as I see Matthew trying to get him to leave.

"Get out, now!" Edward practically shouts at him. "Don't you think you have done enough damage already?"

I see the pain in Andy's bruised and battered face. "Stop everyone please, just stop." I stand up, walk over to Andy, and I slap him so hard across the face. He lowers his head and I know he is just as upset as me about what is happening, so I pull him into a hug.

"I'm sorry Dana." I hear the tremble in his

voice as he wraps his arms tightly around me. "I'm so sorry, I'm a horrible person I know, but I do love James."

"I know, it's okay. How did you know he was here?" I ask.

"I got a voicemail from him. If someone hadn't have knocked me out, I would have been here sooner." He glares at his brother, and Edward just rolls his eyes. "I went straight to the apartment, and no one was there, the bathroom was a mess, and I thought this would be the next best place to look. James told me about his past, and how he deals with things, after that voicemail I knew he was going to do something stupid."

"Well we don't know anything, and we're still waiting for the doctor so you can leave, and someone will call you when we are aware something," Edward injects.

"I'm not going anywhere until James tells me to," Andy replies, with that we all take a seat and wait. Edward puts his arm around me, and Andy holds my hand, the two men glaring at each other.

"She doesn't need you to hold her hand," Edward voices. Andy lets go of me, but I reach out for him again, Edward grabs my fingers instead. "I'll hold you if you need holding."

"Andy needs comforting too, Edward. He's just as distraught about what's happened," I reply and reach back out to Andy. I know Edward hates it, but I can't hold a grudge against someone in such obvious distress, we can deal with all the other stuff after we get some news on James.

"I got us all coffee," Matthew says handing us all one, I sit up and thank him for this much-needed caffeine fix. "Don't thank me yet, it's hospital coffee remember."

I take a cautious sip. "This stuff is vile," I just about manage to say with the face I'm pulling.

All three men start to laugh. "Thank you, for letting me stay," Andy whispers in my ear.

I give him a small smile and shrug my shoulders. "I'm still mad at you but this isn't about me, and I know you love James almost as much as I do." I try lightening the mood.

Andy wraps his arm around me and pulls me to him, kissing my forehead as I let out a little giggle. "I have to make a call," Edward stands abruptly and storms out.

Matthew gets up to follow him, I stand too. "Let me," I tell Matthew, and he nods at me. I walk outside and see Edward sitting on a bench, I sit next to him and wait a few minutes. "I know you want me to hate him and I do, believe me, I do hate him for what he did to you, but I can't turn my back on someone so clearly in need of comforting," I say, trying to reason with him.

He takes a deep breath and exhales, he moves closer to me and wraps me up in his arms. He closes his eyes as our foreheads meet. "I know, you wouldn't be you if you didn't care about everyone. I've also been thinking about how I would react if I were in your position, and I do understand. I just hate him so much, and when he touches you it makes my skin crawl," he says, clearly uncomfortable with his admission. He kisses my hand, and we sit there for a while in silence. "Come on, let's get back inside," he finally says.

As we enter, I see a doctor standing with Andy. "What's going on?" My voice is shaking.

"He won't tell me anything because I'm only the boyfriend and not family," Andy says glaring at the doctor.

"I'm his sister, how is he?" Please say he's okay.

"He's stable now, and his body temperature is rising. He's still unconscious, so we will have to keep an eye on that, but we expect him to make a full recovery." I finally relax, letting out the breath I didn't realize I was holding and when I do I break down. Andy takes me in his arms, and we cry together. "James will need a mental health assessment done when he wakes up, and we will be recommending he see a psychiatrist for counseling." The good doctor sounds like a know it all.

"That didn't work before, and it won't work now, it's fine I'll help him," I inject snottily.

"We'll see how the assessment goes, he tried to commit suicide. It's mandatory for him to spend seventy-two hours in our psychiatric ward for observation before we will even consider discharging him. If we think James is going to harm himself or anyone else we may need to have to have him committed to a psychiatric hospital. It will be a lot easier if we have permission from a family member than to have a court order," he states sensitively.

"He is not a nut case!" I shout.

"Hey, hey, hey." Andy turns me to look at him. "It's okay, I'll take care of this, I promise, and I don't make promises I can't keep."

I take a deep breath, nodding at him and drop the subject. I look towards Edward, he looks so helpless right now. "When can we see him?"

"Only two of you can go in, and only one of you can stay tonight, so someone is here if he wakes up, he needs his rest and visiting hours are over until

314

the morning," the doctor replies.

"Andy and I will go in," I state firmly to the group. Edward's face hardens, he turns around and leaves without even saying goodbye. I know he wants to be there for me, but this is about being there for James.

"He's just worried about you, he'll be fine by the morning," Matthew says, kissing me on the cheek and following his brother out completely ignoring Andy.

"They really hate you, don't they?" I turn to Andy, as the doctor leads us to James' room.

"Yep, I'd rather that than the alternative," he states.

"What? To them loving you?" I'm confused now.

"No. To what could have been. They're my brothers I will always protect them, whether they know that or not," he says dispiritedly.

I'm about to question him further, but we arrive at James' bedside. I move straight to his side, taking his hand in mine. "Oh god, James what did you do? I promise not to lecture you till you're out of here, but I'm removing the lock on the bathroom door when I get home," I say to his sleeping body.

Andy moves round the other side and strokes his cheek. "I'm sorry, I never wanted this. I love you so much handsome, please don't leave me," Andy whispers in his ear, but I can just about make it out.

We sit there for an hour talking to James and each other about anything funny that we can think of when the doctor comes in. "One of you will need to leave now, I'm sorry."

Andy goes to stand, and I stop him. "I'll go," I tell him, he looks at me confused and scared. "James knows I'll forgive him, you're the one that he'll want to see. He'll want to ask you a lot of questions, so be prepared to be honest with him."

"Are you sure?" he asks, I nod and smile. "Thank you, Dana." His eyes are glassy with tears as he hugs me.

"Don't get all sappy on me." I joke with him.

"I'll be here first thing, keep me updated whatever the time." He nods. I kiss James on the head. "I love you, and I'll see you in the morning." I kiss James one last time and leave.

Outside the hospital, the cold night air of October bites against my skin. I hail a taxi as quickly as possible. "West 67th Street, please," I say to the driver and sit back in my seat, the adrenaline that's been pumping through my system all night now has no release, and I start to shake. As I walk into my apartment, I'm overwhelmed by the scene in front of me. I walk to the bathroom, seeing the door hanging off its hinges and James' quilt on the floor that is still soaking wet, causes me to collapse. I gather the quilt and cry quietly into it, the severity of the situation becoming unbearably apparent. I run to the kitchen and open the fridge, pulling out the bottle of wine I down a third of the bottle in one go. It's going to be a long night, I flop on the sofa and turn on the TV still drinking the wine out of the bottle. *Classy Dana, real classy*, I tell myself.

I make my way through two bottles of wine, the pain still aching in me. "Why won't you numb?" I cry to myself. Making my way to my room and finding the razor blade, I lower it to the sensitive skin on my thigh. After fighting the urge all night, I sit there for what seems like forever, but I can't do it, I made Edward a promise. Then I remember he also made me a promise and with a new sense of hope, I grab my bag with Edward's key and make my way back out onto the street to hail a taxi. "Greenwich Avenue please." We pull off, and I know in twelve minutes everything will be okay again.

I check in with the reception desk and using my lift key, I put it in the panel and press the button for the penthouse. As the doors open into the living room, I gingerly step out. Edward is not in the main room or kitchen. He will be in his office or bedroom, I decide to check his office first. "Dana, you scared the life out of me. What are you doing here in the middle of the night?" I just stare at him willing myself not to

318

cry. "Dana, what's wrong? Is James okay?" I nod, and a tear escapes my eye.

Edward lifts his hand and wipes my cheek gently, and I lean into it. "Help me," I manage to whisper.

He grabs both of my arms and checks my wrists. "What do you need?"

"I need you to take the pain away, please," I beg him.

"Okay." He reaches into his pocket. "This is the key to the room we were in before, go in there and get ready I will be with you in a second."

I take the key and unlock the door to Heaven's waiting room. I remove my top and bra, falling to my knees with my head bowed and my hands in my lap, I wait.

# Chapter 16

"Get up!" I hear Edward's stern voice. I stand, feeling a little anxious. This isn't what I'm used to. He pulls the ottoman from the end of the bed to the middle of the room. He comes to me and without saying a word removes my jeans and panties. He leads me to the Ottoman and bends me over it, so my belly is flat on the top. "Reach your arms out in front of you and hold onto the edge. If you move, I will restrain you." My heart rate rises with his words, that's the last thing I want. I'm facing the mirror, I can't look at myself like this. "Open your eyes, Dana," Edward says as if reading my mind.

"I don't want to," I say my voice trembling.

"I told you, you can have all the pain you want, but you have to watch yourself. Now do what I say, or I'm leaving the room." His voice sounds cold, I gingerly open them and instantly blush at what I see. "I will use my belt," he states dominantly. "You will count them and thank me for each one." I don't think I could feel more degraded at that moment.

"Don't we need some sort of safe word?" I ask.

"Remember your place, Dana, what was missing in that sentence?" He grills me.

I rack my brains, and I hear Edward becoming impatient. "Sir," I announce quickly.

"Good girl and no you don't need a safe word with me, sweetheart, if you say stop I will stop," he says this reassuringly, a smile playing on his lips. I'm relieved, I didn't need the extra embarrassment of having to scream out a ridiculous word if it gets too much. "Are you ready?" He challenges, all traces of his smile have been eradicated.

"Yes." I nod

"Yes, what?" He grabs my hair pulling my head up and looks into my eyes in the mirror. I stiffen at his angry tone, this is not what I want.

"Yes sir," I tremble.

"Do I scare you Dana?" he asks, and I shake my head. "Answer me!" His voice is raised again.

"No sir," I reply as powerfully as I can manage.

"Why?" he asks.

"Because I trust you, sir." I realize by saying the words out loud that I do honestly trust him.

"Good, this kind of relationship is based on trust. If there is even the slightest doubt, it won't work. You will get five lashes."

The bite of the belt as it comes down across the backs of my thighs makes me scream out in pain, but it feels so good and is the release I've been craving. "One," I start counting.

Edward waits, staring at me in the mirror. "You need to start listening to me Dana, you've forgotten something already."

I start searching my brain for what I may have forgotten, it's too clouded, and I can't remember. I feel his fingers playing in the creases of my labia, oh god that feels good, but it's distracting me. He pushes one finger into me and starts to stroke my sweet spot as his thumb massaged my clit. He stops, and I feel bereft of his touch then he plunges two fingers in, and his movements on my sensitive nerve endings begin again. I can feel the build up, I can feel release on the horizon, it's so close, but he won't let me get any closer. "Please," I beg him trying to move with him.

"Please what Dana? What do you want?" I hear the smile in his voice though his facial expression is unreadable.

"Please sir, make me come," I speak louder, I have never been so wanton.

"It's amazing how you can remember your manners now but you couldn't a little while ago," he states with disappointment in his tone.

Then it dawns on me what I forgot. "I'm sorry sir, I forgot to thank you," I say looking back into his eyes.

The smile on his face looks like the cat that got the cream. "Well done sweetheart," he says stroking my wet lips again. "You are so aroused. I told you, you were a born submissive, why won't you embrace it?"

His question throws me, along with the soft, continual strokes of my private parts.

"I told you why I can't do it again, I will not let another man take my power from me," I answer defiantly.

"You're letting me do that now," he states.

"This is different. I'm not restrained, I'm free to leave, and you're not forcing yourself on to me." I stop before I get too carried away and tell him it's different because I love him.

"Fair enough. Just so you know, you are the one with all the power. "Are we ready to start again and let's remember those manners this time."

"Yes, sir."

"Good girl, now keep those eyes open and watch."

The belt comes down across the back of my thigh, just above where he hit before. This time I'm more prepared for the sting and manage to breathe through it. "Two, thank you, sir." My face turns a dark shade of crimson. I feel Edward's hand soothing the stinging area, there is a small pause, and then I feel the sting again. I gasp and grit my teeth. "Three, thank you, sir." My breathing becomes shallow, and I'm struggling to regulate it by the time we reach five.

"With that, he plunges both fingers back into me, and as soon the pad of his thumb touches my clit, my orgasm comes fast. It's so intense, I don't think I have ever climaxed so quickly, and Edward can tell because he gives me a moment to gather myself.

"Well done sweetheart, you can relax now. Long, deep breaths beautiful." His soft voice calms me. "Tell me, how you feel?" he asks.

I take a deep breath. "Humiliated, ashamed, and debased," I mutter and look away from myself.

"That's what's on the surface, tell me how you feel deep inside," he asks. I stay quiet, I can't answer that, it's wrong. "I won't judge you or laugh at you Dana," he says, sensing my inner turmoil. "There is no right or wrong."

"Aroused, empowered, and fulfilled," I say quickly, closing my eyes in embarrassment.

I feel Edwards hand on my chin, lifting my face to look at him. "That's what I thought." He says gently, "This is how you should feel. You should feel pleasure in humiliation. You should feel honor in shame. You should feel fulfillment in submission. You should never feel scared or used, look at how beautiful you are when you let go and submit." I look back at myself in the mirror, and I realize Edward's right. There is no right and wrong, to Edward and I this is right, that's all that matters. "You can let go now," he says helping me to stand up from the ottoman, I'm a little achy, and my fingers feel like they were locked in place from how tight I held on. "Do you feel better?"

I smile a genuine smile. "Yes I do, thank you, Edward."

"You're welcome, now go look at yourself and take some time to actually *see* yourself. I'll meet you in the kitchen, don't worry about putting your clothes back on." I frown at him in confusion, and he just smiles back. What is that man up to?

I leave Heaven's waiting room and make my way to the kitchen island. "Hey beautiful, let's go have a bath," Edward says handing me a glass of wine.

"I thought you didn't keep alcohol in the house?" I ask, taking the glass quickly before he changes his mind.

"I thought you might need it after tonight and I thought about what you said before, you're not an alcoholic," he says.

I eye him suspiciously. "So I'm allowed to drink now?" I ask warily.

"As long as you don't use it as an excuse to ignore reality, I can't see why you can't have a glass or two," he explains.

"Now might not be the best time to tell you but I've already had two bottles of wine tonight," I confess.

"I know, I smelt it on you when you came in." I stay silent, this man is an enigma. "It's been a really tough night for you, I'm not going to lecture you. You made progress coming here tonight and asking for my help, instead of cutting yourself."

"I nearly did, but I don't break my promises."

He wraps his arms around me, pulling me to him and resting his chin on top of my head. "You have no idea how glad I am about that right now," he says taking a deep breath and squeezing me a little harder.

"I think I'm starting to understand what you mean now," I say, and he raises an eyebrow confused. "About submitting to the right person. What I just did with you was like nothing I had ever done before. I actually enjoyed it, even though I'm pretty sure I wasn't meant to." He looks like he's pondering what I say as we enter the bathroom.

"Why can't you enjoy it?" he asks as he busies himself running the huge spa bath.

"I did enjoy it, so much so that when you stopped, I felt disappointed that it was over. I'm not sure I understand why? My mum spanked me as a child and believe me, I didn't enjoy that." I feel like I'm confusing myself now.

"This is different... it 's hard to explain, but it's different. I'm sorry I had to stop as I was enjoying myself as well, a little too much." I see his body stiffen slightly. "I find it hard to control my urges during a scene and more so when I'm around you." It's my turn to look confused as he takes my hand and leads me into the tub. "I could've quite easily made love to you in there."

"Why didn't you?" I'm stunned by my own brashness.

"Because this isn't about sex Dana, I tried to tell you this before. We can't become involved sexually like that, at least not yet," he says, his voice becoming quiet.

"You really confuse me. When I left for California, you kissed me and told me you wanted us to talk when I got back. You've been making subtle hints about wanting me, you gave me a key for crying out loud. What's all that about?" I ask feeling disheartened.

"I'm sorry this is all happening so fast, maybe

we should take a step back and slow it down," he says.

"So what was tonight about and the night in your room, we made love then... I think." Was I reading too much into all this? Did I really misunderstand it all?

"That night in my room shouldn't have happened. I told you that there and then, you shouldn't have come in. It's a good job you're on birth control, or we could have made one a hell of a mess of things. Tonight was about me helping you because you asked me to," he answers in such a professional business tone.

"I'm so confused." My thoughts start to process what he just said. "Wait a minute, what makes you think I'm on birth control? I never told you that."

"Well... um, I just thought, you know... a... a sexually active woman, well... she would probably be taking something, for well... you know," he stammers through the sentence making no sense at all.

"You didn't think to ask me? Why didn't you use a condom?" I ask. I knew something wasn't adding up.

"Because I was under the impression that you were on the pill." His voice sounds panicked.

"Why would you think that, when you didn't even ask me?" I'm becoming angry now.

"Why didn't you stop me?" he counters.

"So now this is my fault. Did you see yourself that night, there really was no right time to mention it," I say in my defense.

"No, it's not your fault." He sounds genuine. The cogs of my brain start working, how did I not think about this? *How could you be so stupid, Dana?* "What's wrong?" Edward asks when he feels the tension in my body.

"I might be pregnant." The silence in the room is deafening, after a while it becomes too much. "Say something," I demand, he helped cause this problem.

"What do you want me to say?" I look up at him, disgusted in his response. I climb out of the bath and grab a towel. I hear Edward get out after me. "Dana, wait please." I don't wait, I run, and he inevitably catches me, turning me around in his arms to face him. "If you are pregnant, I will support the child if it's mine."

Wow, that was a slap in the face. "Who else's would it be?" I raise my voice in anger.

"Some people lie, Dana, to get what they want. When the baby comes, and it has been confirmed by DNA testing that I am the child's father, I will be there for you." I blanch at him, I can't believe what he is saying. I walk to my room and close the door in his face. I have complete trust in him. Apparently, he doesn't trust me at all. Why would he think I was on the pill?

I don't know how long I'm lying on the bed, but the sun is coming up, there has been movement through the apartment all night, but Edward hasn't bothered me since I've been in here. I have to get myself together and get to the hospital. After showering and getting dressed I make my way to the kitchen, Edward is nowhere to be seen. He must be somewhere, I heard him not too long ago. I take this moment to gather my things and get out of there. I don't want to see him or talk to him, I can't.

I make it to the street, I feel like I've just done the walk of shame. I can deal with all these other problems later, but right now I need to get to James. I finally manage to hail a taxi. "St. Luke's-Roosevelt Hospital, please," I ask the driver. Settling into my seat, I hear my phone ringing, when I pull it out and see Edward's name I decide to ignore it. I really just need to see James.

When I arrive at the hospital I'm told visiting doesn't start for another half an hour, I decide to get a coffee and head back outside for some fresh air. Exhaustion is taking over me now and I know I really need to get some sleep, but I can't go back to the apartment yet, everything is too raw, and the place needs a good clean. I ring my Mum to tell her what is going on. "Dana, darling how are you?" she asks in her posh phone voice.

"Hey Mum, I thought I should let you know I'm at the hospital-"

"What did you do?" she interrupts me before I finish.

"I didn't do anything, it's James. I found him unconscious last night, in the bathroom with the shower running," I say trying to keep my emotions in check.

"That silly boy," my Mum says, I can tell she is trying not to cry too. "How is he?"

"The doctor says he's going to be okay, but he has to have some sort of assessment done, and that they might want to have him committed to a psychiatric hospital," I tell her.

"Sweetheart I know that sounds bad, but maybe it's what James needs," she says sensitively.

"He's not a nut-nut Mother," I spit back at her.

"You may not think that, but to a medical professional he obviously has mental health issues," she says calmly.

"Do you think that?" I ask not sure if I want to

know the answer.

"Yes I do," she is interrupted by what sounds like a small child. "Dana I'm sorry, I have to go dear," she says hurriedly.

"Who's the kid?" I ask.

"It's our neighbor's grandson, they had an emergency with their daughter and asked us to look after him," she says vaguely.

"Okay fine, well if you need any help you know where I am. Bye Mum, love you," I finish.

"Bye darling, I love you too." She hangs up.

I look back at my phone and see I have a message from Edward.

**It's customary to say goodbye when you leave.**

**Edward.**

Is it? Well, we can just add that to my list of crimes. I'm immature, rude, and can't be trusted. I wonder what else he can accuse me of. I ignore the message, finish my coffee and go to see James.

When I walk into his room, he and Andy are asleep. I pull up a chair and sit by James' bed, taking his hand in mine. "Hey girl," I turn to the raspy voice and smile to see James awake. "Tell me why I woke up to this arsehole and not you," he asks with an amused grin.

"Because you know I love you no matter what," I say squeezing his hand a little tighter. "But this arsehole loves you too, and I thought it would be the best way for you to discuss things when you can't run away."

"You know me too well, and you were right, we had a really long talk last night, and he answered all of my questions. I was very shocked by some things he said but I still love him, and we are going to take it slow," he says searching my face for a reaction.

Did Andy tell him what he did to Edward? He denied it at the hotel, but that doesn't mean it's not true. I believe Edward or maybe I trust him too much? It's a shame he can't return that trust to me. This is not the time to start second guessing everything he ever told me, but he is hiding something. He knows too much about me, he thought I was on the pill. He had to get his information from somewhere.

"Penny for your thoughts," I hear James' voice.

"I'm sorry, I've just got a lot on my mind," I say trying to shake it off.

"A problem shared is a problem... I don't know the rest." James and I burst out laughing, then Andy stirs.

"Good morning," Andy says while stretching, I can't help staring at his firm chest as he does. As I look at him, I wonder how I never worked out he was Edward's brother.

"Morning, sorry if we woke you," I say.

"It's okay, it's good to hear Jimmy's laugh again. How are you this morning?" he asks James.

"Better," James says. "I'm so sorry to both of you, for putting you through what I did."

Andy and I stay quiet and just comfort him. "Dana, have you actually slept?" Andy asks, worried.

"Do I really look that bad?" I answer his question with a question, not wanting to get into all the events of last night.

"I mean this in the best possible way, but you look like crap." I laugh because I know he's right.

"It's been a *long* night," I say plastering on a fake smile.

"You don't fool me, Dee," James says. "What's going on? Other than the obvious."

"It's nothing honestly, I'm just worried about you," I say.

"When I get out of here, we will be talking," James demands.

"Too bloody right we will, did Andy tell you what the doctor said last night about you possibly needing to go to a psychiatric hospital?" I say watching James' face drop.

"No, he didn't." James looks to Andy for an answer to his unasked question.

"I didn't think now was the right time to tell you. Besides once he's had this stupid three-day assessment done, they will know he's fine and was just overwhelmed," Andy replies.

"I hope you're right," I say.

"Good morning Mr. Ward," the nurse says when she enters the room. "I'm just going to check your vitals. This is Dr. Murray he will be the one assessing you." She smiles at James warmly.

"Good morning Mr. Ward-" Dr. Murray begins.

"Please call me James," he says.

"Very well." The doctor shakes James' hand and picks up his chart. "I will be starting your assessment later this morning, but right now I would like us to have a chat, get to know each other, so you won't be so nervous later," Dr. Murray states. "I should stress that visitors are not permitted throughout the assessment period." We all nod in agreement.

I see Andy gesturing to the door, I nod at him, and we both stand. "We're just going to grab some coffee, we'll see you in a bit," Andy says, leaning down to give James a kiss.

"Okay, can you bring me one please?" James says batting his eyelids.

I burst out laughing and give him a kiss myself. "No need for the puppy dog eyes, you know I'll grab you one," I tease him.

"Thank you, see you in a bit," James says as we leave.

Once outside, Andy doesn't even attempt to beat about the bush. "What's going on Dana?" he asks me.

"It's a long story and will require a lot of caffeine before I can even begin to explain." Andy laughs and puts his arm around my shoulder.

"Well, what are we waiting for, let's go get some coffee." I wrap my arm around his waist, and we head to the hospital canteen.

I find us a table while Andy gets the drinks, and when I'm seated, I cautiously check my phone. The last time I didn't answer the phone to Edward, he came crashing in the front door. Seventeen missed calls, three voicemails, and a text message, it's only been an hour. I would be impressed if it wasn't so creepy. I decide to leave the voicemails till later, I know that if I hear his voice, my body will follow his every command even if my brain doesn't agree. Curiosity gets the better of me, and I check the text, then I remember how well curiosity worked out for the cat. The message isn't from Edward, and it's not a number I recognize, I'm staring at the screen in shock at what I'm seeing. The word 'MURDERER' in big bold capital letters.

"Dana, what's wrong? You're shaking, and you look like you've seen a ghost," Andy says returning with the hot beverages.

I look up at him stunned. "I'm fine, sorry don't worry."

"You really expect me to believe that?" Andy replies. I show him my phone and the message that it displays, Andy narrows his eyes. "Who sent that and what does it mean?"

I'm struggling to reply, the only person who knows the truth is James. "I don't know who sent it, but it means somebody knows what I did."

# Chapter 17

I leave Andy sitting baffled in the canteen, and I do what I'm best at, running away. I exit the hospital and don't even wait for a taxi, I walk the forty-five minutes down Amsterdam Avenue towards home. I bump into nearly everyone, I can't concentrate. Who else knows? Should I be scared? I ring Edward because I really don't know what else to do.

"Where are you?" Edward says when he answers on the first ring.

"I'm sorry." Suddenly I don't feel like I can stand, my whole world is crashing around me, and the tears that threaten to fall have broken the dam.

"Dana, what's wrong?" Edward's voice is becoming increasingly concerned.

"I received a text message from an unknown number. I think I'm being threatened by someone who knows what I did a long time ago." My voice trails off and I let out a cry, the past always catches up with you.

"Where are you?" Edward asks again.

"Nearly at my apartment," I say through choked sobs.

"Wait for me in the lobby, I'll be there in five minutes." With that, he hangs up.

Something washes over me that feels a little like relief. Am I really relieved that Edward is coming to my rescue again, even after the way he treated me last night? I step into the lobby, and the receptionist calls me straight over. "Miss Spencer, this package arrived for you a little while ago. It has no name or address on, but the man said it was specifically for you." I thank her, take the rectangular box and move to one of the chairs and wait for Edward. I don't remember ordering anything, maybe it's not for me. I examine the plain package, for a fair sized box, it's very light. If it hadn't of made a sound when I turned it over I would have thought it was empty.

Edward comes flying through the door and wraps me in his arms. "Don't ever leave without saying goodbye again," he says gruffly. I nod because that's all I can manage. "What's going on? What's that?" he says pointing to the package in my hands.

"This," I say pointing to the same package, mimicking his move. "I don't know, I didn't order anything. The receptionist gave it to me when I got here, I didn't want to open it."

Edward takes the package from me and examines it. "You have no idea what this could be or who it's from?" he asks, and I shake my head. "What about the message you got?"

"I'll show you when we're in the apartment," I answer and press the call button for the lift. We ride up in silence, but I swear my heartbeat can be heard very clearly. First the message then this surprise package, the two have got to be connected. I open the door to my apartment and Edward puts the box on the table. "Do I open it?" I ask warily.

"I can open it if you want?" he replies. I nod

and watch him gingerly as he breaks the seal, his face drops, and I suddenly have no desire to see what's in the box.

He hands me an envelope with my name on, it's been handwritten. I take it and examine it, too scared to see what's inside. "What's in the box?" I ask cautiously.

"Flowers," he replies simply. I'm slightly confused, so I step towards him and take a look for myself. "Dead flowers," he replies again just as they come into my line of vision. "What does the card say?"

"I don't think I want to know," I say.

"What is going on Dana?" he asks me, worry etched into every line on his face. I show him the message on my phone, his expression instantly becomes angry. "Hand me the card," he demands, and I do as I'm told, I watch him open it and then fling it into the box. I look at him, my eyes asking the question that my mouth won't let me.

He picks the card back up, hands it to me and

walks towards the sofa. I open it, and my hand instantly flies to my mouth. In big bold letters the words 'BABY KILLER' are written in red. "Is that blood?" I manage to choke out.

"I think it's just meant to look like blood," he answers. He stares at me for a long time, and I'm stuck for what to tell him, maybe it's time to face my demons.

"It's not what it looks like," I say, trying to open a communication channel between us.

"So you didn't kill a baby?" he asks and continues before I have a chance to answer, "Because your reaction says otherwise."

"I didn't kill a baby, well I did but not in the way you think." I'm rambling now because I know I have to tell him the truth.

"You've lost me," he says, the anger in his eyes is killing me.

"Let me start from the beginning," I say, and he nods, ready to hear me out. I walk over and sit down next to him on the sofa, but he instantly moves away. "Remember when we talked about Grant and when I made the decision to leave him, he wasn't going to allow it, so he locked me up." Edward nods, his silence making me uncomfortable. "That's because I found out I was pregnant." Edwards face suddenly changes, a more concerned look appears. "You already know about Nathan, you admitted that much." He nods, his expression looking guilty. "I couldn't continue staying there, bringing a child up in that environment just wasn't right. So I tried to leave with Nathan, but Grant had already worked out what was going on. He wasn't about to let me go especially with his baby and unborn child inside me." My voice becomes timid as I recall the events of that fateful day. Edward places his hand on mine and I know he is trying to comfort me as I continue. "The only people that knew I was pregnant were Grant and James, who I told when I first saw him again a few days after being rescued. After being brought home, I spiraled out of control."

"That's when you started hurting yourself," he

asks.

"Yes and drinking. I was nineteen weeks gone when I terminated the pregnancy, and it was the worst mistake of my life, but at the time it was better all round. I was in no fit state to be a mother, I was fucked up Edward. I still am now." I stop because I can't carry on, it's too hard.

"So you didn't actually kill a baby?" he asks.

"Not in the way you're thinking of, but yes I did kill a baby because what was inside me was a baby, I had even felt it move." My voice is breaking as the tears begin again.

Edward pulls me into him and rocks me as I cry. "Shhh now, everything is going to be okay," he lulls in my ear. "You did what was best for you at the time, you made the right choice knowing you weren't ready to bring a baby into this world. From what you told me before, I take it the baby wasn't put there consensually either. You did nothing wrong, Dana," he says, trying to help me justify my actions but it doesn't take away the guilt.

"I'm sorry about last night. I know you don't want a baby but please don't ask me to go through all that again," I say referring to our current situation.

"I've never said I didn't want a child. Who told you that?" he demands.

"Andy had already told me about Caroline before your Dad mentioned it last night," I say sheepishly. "He said that when Payton told you she was pregnant, you didn't want a baby."

"Caroline isn't my daughter," he confesses. "Andrew is her biological Father."

"I don't understand, he's gay."

"He's bi-sexual."

"Why would he tell me she was yours?"

"Because he doesn't know," he lowers his eyes when he says this. "I suppose now it's my turn to start from the beginning."

"Please do," I reply, confusion plaguing my expression.

"I broke up with Payton because she was too media obsessed, she started tipping the press off whenever we went out so we could be photographed together. I loved her so much, but she loved the fame and money, the social status she received being seen with me, not so much the actual being with me part. About a month after we split, she told me she was pregnant. I would never deny my child, so I decided to try again with her, and she agreed to keep our private life out of the media spotlight. She understood that it could be dangerous for our child, considering who I am." I nod along saying nothing, wondering where this is going. "We went for a sonogram and I know I'm a man, but I can do maths, the dates just weren't matching up. I gave her the benefit of the doubt and stuck it out till Caroline was born when I got a DNA test done. The test came back that we were related but we didn't share enough genetic markers for her to be my daughter. More likely she was a second-degree relative. So I confronted Payton and asked her which one of my brothers she convinced to get her pregnant. Turns out she told Drew she was carrying my child and that I wanted nothing to do with either of them. He comforted her, they had unprotected sex, she got the required result and tried to pass the baby off as mine when she found out she was pregnant," he says, standing up and walking to the window.

"Why didn't you just tell Andy the truth and let him and Payton get on with it?" I ask.

"After what Drew did to me, I couldn't take the risk. I offered Payton financial security if she kept this bit of information to herself, Caroline is my niece after all. I will make sure she is safe, just as my Uncle Nick did for me," he answers.

"But he seems to have changed, and I don't want to sound insensitive, but maybe he realized the mistake he made." I try to reason with him. "You're both adults now, do you think you could ever move on from what happened?"

"I told my parents, and when they didn't believe me, they shipped me off to boarding school. Would you be able to just forgive and forget?" He starts to raise his voice. "He raped me, Dana," he admits quietly. "I was a child, I would never allow him to be responsible for a child because of that."

"You can't play god with people's lives Edward, I know what Andy did was wrong I'm not defending that, but it was fifteen years ago. He deserves to know he is a Father and has a right to know his daughter," I continue.

"He is an evil man, he's never once tried to apologize for putting me through that, and he continues to press my buttons about how he was believed, and I wasn't. You saw what he was like last night, I can't forgive him, I'm sorry. I know you like him and that he says he loves James." He sighs, running his hands through his hair and with exasperation etched on his face. "I just hope neither of you gets hurt."

I realize that I'm just trying to find a reason to justify why I like Andy, especially after what Edward has said. He's right, we saw Andy's true colors at the dinner, I hated him so much at that moment. I hate the idea of Grant being responsible for a child, and I was of legal age when he forced himself on me, not a child. "I'm sorry, don't listen to me I'm being selfish. You obviously have your reasons, and I swear I won't say anything to him about this conversation. It's not my place to judge you, just as you haven't judged me. I couldn't keep my child because the Father was evil, I don't blame you for keeping Caroline safe from hers," I finish.

"Come here," Edward says pulling me up off the sofa and into his arms. "Thank you." We remain silent with me in his arms for a while, I'm dying here. Why do I continue to do this to myself? his smell is so masculine, and my heart swells a bit more with the feel of his tenderness. He makes me mad and crazy, but I love him. I'm truly madly deeply in love with him, and he doesn't want me. I blink away the tears that come to my eyes and sort myself out, maybe one day he will feel the same. "I think we need to figure out who it is that's threatening you," Edward says pulling me from my lovesick reverie.

"Is there anything you can do?" I ask with not much hope.

"I'm going to hand everything over to my security team and see what they can do, I will need to take your phone too." His words becoming quiet at his request, he knows I don't like giving up my phone.

"That's fine, I'll give it to you later after I've let a few people know I'll be unreachable. Then I can use my new necklace if I need to get hold of you," I say, smiling for the first time since last night. "I meant to ask you, is it waterproof?"

"Yes you can wear it in water, so please don't ever take it off no matter what. Promise me?" he says.

"I promise," I answer with a smile.

"Also it's for emergency uses only, I don't want to be breaking down any more of your doors," he says with a lopsided smile, he really is ridiculously handsome.


Edward drives me back to the hospital, so I'm not walking the streets on my own. "Dana, if you are pregnant, we'll deal with it." His voice sounds genuine. "There is no point getting ourselves worked up over it when we don't even know if you are or not."

"You're right," I say with a sincere smile. "Just for the record, I'd understand if you'd want a DNA test."

"Thank you," he says placing his hand on my thigh.

Andy comes flying at the car door. "I've been pulling my hair out Dana, what the hell happened in the cafeteria?" His voice is frantic with worry. "I tried to call you."

"You have no idea how alike you two are," I say to both Edward and Andy. "My phone is on silent, I'm sorry. I'm okay now, Edward is helping me."

"What with? Is this about the message you got," Andy quires.

"I think I'm being threatened. Someone sent me that text message and then sent another message with dead flowers to my apartment," I answer trying not to say too much.

"What did the second message say?" His brow furrowed.

"It doesn't matter, Edward is dealing with it." I try brushing him off.

"I'm just saying that my job involves this sort of thing, I could do some digging for you," he says.

"I've got it under control, there's no need," Edward says flatly. "Do me a favor, though, don't let Dana out of your sight."

"I don't need a babysitter," I chime in.

"That's not a problem," Andy answers as if I said nothing.

"I'm trusting you, Andrew," Edward says with disdain. "Eyes on her at all times."

"Hello? I'm still here," I say, getting annoyed that they are talking about me as though I'm not here. They both turn to look at me finally. "I don't need looking after, I'm not a child," I say to Edward.

"It's Andrew or I hire Carl as your bodyguard, your choice." I narrow my eyes at him. "Could you close the door please I need a moment with Dana," he says to Andy, who nods and does as he's told. "I can't have you out there on your own, at least until we know who we're dealing with."

I place the palm of my hand on his cheek and rub gently. "I understand, why Andy?" I ask, and he knows exactly what I mean.

Edward takes a moment before answering. "Because you were right, what happened with Drew, happened a long time ago. Maybe it's time I let it go of my hatred." He sees the smile on my face and continues, "This doesn't mean I like him or forgive him, but I'll tolerate him for you."

My heart constricts. "At the risk of ruining whatever this is," I say, gesturing my hand between Edward and me. "How can you care about me so much but not want anything more. I really like you, but you're so hot and cold all the time. It's hard to know where I stand with you," I say looking away from him.

"Oh Dana, I do want so much more with you. It's just a bit difficult right now. There are still some

358

things I need to tell you, and I don't think you'll like me very much afterward." His voice sounds shaky, what's he hiding now?

"I don't care because it won't change how I feel about you, I love you, Edward," I blurt out meaning every word.

He pulls me into a tight hold, resting his forehead on mine and looks into my eyes. "Oh god, I love you too sweetheart, from the first time I saw you." His voice cracking as I let out a breath that I didn't realize I was holding. "We need to talk tonight, I need to tell you everything. I don't want secrets between us."

"Okay, I'll meet you at the penthouse at five tonight," I say breezily. He nods and plants his lips on mine. I've been longing to feel these lips since I walked out on him this morning. I push my fingers into his hair to try and draw him closer to me, as he pushes his tongue between my teeth to find mine. He eventually pulls away, and I feel bereft of this touch.

"I'll see you tonight." His eyes gleaming with

happiness as he smiles and I'm sure my face must share a similar expression.

Andy helps me out of the car once I open the door. I turn back to Edward. "Thank you for trusting Andy for me." I smile my appreciation.

Edward shrugs. "I don't know why. He hits like a girl and goes down with one punch, but he looks big and scary enough to deter anyone from approaching you." He turns to me and smiles.

I shake my head and roll my eyes. "See you later, I love you," I say, loving how those words sound and how much they mean saying them to Edward.

"I love you too sweetheart." I close the door, and Edward drives off.

My brain starts to go into overdrive, I turn my attention to Andy. "You ready bodyguard, I wish to go see James."

Andy laughs at my mocking tone. "Lead the way, Miss Spencer." I stop suddenly. "What's wrong?" Andy asks, cautiously looking around.

"What is it you do for a living again?" I query. I

know what I'm about to ask is awful, but Edward wants to talk, and I want to be at least a little prepared for what he's going to say. Especially if it's what I think.

"I'm an inquiry agent," he answers.

"That's just a fancy way of saying private detective, right?" Andy nods. "How much do you charge for personal, on the side work?"

"What do you need?" He sounds perplexed.

"Do you remember I told you I found a cheque on Edward's desk from my stepfather?"

"Yes, have you not asked either of them about it?"

"No," I say matter-of-factly. How can I? Then Edward would know I was snooping through his office. "I need to find out what Edwards connection is to Richard and my Mum, and I need to know before five o'clock this evening."

"Are you sure you want *me* to do this?" he asks uncertainly.

I nod my head determinedly. "I think they're

361

working together, and I need to know why the people

I love are conspiring against me."

# Chapter 18

"Dana, wait!" Andy calls after me as I walk off through the hospital corridors, to James' room. "Dana, stop!" Andy commands as he grabs hold of my arm and halts me, I turn and look up at him. "What makes you think people are conspiring against you?"

I raise one eyebrow at him and shake my head. "Really? After everything I have told you. Edward knows too much stuff about me, he knows about Nathan for crying out loud. He knew Grant was here because my Mum called him and asked for his help, why would she ask my boss and someone she doesn't know? He thought I was on the pill, the only reason he would think I was on the pill is if someone told him. This brings me to my Mum and Stepfather, they are the only people who think I'm on birth control. They were always on at me about taking precaution, so I lied to get them off my back. Then there's Richards cheque to Edward and the fact that my Mum has barely spoken to me since I started working for Edward, that woman use to ring me three or four times a day and then nothing. Even with Grant turning up, she's been vague on the phone, and you know what I literally only just realized as I got out of the car right now, I don't even know their exact address. I haven't been to the house yet, not once in the last six weeks that we've been here. The one time I was meant to go, she canceled on me at the last minute. Edward, Richard, and my Mum are connected somehow," I say feeling paranoid. "Now you tell me, mister private detective, it's a little strange don't you think?" I say to Andy.

"Yes, it is." Andy looks as if he's contemplating something. "I think I already know what's going on," he replies.

"You do?" I'm taken aback as Andy starts to walk back out of the hospital. "Andy where are you going?"

"I just need to make a quick phone call, I'll be right back!" he shouts back to me before disappearing around a corner.

I carry on making my way to James' room, no doubt he's been worrying. "Hey is it safe to come in?" I ask gingerly around the door.

"That depends," James says. "Are you going to stop running away?"

"Yes," I answer half-heartedly.

"What's going on Dee? Andy came in all panicked trying to tell me about a text message you had received, and then he couldn't get hold of you-"

"Jay, stop," I interrupt him. "Someone knows I had an abortion and now they're threatening me. When I got back to the apartment, dead flowers had been delivered."

"Who else knew you were pregnant?" he asks worriedly. "I swear I never told anyone, not even Andy knows."

"The only other person who knew was Grant," I answer.

"Do you think he might be involved?" he asks.

"According to Edward, Grant is back in England, so I wouldn't have thought so." My brow furrows as I try to work things out.

"What are you not telling me D?" James asks.

I tell James everything I told Andy, he listens tentatively and says nothing when I finish. The room is silent for some time. "Say something. Do you think I'm just paranoid?"

"I don't know what to say. It all makes perfect sense, but at the same time, it all seems a little farfetched. I mean Edward and Richard don't even know each other." He says trying not to offend me.

"They must know each other, Edward had a cheque for one hundred thousand dollars from Richard," I snap.

"Maybe Richard was just donating money Dee, you can't go jumping to conclusions," he tries to reason with me.

"Yes she can," Andy's booming voice is heard before we see him.

"Don't encourage this." James turns to Andy. "She'll drive herself crazy with these conspiracy theories."

"Dana," Andy says, ignoring James, "where is Nathan?"

I turn to James asking my silent question. "I never told him," he says, and we both look to Andy.

"You're in on all this too, that's why you know what's going on," I say suspiciously.

"Dana you need to listen to me-"

"No," I inject, stopping him talking. I stand up and try to leave the room. "Sorry Jay I know I said I wouldn't leave again, but I have to go." Tears forming in my eyes, "Get out of my way!" I shout at Andy, who's standing in the doorway.

"I'm sorry, I'm just trying to help. You can trust me." His eyes pleading with me.

"Obviously I can't because just like your brother, you know too much stuff about me. Now get out of my way," I assert through gritted teeth.

"Call me later, please!" James shouts from

behind me. I don't answer, I don't know who I can trust.

Andy runs out after me. "Dana, please stop." He grabs my arm.

I turn to see his face, a mixture of anxiety and frustration rests upon it, I yank my arm free. "Leave me alone Andrew," I spit through my teeth.

"You must really be pissed at me to use my full name," he says with a small smirk.

"This isn't a joke, don't touch me. I want nothing to do with you."

"I can't tell you everything Dana, but I can tell you some of it if you'll hear me out."

"That's exactly what your brother said, and I still don't know what's going on," I say tears coming back to my eyes in confusion. "But I will find out. Until then, everyone needs to just stay away from me."

Once I'm outside the hospital, I take a deep breath. I can't go back to my apartment, that's the first place Edward will look once Andy calls him. I need to let off some steam, and I know just where to go. I head to the nearest motorcycle rental shop, this is just what I need.

"Hi I'm Scott, can I help you?" the shop assistant asks.

"Hi, I hope you can. I'd like to hire a bike for the afternoon. I've not been in New York for long and haven't had a chance to purchase one yet," I say with a smile.

"What are you looking for?" Scott queries.

"Something sporty and quick," I say browsing the bikes, then I spot it. "Like this," I continue putting my hand on the seat.

"That's a big boy's bike, you might be more comfortable on one of our smaller bikes," he says with a slight chuckle.

"I'm an experienced rider," I snap back in anger. "I'll take the Ducati 848 Evo, please. Also, I need to hire leathers and a helmet." I reign in my frustration and pretend like his comment didn't affect me.

"I need to see your bike license please." He

holds out his hand as I retrieve my license from my bag. It must all check out because after fiddling around with his computer for a bit, he gives my license back with red cheeks. "I'll need to take some credit card details and a deposit."

"Here," I say handing over my credit card and my passport for I.D. "Whatever you need to do, just do it. I'll only need the bike for a few hours. I need to clear my head, and this is the best way," I say trailing off at the end. The poor man doesn't need my life story.

We spend the next twenty minutes filling out the paperwork, and I'm more stressed than when I walked in, this better be worth it. "Let's get you some gear. Will you need a locker?" Scott says. I nod, and he hands me the key. I exit the changing room, kitted up and ready to go. I put all my belongings in the locker, I take out my phone and send a quick text to Edward.

**Can't do tonight, sorry.**

**D.**


"I wouldn't wear that necklace out," Scott says just as I'm about to close the locker.

"I can't really take it off," I reply.

"Can you tuck it in?" he asks.

"No I tried, it dug in when I did my jacket up." I contemplate for a minute, Edward wouldn't know, not that it really matters now anyway. I remove the necklace, at least he can't accuse me of being careless with it. "I don't really know my way around can you suggest a route?" I ask Scott as I place the emerald in the locker.

"There's the five-hour green rural loop," he answers.

"That sounds perfect," I squeal slightly.

He takes out a fold away map and starts marking points on it. Then places the map in front of me. "Okay, well you're supposed to start at the Queens Midtown tunnel, but you can start anywhere on FDR drive. Just keep going north over the Kennedy

Bridge on to Buckner Expressway, all the way up onto Hutchinson River Parkway, following signs to I-684. Exit at S onto Route 172, and then take Route 35 onto Route 102, you with me so far?" he says. I nod and smile, I have no idea what he's talking about. "When Route 102 runs into Highway 7, go right and get on Route 107 until it runs into Route 53. Here take a right and head past the Saugatuck Reservoir till 53 meets up with Route 57. Then head south onto Route 15, take a right and head down to Rye Brook. You'll complete the loop when you reach Hutchinson River Parkway and then just follow the original route back to the Queens Midtown tunnel, got it?" I give him a big thumbs up, too overwhelmed to speak. Just give me the keys so I can get on my way.

We walk out the front of the store, where the bike I'll be riding has been parked. He hands me the key, and I start the engine. "Thanks, Scott," I say turning back to look at him.

"I hope that you manage to clear your head," he says with a smile.

"What time do you close?" I ask, thinking about the bits I left in the locker.

"Eight. You should be back well before then."

"Cool, I'll see you soon," I say climbing on to the bike, putting it into gear and winding the throttle.

At first, the bike scares me a little, but as I get used to the handling, I start to relax into the ride. It takes me a while to get out of Manhattan with all the traffic, but once I hit the open road, I finally get to see what this baby can do.

I've been on the road about two hours now, and I'm pretty sure I've already gone past the halfway point according to the fold away map that Scott gave me. So far my head is more clouded than when I started, I've thought a lot about everything, but when it came down to it, my mind kept drifting back to one person, Edward. How can he love me when all he does is lie to me? I hate feeling so out of control. *So much for your submission theory Edward*, I think to myself. I like control, I hate to give it up, why has he done this to me? I knew I shouldn't have let him in, I should have run away and got another job when I had the chance. I think back to earlier in the week when I was in California with Cain Cunningham, the fun we had and how easy it was. Why couldn't it be like that with Edward? Why did there have to be all these secrets? For one fleeting moment I wish Edward was Cain, and then I shake that thought from my head. I should really call Cain and wind him up a bit, tell him we are printing the picture of him pouting that I took on the beach, he would kill me. I'm trying everything I can to take my mind off Edward. I chuckle to myself as I remember those two days I spent with him, and how just knowing Edward, had even ruined that fun. Then my mind is back on him again, I can't keep blaming Edward for all my troubles, this is my fault. It's my paranoia and over thinking that has landed me at this point, but I can't help that niggling feeling that they are all hiding something from me. All of them, Richard, Edward, my Mum, Andy and maybe even James. I pass a sign that's advertising a roadside diner two miles ahead, and I decide I need to take a break, empty my bladder and get a coffee.

I pull off the road and park, remove my helmet and take in my beautiful surroundings. I walk around the car park for a bit stretching my legs and then head inside, taking a seat in one of the booths. "What can I get you?" the waitress asks.

"Cup..." I cough realizing how dry my throat is. "Sorry, cup of coffee and-" I continue, looking down the menu, "a burger and chi- fries please," I correct myself.

She writes down my order and without a smile or any customer service skills whatsoever, she turns and stalks off. I sit in a comfortable silence, trying not to think of anything until she brings my coffee back. "There's a bit of a wait on the food, we have a new chef," the waitress says with no expression on her face at all. "It could be twenty to twenty-five minutes."

"That's fine, thank you," I say. I can hang around for a bit. I'm at least half an hour ahead of schedule anyway. I start to think about Edward again, and what I'm going to do. I can't be with him if I can't trust him, but I do trust him. God, I'm so confused, how can I trust him not to hurt me if I can't trust him not to lie to me, don't the two kind of go hand in hand? I need to stop, this all needs to stop. Edward is a mistake, New York was a mistake. Then I have an idea, and my mind is made up, I'm going back to England, and I'm going to find Nathan, he's the only one that matters to me, he's my priority. With that, I head to the ladies room before my food arrives. As I make my way back to my table, I'm stopped in my tracks. What the hell is he doing here and how did he find me? Edward just stares at me, his facial expression is scarily calm, but his eyes are full of fury. I gingerly make my way over to him, he doesn't say anything just picks up one of my chips and eats it. "You could ask," I say, breaking the extremely uncomfortable silence that surrounds us.

"And you could do as you're told." His voice is harsh and his eyes cold.

"I needed to get away and think," I answer as

calmly as my shuddering breath will allow.

"You took your necklace off, even after you promised you wouldn't," he counters.

"I thought it would be safer in the locker-"

"It's safer around your neck!" he shouts back at me, slamming his fist on the table making me jump. "We're going now, grab your stuff."

"No, I'm eating and then I'm going to finish my ride," I answer defiantly.

"Will you ever do as you are told?" he hisses at me.

"Not if you're going to keep treating me like a child," I snap, letting stubbornness take over.

He grabs me by the arm and starts pulling me towards the door. "We're leaving now," he says after throwing a twenty on the table.

I yank my arm free. "Get off of me!" I shout. We are starting to draw attention to ourselves. "Leave me alone!" I continue screaming, hoping he will become embarrassed and leave.

He doesn't, he just steps closer. He leans in,

looking me directly in the eye. His eyes bore into me, pinning me, letting me know he is deadly serious. "Dana, get outside now or so help me god, I'll take you over my knee right now."

I don't know why but my thighs instantly become wet as my sex throbs. "You wouldn't dare," I say, knowing this is a battle of wits I won't win.

"Call my bluff. By all means, please do," he says, staring at me with a cocky grin on his face.

I concede, picking up my helmet and heading outside. I'm so furious right now but extremely aroused too. I hate what this guy does to me.

"We'll go back to my penthouse," Edward says as I start up the bike.

"I have to take this back to the bike shop," I answer him smugly.

"No need, I've paid for you to keep it until tomorrow." His lips trying to hide a smirk. "And before you say anything, I already have your things that were in your locker."

"How the hell did you manage that? You could

378

have been anyone." I think I'll need to have a word with Scott tomorrow.

"Scott was very cooperative after a little persuading." Edward's eyes are alight with power, telling me not to mess with him because I won't win.

"What did you do to him?" My mouth gaping in shock. "How did you know I'd gone to the bike shop anyway?"

"I have my ways, Dana. You should know by now, you won't be able to do anything without me knowing about it," he says matter-of-factly like it's normal.

"How dare you keep tabs on me-"

"Don't!" Edward shouts interrupting. "All I asked is that you stayed with Drew and keep that necklace on, but you couldn't even do that. You shouldn't be out on your own, I need to know you're safe. I trusted you, Dana, that was a mistake."

"Well you obviously don't trust me, or you wouldn't have had people watching me!" I shot back at him. I jump on my bike and go before he has a

chance to protest. As I look back in my mirror, I see
Edward throw his hands up in anger and kick his bike.
I can't help the smile that comes to my face, but I pick
up speed just in case he decides to follow me. I have
to get as far away from him as possible, he's crossed
the line this time. I'm losing myself and my freedom
again, I can't let that happen. I'm stronger now, I need
to fight him, and I need to get home to England. I find
myself back on Hutchinson River Parkway and make
my way straight to the bike shop instead of the
Queens Midtown Tunnel.

"Miss Spencer I wasn't expecting you back."
Scott looks a little nervous.

"I don't even have the energy to argue with
you about proper client conduct. If Mister Neurotic
comes back, tell him I went to the penthouse, and I'll
meet him there," I say to Scott in a less than
impressed manner.

"Sure. I'm really sorry, I hope you're okay?" he
says with a small, sincere smile.

I wave my hand over my shoulder and roll my

eyes as I head to the changing room to remove the leathers. I leave them in Scott's capable hands and jump in a taxi back to my apartment. I know I don't have long before Edward realizes I'm not going to be at the penthouse. There is a slight feeling of déjà vu, it reminds me of when I tried to leave Grant. Why am I so scared of Edward finding me? Maybe because I'm afraid to hear the truth, to find out that he has been lying to me and betrayed me. Arriving at my building, I ask the receptionist at the front desk for my spare key and tell her to take everyone off my approved list so no one can come up. I run into my apartment and search frantically for the essentials that I'll need and pack them all in a suitcase when I realize I don't have my phone or passport. They were in my locker that Edward had emptied, fuck! I mentally curse myself for being so stupid, I should have got my things from him before I left. There is only one thing for it, I'll have to go to the penthouse. I leave my packed suitcase in the living room and make my way out the front to hail another taxi. As I reach the lobby Edward is sitting there waiting for me.

The anger in his eyes is a scary thing. "Did you really think I would believe you went to the penthouse?" His argumentative tone daring to be questioned.

I shrug my shoulder and pull my 'I really don't care' face. "I want my belongings," I hold out my hand.

"Why am I not allowed up to your apartment now?" he asks looking a little offended.

"You and your brother have both been removed from my approved list as I don't allow people I don't trust into my apartment. Now give me my stuff." My voice is more forceful this time.

"No," he simply replies.

"Please don't piss me off any more than I already am." I can feel myself losing patience, I won't be able to control my anger much longer.

"What? Don't you think I'm pissed off too? You're going to come to my place so we can talk, then you can have your stuff back," he orders.

My body has stopped complying with him thankfully, stubbornness has taken over. "You're insane. I'm not going anywhere with you. You don't own me, and you're not in control of me. I can do what I want when I want."

"Then I guess you don't want your stuff back." He smirks at me and walks towards the exit.

"Fine," I say feeling defeated and following him out front.

"That's what I thought," Edward replies, his eyes playful.

We make our way to the car parked outside. "I hate you." My deflated voice nearly nonexistent.

"No you don't," he replies arrogantly.

He opens the passenger door for me, I stop and turn to him. "I do, it was a mistake telling you I loved you," I say with disgust as he clenches his jaw. "I hate you *so* much the only reason I'm coming with you, is to get my passport back so I can go home," I sneer at him.

I think I see panic cross his face. "Home?" he

questions.

"Back to London, so I can be as far away from you, Andy, and my parents as possible," I answer confidently, with a determined look on my face.

He closes the passenger door, grabs my arm and opens the back door. "Get in the fucking car!" His face is stony and cold. He pushes me in and closes the door, I try to open it, but he has put the child lock on. He climbs in the front seat as I'm trying to jump over, he pushes me back into the back seat. "Sit the fuck down and put your seat belt on now!" he demands infuriated. I don't say a word to him the entire drive to his place, I'm too irate, and I know I'll lose it.

We pull into the underground garage and a sense of relief washes over me, I need to get out of this car. Edward walks round and opens the door. "Get out," he tells me, I do as he says and wait till he closes the door.

He grabs hold of my arm, and I can't take it anymore, I raise my hand, and it comes crashing down against his cheek. "Get your hands off of me!" I'm furious now.

"Don't slap me, Dana," he responds while rubbing his face.

"Then stop manhandling me." I'm pleading now.

"Fine, get in the elevator." I don't move, and he rolls his eyes. "Please." Well seeing as he asked so nicely, I get in the lift, and we ride to the top. I can feel his eyes glaring at me, but I remain nonchalant. I will not let him get to me, and I pray my body doesn't betray me. The doors open and he gestures for me to exit before him, as I walk into the vast open space I'm unaware of what happens next.

Edward pulls my arms behind my back and starts to push me towards the double doors that lead to Heaven's waiting room. "What are you doing? Get off of me!" I shriek at him.

He opens the door and grabs my hair, yanking my head back. "You need to learn your lesson sweetheart." His voice full of disdain, he pushes me in and leaves the room, locking the door as he goes.

I bang on the door for what seems like forever, I'm begging and pleading with him to let me out. "Edward please let me out, please. Don't leave me here, I'm begging you. I'll do whatever you want, just unlock the door. Please, please, please." My cries go unheard or unnoticed. I'm scared now, too many bad memories come back to haunt me. With floods of tears running down my cheeks, I move to the corner of the room and fall to the floor curling up in a ball. I close my eyes and let fear and anxiety take over, I'm broken, and I don't think I have the strength to fix myself again.

# Chapter 19

I hear the door unlock and I stand up waiting for him to come in. I've been counting since I sat down, one thousand and thirty-four seconds have passed. So it's been nearly twenty minutes since he left the room. His head comes round the door, his eyes locking with mine. He must see the hostility on my face and the malice in my eyes because he instantly looks away. "Come here," he orders, his voice impassive.

I comply, not because I want to or have to, but because it's easier. He pulls me into his arms wrapping them around me, but I leave mine at my side. He pulls back and searches my blank eyes for some sort of recognition or emotion, but I don't respond. Finally, he tries to kiss me, but I don't open my mouth, I don't even purse my lips. He wanted control, I guess it's true what they say, be careful what you wish for.

He pulls my top off over my head, I lift my arms for him. He pulls my jeans and panties down, I lift my feet out. "Are you going to say anything?" he asks quietly. I remain silent, letting him feel the hatred coming off of me. "I'm sorry I have to do this, but you need to learn to do as you're told." I close my eyes and turn my face away. "Fine, be like that." He grabs hold of my wrists and pushes me onto the bed, I'm just about to react but decide against it, that's exactly what he wants. He goes to the ottoman, opens it and pulls out a set of cuffs. It takes everything in me to stop my eyes from widening, he is trying everything he can to provoke me. He turns me on to my stomach, fastens the leather cuffs around my wrist above my head and attaches them to an eye bolt in the wall. I'm petrified, but I'm glad he can no longer see my face. He moves to his wall of spanking equipment, and I wrench my head round as far as I can, I watch as he picks up a leather flogger, hiding my face again as he turns back around. "I think ten should be enough," he says as I bury my head back into the mattress. "You will count and thank me for each one." There is a long sullen silence before he speaks again. "Answer me!" he roars. Staying quiet I realize, is winding him up more than me. Silence is my only weapon, and I will use it to bring him down.

When I don't answer, I hear him growl with frustration and stalk across the room, at first I thought he was leaving me again, so I jump when I hear a loud bang, he has kicked the door closed.

*Smack.*

I wasn't expecting it, I take in a quick breath and grit my teeth. "What is your problem Dana?" he snarls.

*Smack.*

I feel the tears pricking my eyes. "You did this, this is all your fault."

*Smack.*

The pain is becoming too much for me, and my breathing begins to shudder as I silently cry into the mattress. "I only asked for you to stay with Drew and keep the necklace on."

*Smack, smack, smack.*

"Do you know what was going through my head when Drew called me and said you ran off?"

*Smack, smack, smack.*

"And then the pager went off, letting me know the GPS in the necklace had been activated. God, Dana!"

*SMACK!*

I cry out as the pain from the last stroke is too much to bear. He sits down on the edge of the bed, throwing the flogger on the floor and putting his head in his hands. "My heart felt like it had stopped. I didn't know what I would have done if something had happened to you. It hurt so much to think you were in trouble and I wasn't there. The crushing feeling in my heart was more pain than I've felt my entire life." He got the reaction he wanted, he needed me to feel the pain he felt, to be as scared as he was. He leans over me and unlocks the cuffs releasing my hands. He turns me over, and with tears running down my face, I start to laugh. "What's so funny?" His face becoming angry again.

"You," I manage. "You know, I thought you were just like Grant." His expression hardens. "Then I realized that wasn't true." He furrows his brow. "You're worse." He tries to move closer to me putting his arms around me. "No, get your damn hands off of me, don't touch me!" I yell at him, as I manage to fight my way out of his arms and move off the bed. "At least Grant didn't lie to me." I start laughing hysterically again as I pick up my clothes and head to the room Edward gave me for when I stay. I lock the bathroom door before I get in the shower, I don't want any unwanted visitors. I start to scrub my skin, I need to get him off of me.

After standing under the water until my skin is bright red, burning, and sore from scrubbing, I get out and towel myself dry. I put the toilet seat down and just sit on it, contemplating what I'm going to say to Edward. I don't have to wait long, I hear him knock on the bathroom door, but I ignore it. "Dana, please talk to me," I hear him call through the door, he sounds upset and scared. I still don't say anything not because I'm being stubborn now, but because I really don't know what to say. "I'm sorry, I shouldn't have done what I did. I have no good excuse for it, but I was angry and scared. Please talk to me, please just let me see you." I hear his voice cracking.

My heart breaks for him, it shouldn't, but it does. I open the door and have to jump back when he comes falling into the bathroom and stumbling over. I chuckle a little, I can't help it. "You could have told me you were leaning against the door." I try suppressing a grin.

"I didn't think you were going to open it, it's good to see that smile again," he says weakly. He looks at me, searching my face for how I'm feeling or what I'm thinking. "Would you like a drink? I went out when you came in here and got you a bottle of wine, or you can have coffee."

"I'm okay thanks. I would like my stuff back

please," I ask as nicely as I can.

"Can we at least talk?" he pleads with me.

"Yeah we can actually, I have some things to say too," I answer, and his facial expression turns worried.

We move to the living room and take a seat on the sofa. "Are you sure you don't want a drink?" he says, and I think he's just trying to delay things.

"Edward, just sit down," I balk at him.

He does and takes hold of my hand, rubbing his thumb over my knuckles. I try not to pull away, but he can tell I'm uncomfortable. "I'm sorry, I don't know what came over me," he starts.

"What are you and Richard up to?" I ask bluntly, ignoring his apology.

His face whitens. "You know?" His brow knitting.

"I know something is going on, the only people who thought I was on the pill were my mum and Richard. Plus, I saw the cheque Richard gave your charity, one hundred thousand dollars is a very generous donation." I stop and let him absorb what I'm saying.

He lets out a heavy sigh. "Richard came to me about seven weeks ago, just before you and James arrived in the states. He told me you had applied for the photographer position at Mode, he asked me to personally look at your portfolio and to consider hiring you. He knew about the charity and about what we do, and he told me a little of your backstory." He pauses for a moment.

"So everything I told you when I thought I was opening up to you, you already knew," I say.

"The basics only, about Grant and Nathan and about you hurting yourself and he told me about James too. I also knew that Richard had people looking for Grant," he says. "When Richard showed me a picture of you I knew I had to meet you. I loved your work, and I instantly wanted to personally help you get your life back on track. Richard donated to the charity for my help and for me to report back to him."

"So you know Nathan is missing and understand why I need to go home. What is Andy's involvement in all this?" He looks at me confused. "When I expressed my concern to James earlier, Andy went to make a phone call. When he came back and asked me where Nathan was like I would know," I clarify.

"I have no idea what role Andy is playing here, he's not working with Richard or me," Edward answers, which means Andy is working for someone else.

"What do you mean you were reporting back to Richard?" I frown.

"They needed to know that you were being responsible, that you weren't hurting yourself anymore and that you weren't drinking," he answers.

"Why?"

"I can't tell you."

"So you're still hiding things from me."

"Dana you have to understand I signed a confidentiality contract. I could tell you all the stuff I just did because you had practically already worked it out, but I can't tell you any more than that. I'm sorry, please trust me." His voice has become frenzied.

I realize then what has to be done, for me if not both of us. I look at him for a moment, this is the last time I'll see him here, and I try to take all of him in. "I can't trust you, Edward, I'm sorry," I say honestly.

"Dana, please." His eyes are so sad.

"If I'm honest this has nothing to do with your arrangement with Richard, or that you're having me followed and keeping tabs on me," I say pensively.

"What is it then?" he asks, dazed.

"It's what you did when we got here. That wasn't love Edward, that was revenge," I say.

"Dana I don't know what came over me, I was in so much pain." He grabs hold of my hand and gets down on his knees.

"I know, and I think I understand. You wanted me to feel your pain, to feel how scared you were. I get it, but that was abuse, Edward. Doesn't that go against everything your charity stands for? You told me I should feel fulfilled, but I didn't, I was just petrified," I say truthfully.

"Why didn't you say stop?" he questions.

"I shouldn't have had to. Besides after what I told you about Grant, you went and locked me in that room, in the dark for nearly twenty minutes and ignored me." I see his face pale, he goes to speak, but I stop him. "I felt no pleasure from what you did I only felt debased, you betrayed my trust." He clenches his jaw, and I continue before he can interrupt. "You spun me that stupid lie about never disciplining me in anger, how it was wrong to do that. You said you would never allow me to be scared of you and should always be able to trust you. Everything you told me was a lie to get what you wanted, and that's what makes you worse than Grant. At least he didn't try to make me believe what he was doing was right, he was just so fucked up he made himself believe I was enjoying it."

"Give me another chance please, it was a

mistake. You wound me up so much I lost control," he begs.

"It's all my fault, that's what you said when you were *spanking* me, and that's what you're saying now," I say sombrely.

"No, it's not what I mean." His voice is becoming frantic, and tears are welling up in his eyes. My heart is breaking. "I told you, I don't know how to do this, and I need you to bear with me."

"You've had relationships before so you should know the basics. Please don't make this harder for us," I ask.

I can see his brain working overtime. "Marry me?" he asks as if it's the answer to everything and I'm shocked.

"No," I say simply. "I'm going home, and I don't want anything to do with you anymore. You're hurting me inside and out. I'm not strong enough to deal with this. Please, can I have my stuff? That's what I came here for."

"What if you're pregnant? That's my baby

too." He's clutching at straws now.

I can't help but laugh a little. "So now it's your baby, what happened to 'I want a DNA test, people lie Dana'?" I say in a mocking tone. "You won't be having anything to do with my child *if* there is one."

"You can't do that." He starts to raise his voice. I roll my eyes as he walks toward his office. When he comes back, he's holding my phone, purse, and that damned necklace.

"Where's my passport?" I ask, getting frustrated.

"Two weeks," he states.

"Huh?" I'm confused.

"We wait and see if you're pregnant, if you're not and you still want to go back to England, then so be it. I'll have no right to protect you if you don't want me to, plus I'll know your decision is because you want to go home and not a spur of the moment decision because you hate me," he answers.

"And what if I am pregnant?" I ask cautiously.

"Then you have to understand, that while

you're carrying my child, I won't be letting you out of my sight," he says firmly with no room for argument.

"Let's hope I'm not pregnant then," I respond with a bitter smile. Edward hands me my phone and handbag. "Thank you," I say, rummaging through my bag for the lift key so I can get the hell out of here. "I guess I'll see you in two weeks with a pregnancy test," I say through gritted teeth and a false smile before turning to leave.

I feel his hand on my shoulder as he talks to the back of my head. "Let me give you a lift back to your apartment." He is almost pleading with me, but I can't handle this for any longer than necessary.

"No thank you," I say shaking my head. "I'll get a taxi."

"I'll see you at work on Monday?" he asks and I'm surprised it's not a command.

"I still need to work, so yes. I would really appreciate it if you didn't approach me and just let me get on with my job. I'm sorry it's come to this." Silent tears roll down my cheeks, and I'm unable to stop them, this is so much harder than I thought it would be. "I do love you so much, I'm just not strong enough for this." I break down and sob.

I see tears fall down Edward's cheeks too. "I can be strong enough for both of us, please don't leave like this. You haven't even given us a chance. You know the truth now." He is literally begging me.

"Not everything, you're still hiding things. I need to be strong on my own. I can't lean on you entirely. What happens if you can't be strong anymore, then we will both come crashing down," I say, trying to get him to understand.

"Please wear the necklace." I shake my head and start to object, but he stops me. "Please, even if you hate me, always know that if you're ever in trouble, I'll be there to rescue you. Or, if you want, I'll give the pager to Peter. He's head of my security team, so you won't really be asking for my help." I nod, and I let him put the necklace back on me. "Don't take it off."

"That's how you knew I'd been to the bike

shop," I say as I start to figure things out. "If I take it off, it activates the GPS, doesn't it?"

"You are such an intelligent woman," he says with a small smile. "Yes, and before you say anything, I didn't tell you about it because I didn't think you would take it off. It was more for my piece of mind, so if for some reason it was stolen it could be tracked."

"Okay, I'll keep it on for the next two weeks. If I'm not pregnant, I'll need to give it back." I decide as his brow furrows. "I don't want anything to remind me of you, or I'll never move on."

"If that's how you feel, I guess I'll have to understand," he answers, defeated.

"I hope that maybe one day we can be friends. I'm going to miss you and the fun we did have." I choke back the tears that threaten to come again. Edward says nothing and I can see he is attempting to hold back his own tears. I put my key in the lift panel and press the call button. I don't remove the key from the panel, I've no need for it anymore. I just step inside and push the ground floor button. "Goodbye

Edward." There is such finality in that word.

He walks toward the lift. "Goodbye sweetheart," he manages softly and the doors close on Edward's defeated face.

I manage to get a taxi quickly and get back to the apartment. Once I'm inside, and the door is closed, I crash to the floor and let my emotions overcome me. I'm quickly brought back to reality when I hear a loud bang come from my room, I stand gingerly. "Hello, who's there?" I call out cautiously. I reach my room and stop at the sight of two people, one who shouldn't be here and the other I don't even know. "Andrew, what are you doing here? Why are you in my room? And who the hell is this?" I exclaim.

"Dana, I can explain." He starts. "This is Payton."

Payton. As in Edwards ex-girlfriend that tried to trap him with a baby that wasn't even his, Payton. Why has he brought her to my apartment and why is she in my room? The evil grin crossing her face tells me this is not a good thing.

# Chapter 20

"Start explaining Andrew." I'm starting to lose patience with the Day brothers now.

"What's wrong? You've been crying, Dana what's happened?" Andy looks genuinely concerned, but the fact that he is in my room with another woman going through my things has my guard up.

"Did he dump you too? It never takes him long. I wouldn't worry about moping over him, Edward and I have been talking about getting back together," Payton speaks, but all I hear is blah, blah, blah. I know that everything she's saying is complete rubbish.

"Really?" I ask with a slightly amused smirk.

"It was his idea, he said he wanted to be a proper family for his daughter's sake. You know he has a daughter, right?, Her name is Caroline. We named her after his Mother, she'll be six next month. God how time flies." Her voice is like nails on a chalkboard. I want to slap that smirk off her face, but I already have the upper hand on her because I know the truth.

"Yeah, Edward told me all about Caroline and you, how you tried to trap him with a baby. I also know the rest of the truth, so if I were you, I'd shut the fuck up." I give her my 'screw you' look and her face pales instantly.

Andy looks between Payton and me. "Did I miss something, what's going on?" he asks.

"I've just had to tell the only man I've ever truly loved, that we can't be together because I don't trust him. Now you answer me, why are you in my room?" I assert again, trying to change the subject back.

"Please hear me out before you jump in." I consider his request for a moment. Eventually, I nod and let him continue. "You might be in danger-"

"What?" I start.

"Dana, please," Andy says.

"Sorry, carry on," I concede.

"I'm sorry I've had to keep things from you, after what you told me at the hospital I knew something wasn't adding up. I've been hired to find Nathan," he says slowly, letting what he's saying sink in. "No one can seem to find him, and I had to rule out the possibility that you knew where he was."

"You're working for Richard too, aren't you? This is getting stupid, I have no idea where Nathan is and believe me I want to find him more than anyone. Why is she here?"

Payton narrows her eyes at me. "I've been hired to help too," she sneers. Really? Is everyone in on this but me?

"Well I can tell you now, you're not going to find anything because I haven't seen him in a year and a half," I snap back at them. "Now get out of my apartment and don't come back. I'm serious Andrew, if I see you in here again, I'll call the police."

"I'm trying to help you." Andy's voice becomes

frantic.

"I can deal with my Stepfather, you just stay away from me," I warn him.

I watch Andy and Payton leave, and then I let myself break down again. I'm so tired I just want to sleep, I'll speak to Richard when I've calmed down. I climb under my cover and check my phone, nothing. There are no messages, missed calls or voicemails, it makes me feel kind of empty. As neurotic as Edward was, it was nice to know he cared. I don't get a chance to think about anything else, exhaustion takes over, and I fall into a deep sleep.

*"Edward! Edward! Where are you?" He stalks towards me with a smoldering look, he pulls me into his arms tightly and strokes the hair on the back of my head.*

*I'm startled by the sudden yank on my hair. "Get on your knees." A familiar voice snarls, it's not Edward's voice, but it's his lips I see moving. I'm pulled to the ground as he holds his cock just inches from my face. "Suck it, whore." That's not Edward, whose voice is that? I'm searching my brain, trying to put a face to the voice. Just as I realize who it belongs to, Edward's face changes and Grant is standing over me.*

I'm jolted awake and sweating. What an awful dream. Why would my brain associate Edward with Grant? They are nothing alike. I know that's not true, but I still want to believe it. The time on my phone says it's five-thirty, I try for a while to get back to sleep, but it's evading me. I decide to get up and go for a run. By the time I'm dressed and have my iPod set on Eminem, it's just after six. I walk out of the lift and find Edward sitting in the lobby. Really? This guy knows no bounds. I ignore him and turn my music up as loud as it will go, he rises when he sees me but doesn't approach me. Once I'm outside I pick up the pace and head to Central Park. I enter the park by the Tavern on the Green, there is a one and a half mile loop I like to run when I find the time. As I start on my path, I can see Edward in my peripheral vision making his way into the park. I don't have the time to worry about what he wants right now, even if he does try to speak to me I won't be able to hear him. I decide to stop thinking and just sing along in my head to the music playing in my ears. I'm on my third lap, and I'm not tiring, Edward is perched on a bench I have to run past. I continue to ignore him as he watches me. By the time I finish my sixth lap, I'm surprised to find I'm still full of energy, but I'm stopped in my tracks by Edward standing in my way. I try to move around him, but he steps in front of me. Finally, he holds up a bottle of water.

"Thank you," I say turning off the music, pulling my headphones out and taking the bottle.

"You shouldn't be over exerting yourself," he says.

"I was hardly over exerting myself, I could quite easily have done another six laps," I reply.

"You have just run 9 miles, please think of the baby," he says softly.

"There probably isn't even a baby, for god sake. Edward, why are you here?" I'm exasperated.

"I couldn't sleep, so I decided it would be a

better use of my time to make sure you're safe." His calmness is unsettling.

"You need to stop this, please just back off. It's too much, I can't take it," I concede. "By the way, Andrew is working with Richard and so is Payton. I had the pleasure of meeting her last night, the snot-nosed cow. The pair of them was searching my room for information about Nathan."

"I don't understand why Richard would hire them to find Nathan." He trails off as if he's figured something out. "I thought Richard would have told me if they were working for him, maybe he just didn't want to upset me."

He's hiding something again. "Whatever, I don't care. Just all of you, please leave me alone," I say, then turning on my heels I head for home and straight into a steaming hot shower.

I spend the rest of Sunday tidying up the apartment, we're not allowed to see James till Tuesday while he's in the psych ward, so I'm stuck doing nothing with no one to talk to. I really don't want to call my Mum or Richard right now, I feel too betrayed by them, and I don't understand why they think I would know where Nathan is. Why haven't they just asked me themselves? Instead of hiring people to snoop around behind my back.

After spending the afternoon cleaning, watching TV and doing anything else to distract me, I'm still on edge. I can't relax, and I need a drink, so I get myself ready and head to the usual bar James and I frequently attend.

"What is a beautiful girl like you doing here all on your own?" a strange masculine voice comes from beside me.

I'm nursing my second glass of white. "Do I need an excuse to be on my own?" I ask back without looking at him.

He gives a small chuckle. "No, but you seem like you could use the company," he says.

"If I wanted company I would have brought someone with me," I say still not looking up. "No offense, but could you leave me alone please?"

The strange man places a hand on my shoulder, in a gentle, reassuring way. "I'm sorry I bothered you. You seemed upset. If you would like some company my name is Doug and I'll be sitting just over there on my own." He pats my shoulder and heads off.

Now I just feel bad, I wanted to make friends and the first person who tries, I brush off.

I work my way through to my fifth glass of wine, and I'm starting to feel a lot better. I feel lighter and freer like nothing really matters. I turn and see Doug still sitting on his own, caressing a pint.

"What's a handsome man like you doing here all on your own?" I mirror his words from earlier.

I receive a smile as he kicks the chair opposite out from under the table. "Have a seat." Such a gentleman, I laugh to myself.

"I'm Dana, So what's your story?" I ask.

"Long day at work, underappreciated by my boss. Walked in on my girlfriend with my best friend, you know the usual stuff," he says flippantly.

"Oh god, I'm sorry." My hand flies to my mouth, and I feel even guiltier about my earlier brush off.

"It's okay, I'm always underappreciated by my boss," he says, and we both laugh about it. "What's your story?"

"Everyone I love is hiding something from me, my best friend tried to kill himself, I might be pregnant. The usual stuff, you know?" I say.

"Should you be drinking?" he asks.

"It was my best friend who tried to kill himself, not me," I say with a small but sad smile, he nervously laughs at my morbid attempt at humor. "I probably shouldn't be drinking, no. I don't know if I am or not, but trust me I won't be thrilled about it if I am."

"I don't want to sound like your Dad, but you know there is such a thing as a condom," he says with a smirk.

"Yeah, I'm not stupid." He holds his hand up in mock surrender. "It's a long story, I'm sorry I didn't mean to snap."

"Let's change the subject," he says, and I nod. "I noticed your British accent, how long have you been in New York?"

"Just over six weeks now, it feels like a lifetime. So much has happened and I've been thinking about going home to England," I answer.

"Why's that?" he continues probing me.

"I met someone only two weeks ago and everything that's happened since I met him, should never have happened in such a short space of time. It feels like an entire lifetime, and not in a good way either," I say, hurt lacing my voice.

"So where is he tonight?" he asks.

"He can't be trusted, and I've had to end things," I answer angrily. "Do you want to dance?"

I spend the rest of the evening getting very drunk to the point of not being able to walk straight, and my vision is completely disoriented, this is exactly how I need to feel. I danced the night away with Doug, who despite being such a gentleman – not. He didn't even bother putting me in a taxi to make sure I got home safely.

I wake up Monday morning, and my head feels like it's been clamped in a vice. My mouth feels like sandpaper, my hair looks like I've been dragged through a hedge backward, and I swear I'm still drunk. After checking the time I realize I only have an hour before I have to be at work. I run around the apartment, turning on the shower so it will be hot when I get in and make a cup of coffee. I jump in the quickest shower on record, throw on a bit of make-up and tie my hair up in a French twist, so I don't have to dry it. After quickly getting dressed and drinking the coffee I made before getting in the shower, I run out of the building. Luck is not on my side today, there isn't a taxi in sight. I have fifteen minutes to get to work, *crap!* I start running, and I manage to get to work with a few minutes to spare. I wait outside the Daylight tower as I gather myself and steady my breathing, once I straighten my clothes and sort hair out I head inside. I start to walk toward the bank of lifts when an older woman steps in my way.

"Sorry," I say as I try to side-step the woman, but she mirrors me, and I look at her confused.

"Dana Spencer?" she asks.

"Yes, can I help you?" I say.

"I'm Caroline Day, Edwards Mother." I instantly want to slap this woman, but I decide to remain polite.

"It's nice to meet you. Sorry, I must go, I'm late," I say.

She grabs the top of my arm, what is it with the Day family and arm grabbing? "Just a quick word," she says in her very fake posh voice. "Edward and Payton are working on reconciliation, they do have a daughter together after all."

"What's this got to do with me?" I snap, interrupting her. The expression on her face tells me she didn't appreciate the interruption.

"I think it will be best if you try your gold digging techniques on someone else. Edward should marry Payton, he'll disgrace the family name if he doesn't. It's bad enough he had a love child with her, but Payton is a lovely girl who comes from money. She has social standing too and knows how to behave in public." I want to wipe the smile off her face, but I remain passive. "You should move on now, you've had your fun with my son-"

"Your son?" I laugh at her brash statement. "You have the cheek to call him that," I start raising my voice.

"Excuse me?" She gives a nervous giggle.

"Well he wasn't your son when you shipped him off to boarding school after your other son raped him, was he?" I grit my teeth to reign in my anger.

"Edward was a troubled boy, who liked to make up stories to get attention. We got help for him, and we were told by professionals that it was very common for a sibling born in the middle to feel left out and to start making stuff up. It's also more common for siblings all of the same sex, it's called middle-child syndrome," she replies matter-of-factly.

"So you sent him away instead of showing him more love, or did you send him away because you were worried he was telling the truth and what people would think of you if it came out? You have no right to call yourself his Mother." I manage without shouting.

"Please escort Mrs. Day off the premises," I hear Edward's booming voice and feel the tension leaving me quickly as I start to relax.

"Edward, stop being so dramatic," she half laughs, as if he's being ridiculous.

"I have nothing to say to you, and I don't appreciate you harassing Dana," he barks at her.

"You're defending this tramp-"

"Enough, Mother! Leave now," he cuts her off. He places his hand on the small of my back and leads me through the lobby. I can feel the heat from his hand through my top, and I instantly feel the spark from his touch, damn my body betraying me again. "I'm sorry about her." Edward turns to me. "I spoke to Payton last night regarding her being in your apartment, and she took it upon herself to call my parents, telling them you and I were no longer together and that I was considering taking her back."

"We aren't together, so there was no need for her to call your Mother," I say cattily. "Why was she here anyway?"

"To give me my Grandmothers engagement ring. She wants me to use it to propose to Payton," Edward practically spits.

"Your family is confusing," I say honestly.

"My family likes publicity and social status, they will use anyone they can to climb the social ladder," he says. "Dana, I've been doing a bit of digging, and there is no way Drew and Payton are working for Richard."

"Are you sure?" I ask worriedly, and he nods. "So who are they working for?"

"I haven't worked that out yet," he says as the lift car arrives, he steps in, and I stay outside. I need to distance myself from all the energy passing between us. "There is plenty of room for both of us Dana."

"I don't think that's a good idea," I say as

Edward steps back towards me. "Thank you for saving me from that vile woman, but you said you would leave me alone at work to get on with things." As I say this, Edward's brow knits. "What's wrong?"

"Are you drunk?" he asks, "Because you smell like a brewery."

"I'm hung-over, that's all," I reply, not making eye contact with those beautiful emerald eyes that I swear can see right into the depths of my soul.

"Dana, if anything happens to my baby, so help me-"

"What baby?" I shout, cutting him off. "There probably isn't even one. Get a grip and leave me alone, you said two weeks." I see his jaw clench and his shoulders square, he stares at me for some time before turning on his heels and leaving me standing on my own in the lobby. This is going to be a really long two weeks. "Oh come on Dana," I mumble to myself, "how bad can it be?"

# Chapter 21

I head to my desk as quick as I can, I just want to get started on today's task, and then I can get home. Maybe Doug will be at the bar again tonight so I can apologize for last night's behavior. But then again if he wanted to see me, he would have left me his number. Do I even really want to see him again? I've got too much going on right now. Getting involved with another man would be the wrong thing to do, especially when I'm still in love with the last man.

"Hey, woman to the stars," Simon comes bouncing over.

"Please don't even joke," I say, amusement lacing my voice.

"I'm all yours today, do with me what you will," he replies.

"I was just going to upload the photos from the shoot last week and do a bit of editing, you're welcome to half the workload." I smile innocently at him.

"I suppose I could do that." His face doesn't look impressed at all. I laugh at him, I can't help it. Simon has always been good at lifting my mood. "Mr. Day is in an awful mood today, any idea why?"

"None whatsoever," I say. "Edward's business is none of mine." I swiftly gather the bits I want Simon to work on so he won't ask me any more awkward questions.

As lunch time approaches, I'm impressed with the amount of work I've gotten done. In the future, if I need distracting, I'll just edit some photos. I really love my job, photography is the only thing I dreamed of doing since my Dad gave me my first camera at the age of eight. It's times like now when I really miss him. When I remember all the things he taught me. I miss you so much Dad, I can't believe it's been nearly ten years since I lost you. I feel a stray tear fall down my cheek, and I wipe it away quickly. Shaking my head, I get back down to business. "I'm going to the deli for lunch." Simon approaches my desk. "Do you want to come? Or I can just bring you something back."

"Thanks, Simon but I'm not hungry, I'm just going to finish up here, enjoy your lunch," I answer him. Maybe if I work through lunch, I can have all this done by the end of the day. I'm startled by the sudden sound of my desk phone. "Dana Spencer," I say into the speaker.

"Are you going out for lunch?" Will this man ever leave me alone?

"No, I'm working through lunch, goodbye." I hang up the phone immediately and ignore it the next two times it rings before Edward finally gives up.

I hear the lift doors ping, but I don't pay attention to the people getting on and off. That sound used to have my neck snapping up to look, and now I barely notice it. A paper bag and smoothie are placed on my desk, when I look up, I see the back of Edward as he walks away without saying a word. I read the note attached to the bag.

*Just in case.*
*Edward xx*

I feel a small smile playing on my lips, he will make an amazing Dad one day. We don't even know if I'm pregnant and he's being like this, imagine what he would be like if I were. My eyes go wide at the thought, he would probably have me chained to the bed. I chuckle to myself, I wouldn't mind if it were Edward's bed. Stop it! I tell myself, stop doing this to yourself, he can't be trusted. I grab my phone and send him a quick text.

**Thank you,**
**D xx**

Inside the bag is a chicken and bacon salad with vinaigrette, Caesar dressing, and croutons. He has also brought me a strawberry and banana smoothie, he's making sure I'm eating healthy, just in case. I shake my head with a small chuckle and prepare my lunch.

When Simon comes back, he looks at me suspiciously. "I thought you said you weren't hungry?" His face showing his confusion.

"I wasn't, I'm being force-fed," I reply.

"Okay then," he says. "I've finished everything you gave me, do you need me to anything else?"

"I don't think so, I'm nearly done too. Bring all your work over, and we will go through all the photos together. Simon heads back to his desk, and I get to my last photo, it's of Cain posing with his pouty face. I burst out laughing, remembering the fun we had that night on the beach. I won't be putting that in the compilation for Vanessa, so that's it, I'm done as well.

Simon and I spend the next few hours going over all the photos from the shoot and picking out the ones we think should go in the magazine, with the interview Cain did. When we're done, I head straight to Vanessa's office and hand her the memory stick with everything on it.

She goes through the photos herself, occasionally nodding and "mm-hmm"ing. Finally, she's finished. "These are great Dana, you were definitely the right person for the job. The magazine goes to print tomorrow night, I will narrow it down to about half the amount you've given me." I smile feeling like something is going right for a change. "When you come in tomorrow, you can check the ones I've chosen and let me know if you agree?" she says.

"Really? Wow, thank you." I'm almost speechless.

"It's your work Dana, you've done a fantastic job, and I wouldn't want to mess that up by picking the wrong photos," she says simply. "Go home and get some rest, you look a little pale today, I'll see you in the morning."

"Thanks again Vanessa, I'll see you bright and early." I smile at her. Once back at my desk, I gather all my stuff so I can get home. I feel so proud of myself for what I have accomplished. When I'm finally outside the Daylight tower, I thank my lucky stars that I didn't bump into Edward. I hail a taxi, once inside the backseat and bound for home, I check my phone. There's a message from Mister obsessive.

**What are your plans tonight?**
**Edward xx**

None of your business I think to myself, but then decide against sending that. He will only come over and check on me.

**Dinner, bath and an early night.**
**D xx**

Hopefully, that will satisfy him.

**Is that what you're really doing?**
**Or are you just telling me what I want to**
hear?

**Edward xx**


His reply makes me laugh, he knows me too well. I stop laughing when I remember he does know me too well.


**Maybe, is poor Eddie worried I'm not telling the truth?**

**D xx**


I know I'm goading him, but I can't help it, he makes it too easy. My phone starts ringing, and I shake my head when I see his name on my screen.

"Did you get bored of texting?" I say when I answer the phone.

"Don't ever call me that!" He growls at me, is he really pissed off because I called him Eddie.

"Oh my god, you need to chill. It was a joke. Get a grip yeah?" I reply. "I don't even know why I bother. I'm trying to understand this incessant need you have to keep me safe even though it's none of your concern, you could at least meet me halfway."

"Dana, I'm sorry I really hate that name." He relaxes a little.

"Don't ever speak to me like that again. You know, today, I thought maybe we would be able to be friends. Obviously, I was wrong." I hang up the phone, fuming at him for ruining my good mood again.

When I get back to my apartment, I run a bath straight away. Sod it, I'm going out tonight. I end up putting my phone on silent, Edwards constant ringing is doing my head in. I manage to relax in the bath for an hour, with a good book and glass of wine. I really start to feel the tension leaving me, I may just have to stay in here all night. When I finally decide that I look enough like a prune, I get out and start getting myself ready for the evening. I check my phone again, there is missed call after missed call from Edward. I wondered for a moment why I thought I missed this, this is not caring it's stalking and obsession. I notice my phone battery is almost dead, thanks to him. I'll just leave it on charge at home, I shouldn't need it tonight. I really can't wait to see James tomorrow, I've missed him so much.

I've been in the bar about thirty minutes, there is no sign of Doug, and I'm already on glass number three, not including the two I had at the apartment. Edward was right, I do drink too much. I wouldn't be surprised if Doug never comes in here again, just to avoid me.

"I don't know what you said to Mrs. Day today, but you really pissed her off." I turn and see Payton sitting next to me, gloating. "Thanks for making it so much easier for me."

"What do you want, Payton?" I ask completely uninterested.

"To thank you," she replies. "For leaving Edward alone."

"I didn't do it for you Payton, I did it for myself." I give a snort of derision. "He doesn't want you, though. And don't pretend like you have something between you. I know Caroline isn't his, she's Andy's." She turns her head from me.

430

"He really did tell you the truth," she says, and I just nod, not knowing what to say. "He's never told anyone else, he really must love you." She sighs, sounding defeated. "When I spoke to him yesterday, he said you were carrying his baby. Is that true?" she inquires, looking from me to my empty glass.

"Not entirely, we don't know yet," I answer honestly, and then call the barman over to refill my glass.

"Why don't you want him?" Her question stumps me. "He's rich, you would be well looked after. He's Manhattan's most eligible bachelor, girls would kill to be in your position."

"I guess I just don't care about all that stuff," I reply with little enthusiasm.

"Every woman wants a man who can take care of them," she claims matter-of-factly. "The fame, the money, you really wouldn't want it?"

"If I wanted all that, I'd just hang around my stepfather," I sneer at her, disgusted that she would be happy being a kept woman. "We're not that much different really Payton, I just choose not to stand in the limelight flaunting it all for the world to see."

She narrows her eyes at me. "Don't judge me, you don't even know me."

"I know enough that you were using Edward to climb the social ladder, just like his parents," I argue.

"Do you blame them for being the way they are with him? He lied about something so serious it could have ripped their family apart." She sounds saddened.

"Did you ever sleep in the same bed with him?" I ask.

"Yes, all the time," she answers a little too quickly.

"That's a lie right there, Edward doesn't share his bed." I shake my head at her.

"Maybe that was just you," she replies smugly.

"No." I laugh at her audacity. "Because if you did share his bed, you would know he has extremely bad night terrors. When I experienced him having

one, it broke my heart watching him in so much pain."
My voice filled with disdain for the woman sitting in
front of me, I down the rest of my drink and signal for
yet another refill.

"You've shared his bed?" She looks at me with
so much hurt in her eyes.

"No I stayed in his spare room, but he
managed to wake me with his screaming," I say
sympathetically.

"He let you stay?" She sounds like her heart
has just shattered into a million pieces.

"Yeah, are you telling me you were in a
relationship with him and never stayed at his place?"
She doesn't answer me, she just continues staring at
the bar. "I'm sorry, I didn't realize. Wow, the guy
really does have issues."

"Maybe, but I really love him," she mumbles.

"If you don't trust him and he doesn't trust
you, then the possibility of you ever having a
successful relationship with him is slim to none." I try
to make her see sense.

"I do trust him, and he will learn to trust me again, he's taken Caroline as his own, he must love us," she says hopefully.

"He loves Caroline as his niece, Payton. That's all." I try to be straight with her.

"He told you this?" she asks unconvinced.

I nod, and my face softens. "I'm sorry." I finish my drink and realize I'm rather tipsy. I look at the time, it's almost eleven. "Look I'm sorry, but I have to go. I've got to go to work in the morning. I hope you manage to sort things out."

"Do you want another drink?" She tries to tempt me.

"The bar's closing soon," I answer confused.

"My place is just a few blocks from here, I've got some white and red wine and some harder stuff too," she says with a side smile. "Come on, I've actually enjoyed your company tonight. You're nothing like I thought you would be."

"Believe it or not, neither are you," I reply. "Fine, one more won't hurt." We giggle together as we exit the bar arm in arm. I wonder how Edward would react to us being friends.

While we walk I decide to probe Payton a bit about Saturday. "Why were you in my apartment?" I ask carefully.

"Look, Dana, if I'm honest, I don't really know. I was hired by Drew to help, he wanted a woman's perspective. I don't know who hired him, or what they want him to do," she answers.

There isn't much I can say to that, she sounds genuine. Besides Andy is the one I really need to talk to. "That's okay."

"I'm sorry we were there. If I could give you more answers, I would. This is me," she says pointing to a small apartment block.

"I didn't expect this," I say trying not to offend her. "I imagined you in a huge penthouse suite." I give a small chuckle.

"I guess you got me wrong, we're not all after men with money and some of us like to pay our own way in this world, not live off our trust funds." She gives me a small smile.

I narrow my eyes slightly. "But I thought... all that stuff you said in the bar about having a man to look after you and all that," I say.

"Please don't hate me now," she says looking worried. "I was trying to test you, to see if what Mrs. Day said was true about you being a gold digger."

"Well, I guess we both got each other wrong." I half laugh.

"Clean slate?" she asks hopefully.

"Clean slate," I confirm. "Shall we?" I gesture for her to show the way.

We enter Payton's apartment, and I'm shocked at how small it is. It has a small living room with very outdated furniture, a small hallway that leads to a box sized bathroom and a modest sized bedroom. The kitchen is on the other side of the living room. I instinctively reach up for my necklace, something is off, there is no way Payton lives in this dive. If she has a child, where is the second bedroom? "Please make yourself at home," she says gesturing to the old tatted sofa. "That's a beautiful necklace."

"Edward gave it to me," I reply.

"Let me guess, it's a locket that has a manually activated GPS tracking system in it," she says.

"Yes, to be used for emergencies," I answer her confidently. Hopefully, she understands I will use it if I need to. Edward must have given her a similar necklace, I think to myself.

"What would you like to drink?" she asks, seemingly letting the subject of the necklace go.

I begin to relax, maybe I'm just being paranoid. "White wine, please?" I answer, and she heads off into the kitchen.

"Jesus!" I hear her scream.

I go to stand from the sofa. "Are you okay?" I shout as I get up.

She appears in the doorway instantly. "Sorry I thought I saw a rat." My mouth gasps in shock. "No, no. It's okay it was just my fur hat that I wear in winter, must be karma. Wear an animal on my head, and they will haunt me for life." She gives a little chuckle.

"Okay," I answer with a smile, something's not right. Why would someone that owns a real fur hat, live in this dump? I reach for my necklace again, please don't make me use it. I decide to stick it out, there has to be a reason she brought me here.

"Here you go," Payton says, returning with our drinks.

"Thank you," I say as she passes me a glass and I take a large sip to settle my nerves, she sits next to me with her glass of red wine.

"Are you okay?" she asks. "Would you like me to just bring you the bottle?"

I realize I've downed my entire glass. "No thank you. I'm fine, just a bit nervous," I say without thinking.

"Why are you nervous?" she continues.

"I'm sorry Payton, please don't take offense to what I'm about to ask. Do you really live here?" I try to hide my embarrassment.

"No, I don't. You really thought I'd live here?"

438

She starts laughing heinously, and my guard goes up. I knew it.

"So why are we here?" I try my hardest to keep the terror from my voice.

"You're here because we need to talk to you." I turn around at the sound of the familiar masculine voice.

"Andy, what's going on?" I ask. At that point I start feeling dizzy, my eyes starting to blur.

"Dana, are you okay?" Andy asks as I stumble trying to stand from the sofa.

"Something's wrong, I can't-"

"I drugged her." My heart rate suddenly increases tenfold at the interruption of another familiar masculine voice, but this one scares the hell out of me.

"You said you were working for Richard," I say to Andy.

"No you said I worked for Richard, I just didn't correct you," he replies.

"I swear I knew nothing about this," I hear

Payton pleading from the tatty sofa. "This wasn't in the plan Drew."

"I need her Payton, you wouldn't have helped if you knew what I had planned." The voice from my nightmares replies. My head is spinning, and I can't focus properly on what's being said. "Hello, Dana." He puts his hand on my face and rubs his thumb along my jaw line. "It's good to see you again Angel."

I just about manage to look up. "Grant," I say, and he smiles his chilling, eerie smile. "Where is Nathan?" I ask trying to raise my voice from a mere whisper.

"I don't know Dana, why don't you tell me?" he says coldly.

My head is getting cloudy fast, what game is he playing? "Grant, where is my son?"

I can't hold on anymore, darkness takes me.

# Edward

# Chapter 22

Why can't I just be normal? Why when it comes to her, do I find myself losing my head? I don't know what to do. Do I go to her apartment? No, she won't appreciate that, but if she doesn't answer her phone soon, I'm going to have to do something. She can't keep doing this to me, I know she's a stubborn woman but really? Ignoring me for six hours is going a bit overboard. I will definitely talk to her in the morning about this. She must be okay, I've checked the pager that receives the signal from her necklace about a million times, if she were in danger, she would have let me know. I'm pulled from my train of thought by the ringing of my phone.

"What is it, Peter?" I ask my head of security,

slightly agitated at the late night call.

"I'm afraid it's a matter of urgency that requires your immediate attention, sir," he replies.

"What's happened?" He has my full attention now.

"You have received a letter Mr. Day, which we believe to be a credible threat," he answers. "I will be with you shortly, I'm close by."

"Okay Peter, I'll be in my home office," I say and hang up. What the hell is so damn urgent that he needs to see me now?

"Good evening, sir," Peter says as he enters the office.

"Let's see the letter," I say getting straight to the point.

"Of course." He hands me the letter, and I open it, re-reading it several times to try and make sense of it.

*A life for a life, for a life, for a life.*
*I want what is mine, and I won't stop until I get*

*it. I'm halfway there, bring me the rest and no one will*
*get killed. If you don't, I will make it as slow and as*
*painful as possible, until every drop of blood is drained*
*from their bodies.*

"I don't understand how this is for me?" I say
to Peter, who looks just as confused as I do. "What
does this mean? A life for a life, for a life, for a life?"

"I believe that statement to be referring to
four people sir, the rest we have no clue on," Peter
replies hesitantly.

My phone rings again, and I grunt when I see
her name on the screen. "This better be important
Payton," I growl at her, angry at what she put Dana
and me through with my Mother this morning.

"Edward, are you home? I really need to see
you, it's urgent." I can barely hear her, she's so
hysterical.

"Payton where are you?" I ask concerned.

"I'm outside your building, please I need to see
you before he finds me." The panic in Payton's voice is

scaring me.

"Before who finds you?" I ask quickly.

"Edward please, I don't have a lot of time." She's frantic, I call down to the front desk and inform them to let her up.

I'm at the elevator door just as Payton is stepping out, she looks a mess. "What's going on? Where is Caroline?" I ramble on.

"It's not Caroline, it's Dana." My heart stops, I knew something was wrong. "Grant has her, he drugged her, and he took her." She manages to get out.

Peter has joined us by the elevator, and he helps me move Payton to the sofa. "Peter, could you grab her a glass of water please."

When Peter comes back, she instantly takes the drink for a long sip. "Thank you," she says.

Peter sits in front of her with his notepad and pen ready in his hand. "Payton, I need you to calm down and tell me what happened," he says soothingly to her.

"Grant hired Drew to track down Nathan. Grant assumed Nathan would be with Dana by now. So Drew got close to James to get to Dana, but it turns out Dana doesn't have Nathan. Drew hired me to help, but we can't find him either, so Grant asked Drew to set up a meeting between Dana and him. I had to help with convincing her to come to the apartment Grant rented for the meeting, when we got there I didn't know Grant had spiked her drink. He was just standing in the kitchen with two drinks ready, he scared the crap out of me. She was unconscious when I left. They had tied her up and were putting her into the trunk of a car.

"They?" I ask, fearing the answer.

"Grant and Drew," she replies.

"And you just left her there?" I can't reign in my anger any longer.

"I'm sorry, I couldn't be a part of it. I have a daughter. I ran away as fast as I could. I knew I had to tell you as quickly as possible. I'm so sorry. I didn't know Grant or Drew was going to do that or I would

446

never have got involved." Payton says pleading with me to forgive her. I extract my hand from hers and shake my head.

"Payton tell Peter everything you can remember and then get the hell out of my sight!" My voice is scaring me, so it's no surprise to see Payton flinch.

I head to my office to make some calls, firstly to Richard Dalton. "Edward, I'm guessing you have received a letter too or have a very good reason to be calling me at this ungodly hour," he says when answering the phone.

"I'm sorry, Grant's got Dana. I'm working on getting a team out to find her," I say, the sadness in my voice evident.

"What are you talking about Edward? We sent Grant back to England." His voice, disbelieving.

"I'm sorry, I've just gotten confirmation that he is back. I also received a letter today, I now believe the letter is connected to Grant," I reply.

"If your letter is the same as mine..." There is a

long pause on the line. "Dana is in grave danger," he whispers.

"I'm afraid that's most likely the case Richard. I will have people out within the hour, searching her last few known locations," I reply calmly.

"She isn't a business deal that's gone wrong Edward, she's my daughter," Richard snaps.

"She's carrying my child, so believe me I know," I snap back.

"She's pregnant?" he asks me uncertainly. "You got my daughter pregnant?"

"We think so, we just never got the chance to confirm it. I'm sorry Richard, we fell in love," I reply. "I told you from the start that we were going about this the wrong way, you should have told her where Nathan was from the beginning."

"I know, we just wanted to let her get settled. Then we canceled the dinner we arranged so we could tell her after you called and said Dana was still harming herself." He sounds tired and crushed.

"You used my updates against her, so she

couldn't see her own son?" I can't hide the disgust in my voice. "Dana will never forgive any of us after this."

"Edward I agree, Stella and I will be talking about this after I tell her about Dana being kidnapped. I assume we are keeping this from the authorities for now?" he asks.

"Yes, I will find her, and I want Nathan ready for when I do. She needs her son Richard, I'm serious," I order. "Did it ever occur to either of you that Dana may have been acting recklessly because she thought she had lost her son for good?"

I hear a long sigh down the line. "I know we've messed this up, and now we may have put Dana in danger because of it. Keep me informed, please. I'll gather my men together too and get them to coordinate with yours," Richard says as he hangs up.

I walk back to the living room as Payton is leaving. "If anything happens to her or my baby, I'll be holding you personally responsible," I sneer at her.

"I didn't know Grant was going to drug her, he

449

said he just wanted to talk," she pleads.

"You delivered her into the arms of a sadistic evil monster, for what? To hopefully end up getting me to yourself. Sorry, Payton, I don't love you, and I'm pretty sure I never did, now I know who you really are." I can't help the cruel words that are coming out of my mouth, at this moment I want to strangle her.

"You don't mean that," she says, stepping into the elevator. She turns to face me, and I can see her eyes swimming with unshed tears, but I don't care. Turning my back on her before the doors even close, Peter and I walk back to my office in silence.

"Miss Channing gave me everything she could," Peter says, sitting down in the chair across from me.

"Give it to me," I say, bracing myself.

"It would appear that your brother has been working for Mr. Baker for quite some time, probably before he ever met Miss Spencer. According to Miss Channing, Mr. Day is still with Miss Spencer and Mr. Baker."

I huff. "Please drop the formalities, Peter."

"Yes, sir. We don't know what Grant plans to do with her. Does the letter make sense to you yet?" he asks me.

"Apart from the fact that he is going to kill her?" I reply. "The four people you referred to I now believe are, Dana, Nathan, the baby she terminated and the baby she is possibly pregnant with now."

"Who else knows Dana could be pregnant?" he asks.

"Only Payton." A chill runs down my spine when I think of the person she has become.

"I know you may not want to believe this, but I really do think Payton was telling the truth when she said she didn't know what Grant and Andrew had planned. I honestly believe she was just a pawn in their game," Peter says bluntly.

"Well if Payton didn't tell him, who did?" I can't seem to get anything straight in my head.

"I have another theory, sir." He looks to me for permission to share his idea, I nod. "He may have taken her, to impregnate her. You did say she terminated a pregnancy, I assume the unborn child was Grant's?" Again I nod, confirming his assumption. "I think that the letter is stating his obvious want. A life for a life: Nathan for Dana. For a life: Dana for the baby she terminated. For a life: The baby she terminated, for the baby he will impregnate her with." Peter stops, letting it all sink in.

"So in a nutshell, he wants Dana and Nathan, and for Dana to give him another child, or he will kill them all?" I summarize.

"I believe so sir," he replies.

"And my brother assisted in her abduction?" I ask, trying to piece it all together.

"Yes, sir." Peter nods.

"There is a small problem Peter." His eyes snap up to meet mine. "What happens when he finds out he can't get her pregnant because she's already pregnant?"

"I believe we have a time bomb on our hands Edward, and we need to move fast because it could go off at any moment." Peter's eyes are deadly serious.

"He's going to kill her if she's already pregnant, isn't he?" I ask already knowing the answer.

Peter doesn't say anything, he just gets out his phone and goes to work. Please be okay Dana, stay alive for me. I'll find you soon, I promise.

Made in the USA
San Bernardino, CA
28 June 2017